凱信企管

用對的方法充實自己，
讓人生變得更美好！

凱信企管

用對的方法充實自己，
讓人生變得更美好！

凱信企管

用對的方法充實自己，
讓人生變得更美好！

凱信企管

用對的方法充實自己，
讓人生變得更美好！

全方位英語大師

英文文法原來如此

易混淆文法
X
程度精進測驗

帶你站在英語語言特性制高點學習，
以原則取代規則、以理解取代記憶，
成功地將文法學習歷程擴及寫作及解題。

暢銷
增訂版

使用說明 User's guide

站在語言學習特性制高點，掌握訊息傳遞溝通原則，文法學習才能成功！

1

八大文法原則一次完整傳授，文法句型認知有系統也更全面。

以獨創的文法原則，含語意完整、主從標示、指涉明確等八大項，破解細碎文法規則，學習更完整有系統也更全面。

Chapter
1.語意完整

語意完整是溝通的基本條件，但是，句式上的完整卻是中英不同。

Chapter
2.標示主從

語意或結構有必要成分及非必要成分，這是主從之分。主從之分可擴大為階層之別，標記主從，辨識階層差異，對於語意、解題、寫作皆相當有益。

Chapter 2.標示主從

2

精選 122 條易混淆文法 + 原來如此精準解析，問題隨查即找，學習最清楚方便。

必學 122 多篇易混淆文法，以單一獨立問題呈現，再以【原來如此】一針見血的精準解析，讓學習一看就懂，不再似是而非。目錄更以索引方式呈現，有任何需釐清的文法疑問，查找更簡捷快速。

Q02. "I came, I saw, I conquered." 為什麼沒有連接詞 and ？

原來如此 這是 tricolon，一些英語教學學者譯為「三節格律法」。接續且長度相仿的三個單詞、片語或子句形成三節格律，該修辭體例源自希臘文與拉丁文的古詩。

◆ 三節格律常使語意漸次增強，為求一鼓作氣，連接詞 and 予以省略。語用上，除了詩、小說、短篇故事，三節格律也常見於口述敘事、電影、廣告或活動標語，以使訊息聚焦而令人印象深刻。

例1 "I came, I saw, I conquered."
我來之，我見之，我克之。
→ 語出凱薩大帝 Julius Caesar，原文是 "Veni, Vidi, vici"，中譯「我來，我見之，我克之。"，中英文皆屬簡潔過癮的押頭韻。

例2 "of the people, by the people, for the people"
民有、民治、民享
Lincoln, Gettysburg Add..

例3 "Friends, Romans, countrymen, lend me your ears."
朋友們、羅馬人，同胞們，請聽我說。
William Shakespe..

must be handsome, ruthles..

Dorothy Pa..

這是 tricolon，一些英語教學學者譯為「接續且長度相仿
該修辭體例源自希臘文與拉丁文

三節格律常使
"I came, I saw, I conquered."
我來之，我見之，我克之。
語出 Julius Caesar

"There is" 是引介句，引介下文，猶如開場白，啟動故事情節，常於一些童話故事，例如：

例1 Once upon a time, there were three little pigs. One pig built a house of straw while the second pig built a house with sticks.
很久以前，有三隻小豬。一隻用麥稈蓋房子，而第二隻用枝條蓋房子

引介句揭開場景，看官與舞台角色初次見面，主詞是不特定對象，搭配不定冠詞，例如：

例2 There is a book on the table.
桌上有一本書。

例 3 定格情景，前無上文，後無下文，作說者明確指出「一本書在桌上」，a 雖是不定冠詞，但表示特定，意思是數量的一本。

例3 A book is on the table.
一本書在桌上。

同樣，例 4 的主詞 "a book of yours" 是不特定，而例 5 的主詞是特定：

例4 There is a book of yours on the table.
桌上有一本你的書。

例5 One of your books is on the table.
你的一本書在桌上。

雖然只是一張桌子、一本書，但是，場景、角色及劇本都不同，若硬把塩調等於那詞，塩就是外行人看熱鬧了！
→ There is a book on the table. 是講第一本書，A book is on the table. 是講特定的一本書。

---

3 **3W 文法層次，以大量例句佐證理論、貫穿文法，學習方能更有邏輯、融會貫通。**

What：了解文法原理；
Why：探討複雜句型；
How：活用文法觀念，
以大量的例句貫穿與說明文法理論，確實提升寫作實力及增強文法能力。

What

◆ There is" 是引介句，引介下文，猶如開場白，啟動故事情節，常於一疊童話故事，例如：
例1 Once upon a time, there were three little pigs. One pig built __ of straw while the second pig built a h__
桌上有一本書。

Why

◆ 例 3 定格情景，前無上文，後無下文，作說者明確指出「一本書在桌上」，a 雖是不定冠詞，但表示特定，意思是數量的一本。
例3 A book is on the table.
一本書在桌上。
__ "a book of yours" 是特定

How

◆ __ books is on the table.
你的一本書在桌上。
◆ 雖然只是一張桌子、一本書，但是，場景、角色及劇本都不同，若硬說塩調等於那詞，塩就是外行人看熱鬧了！
→ There is a book on the table. 是講第一本書，A book is on the table. 是講特定的一本書。

---

4 **特別收錄 129 題文法試題及清楚易懂解析，讓學習溫故知新，並大幅提高解題能力。**

將八大文法原則融會貫通後，再利用全新撰寫的文法測驗試題來確認學習成果，除能藉以複習所學，同時更能藉由測驗加深學習印象，再利用解析延伸學更多、精進解題技巧，寫作也能更有條理，更有深度。

B: I went to the bookstore, _____ some books and visited my uncle.
A. to buy B. bought C. buy D. buying

__97. Few of us get the _____ seven to nine hours of sleep a night, and many who have time _____don't, for fear of spoiling night time sleep.
A. recommended...napping B. recommended ...to nap
C. recommending...napping D. recommending...to nap

__95. _____ into French, words and phrases for congratulations at the wedding party surely became language barriers for those who only knew English.
A. Having put B. Put C. Being put D. To put

__99. _____ her suggestion is of greater value than yours.
A. All things considered   B. All things considering
C. Considering all things   D. Considered all things

__100. In the teaching of mathematics, the way of instruction is generally traditional, with teachers presenting formal lectures and students _____ notes.
A. take B. to take C. taking D. taken

__101. Returning to her apartment late that night, _____

---

cigarette to underage kids.
A. don't allow   B. shouldn't allow
C. aren't allowed   D. not be allowed

解 that 是從的標記，引導同位語子句說明先行詞 law 的內容，shops 是主詞，加接時態動詞，not be allowed 是非限定動詞，不扮演句子的時態動詞，因此不選 D。allow 的次分類是 V: _____ NPtoVP，句中 NP 前移至主詞位置，應選被動語態，A、B 是主動語態，應加接受事者 -patient。

C 20. The bill he had long been opposed _____ at the last session, _____ in more young men being recruited into the army.
A. to being passed...just to result
B. to be passed...only to result
C. to was passed...resulting
D. was passed...having resulted

解 1. 反對 —be opposed to：to 是介係詞，he had long been opposed to 是 The bill 的形容詞子句，to 的受詞缺項，受格關係代名詞省略。
2. 主詞是含形容詞子句的名詞片語 — The bill he had long been opposed to
3. 主詞加接時態動詞，pass 的次分類是 V: _____ NP，受事者 The bill 移至句首，被動語態。
4. 逗號後面是從一片語，result in 主動語意，說明的 the bill 的附帶結果，可改寫如下：
The bill he had long been opposed to was passed at the

作者序 Preface

　　《英文經典文法大全 - 英文文法原來如此》於 2019 年春天初版問世，旋即引起廣大讀者的青睞與回響，掀起「英文文法原來如此」的學習風潮。該書呈現英文的嶄新視角，引領窺見文法的義理脈絡，看見學習的明確路徑，可喜可賀。

　　為了傳揚「英文文法原來如此」的理念與具體內容，翻轉當前「只有規則、沒有原則，只背公式、不談邏輯」的窘況，蘇秦老師開設「英文文法原來如此」網站，發表論述─闡述「what─句型是什麼、why─原因是什麼、how─如何運用於解題及寫作」三層次的文法內涵，深獲眾多教師、學生、進修者的肯定。由於「英文文法原來如此」有助於國高中學生的文法學習，「英文文法原來如此」常成為校園教師研習的主題而使高品質文法教學展現於教學現場。

　　為了使「英文文法原來如此」成為多元創意的教材教法，蘇秦老師特於國立高雄師範大學進修學院開設「國中高中文法精進教學課程」，發表「結構樹狀圖系列卡牌遊戲」，發展「理解融入結構」的文法教學實作，落實學理與教學相輔相成的理念。而此一教學效益也在蘇秦老師親授的勞動部人力發展署台南地區文法教學職訓課程的訓後回饋中得到印證。

　　時值《全方位英語大師─英文文法原來如此【暢銷增訂版】》付梓，回首「英文文法原來如此」在臺灣的推行與精進歷程，衷心祈願增訂版嶄新而充實的內容能夠為這片土地的文法教學開闊視野、增添量能。

目錄 Contents

• Chapter 1. 語意完整

Chapter 4. 鄰近原則

Chapter 5. 指涉明確

• Chapter 6. 結構保留

Chapter 7. 經濟原則

Chapter 8. 語用原則

● 附錄：

Chapter 1.
語意完整

語意完整是溝通的基本條件，但是，句式上的完整卻是中英不同。

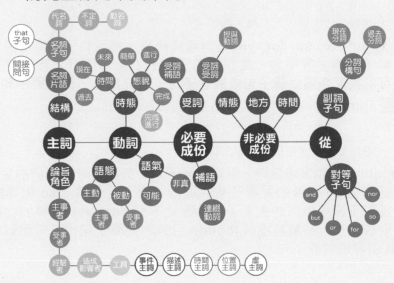

Q01. because 和 so 子句為什麼不可以構成一個句子？

 原來如此 **because 引導從屬子句，搭配不含連接詞的主要子句。**

◆ 陳述事件是句子的主要功能，完整陳述事件的句子可以獨立存在，稱為獨立子句。

例 1 Tom didn't attend the class.

湯姆沒去上課。

◆ 獨立子句連接副詞子句，增添事件的時間、空間、條件、原因、結果等訊息。從屬連接詞引導副詞子句，標示從屬位階及訊息性質。副詞子句不是事件主體，不可獨立存在。獨立子句搭配從屬子句，獨立子句便成了主要子句。

例 2 Tom didn't attend the class, because he was sick.

　　　　　　主要子句　　　　　　　　　　　　從屬子句

湯姆沒去上課，因為他生病了。

◆ and, but, or, so, for, yet 是對等連接詞，標示句子的對等位階及語意邏輯，引導對等子句，置於主要子句的右側。值得注意的是，**一個句子可以搭配多個從屬子句或對等子句，但只能有一個主要子句。**

例 3 Tom was sick, so he didn't attend the class.

　　　　主要子句　　　　　　　　　對等子句

湯姆生病了，所以他沒去上課。

◆ because 是從屬連接詞，引導從屬子句，搭配不帶連接詞的主要子句，因此不與 so 引導的對等子句共同形成句子。同樣，so 引導的對等子句搭配不帶連接詞的主要子句，因此不與 because 引導的從屬子句共同形成句子。從屬連接詞 though 引導的從屬子句也不搭配對等連接詞 but 引導的對等子句。

Q02. "I came, I saw, I conquered." 為什麼沒有連接詞 and ？

 原來如此 這是 tricolon，一些英語教學學者譯為「三節格律法」。接續且長度相仿的三個單詞、片語或子句形成三節格律，該修辭體例源自希臘文與拉丁文的古詩。

◆ 三節格律常使語意漸次增強，為求一鼓作氣，連接詞 and 予以省略。語用上，除了詩、小說、短篇故事，三節格律也常見於口述故事、電影、廣告或活動標語，以使訊息聚焦而令人印象深刻。

例 1 "I came, I saw, I conquered. "

我來之，我見之，我克之。

→ 語出凱薩大帝 Julius Caesar，原文是 "Veni, Vidi, Vici"，中譯 "我來之，我見之，我克之。"，中英文都是語氣遞增的押頭韻。

例 2 "of the people, by the people, for the people"

Lincoln, Gettysburg Address

民有、民治、民享

例 3 "Friends, Romans, countrymen, lend me your ears."

William Shakespeare

朋友們、羅馬人、同胞們，請聽我說。

例 4 "I require three things in a man: he must be handsome, ruthless and stupid."

Dorothy Parker

我要求男人三件事：他必須是英俊、無情和愚蠢。

例 5 Every gun that is made, every warship launched, every rocket fired signifies. It is spending the sweat of its laborers, the genius of its scientists, the hopes of its children.

Dwight Eisenhower

每一把製造出來的槍，每艘下水的戰艦，每一枚發射的火箭都很重要。它正消耗著勞工的汗水，科學家的天賦，以及孩子們的希望。

例 6 With malice toward none, with charity for all, with firmness in the right as God gives us to see the right,...

Abraham Lincoln

不對人心懷惡意，對所有人寬厚，神讓我們看見正確的一邊，我們就堅信那是正確的一邊……

例 7 And when the night grows dark, when injustice weighs heavy on our hearts, when our best-laid plans seem beyond our reach, let us think of Madiba and the words that brought him comfort within the four walls of his cell.

Barack Obama

當夜晚變得黑暗，當不公不義在我們的心裡出頭，當我們精心策畫的計畫超越我們所能達到的，讓我們想想曼德拉，以及他在監禁時帶給他安慰的話語。

Q03. 為什麼"The man whom I talked to just now is my colleague."的形容詞子句不可以縮減為分詞片語？

原來如此 形容詞子句的主詞是名詞，新訊息，不可省略，因此，不可縮減為分詞片語。

◆ 依照經濟原則，不會造成結構混淆或語意不清，子句結構的修飾語可以縮減為片語，因此，形容詞子句可縮減為介係詞或分詞片語。

例 1 The professor who is from London is an expert on viruses.

→ **縮減：The professor from London is an expert on viruses.**

來自倫敦的那位教授是一名病菌專家。

例 2 The lady who said hello to me is my niece.

→ **縮減：The lady saying hello to me is my niece.**

向我打招呼的那名女子是我姪女。

◆ 例 1、例 2 的形容詞子句主詞是關係代名詞，指涉先行詞，屬於舊訊息，可以省略。但是，省略之後，形容詞子句違反句子主詞不可缺項的原則，因此縮減為片語。例 1 的形容詞子句的"is"是聯繫動詞，無詞彙意義，應予省略；例 2 的形容詞子句的限定動詞"said"是持續動作，降為非限定動詞"saying"。

◆ 例 3 的形容詞子句主詞是"I"，新訊息，不可省略，因此形容詞子句不可縮減為分詞片語，僅能省略表示舊訊息的受格關係代名詞：

例 3 The man whom I talked to just now is my colleague.

剛才跟我談話的男子是我的同事。

→ **省略受格關係代名詞：**

The man I talked to just now is my colleague.

◆ 值得注意的是，即使主詞是關係代名詞，形容詞子句縮減為分詞片語仍有一些限制，例如現在分詞表示持續，不可以現在分詞呈現非持續的動作，也就是說，形容詞子句的動詞是非持續性質時，不可縮減為分詞片語。

例4 The man who arrived in Mengaluru from Dubai Sunday night was hospitalised for suspected coronavirus.

誤 The man arriving in Mengaluru from Dubai Sunday night was hospitalized for suspected coronavirus.

周日夜晚從杜拜抵達班加羅爾的男子因疑似感染冠狀病毒而被送進醫院。

◆ 分詞片語與主要子句的動作同時或接連發生，形容詞子句所述事件若是較早發生，不可縮減為分詞片語。

例5 He voiced his appreciation to those who had helped him.

誤 He voiced his appreciation to those having helped him.

他對那些幫助過他的人表達感謝。

◆ 以例 6 而言，形容詞子句若要縮減，應將單詞過去分詞置於名詞左側，前位修飾的詞序，如例 7。

例6 The car which was stolen has been discovered by police.

遭竊的汽車已被警方發現。

例7 The stolen car has been discovered by police.

Q04. "I bet you a steak that the school team will win the semifinal."是什麼句型？

 bet: _____ NP NP S，動詞加接三個受詞的句型。

◆ 句子陳述事件，動詞是事件的核心，語意展開並投射出主詞、受詞、補語等必要成分。句子是動詞語意的鋪陳，了解動詞在句中的語意便能預測、決定句子的必要成分，例如：

例 1 My boss usually goes to the races and bets heavily.

　　我老闆經常去賽馬會，而且都下重注。

　　→ bet 僅表示下注，不加接受詞，必要成分只有主詞，bet 是一元動詞（one-place verb）。

例 2 I bet that the meeting will be cancelled again.

　　我打賭這場會議將再一次取消。

　　→ bet 表示打賭什麼事情，加接名詞子句作為受詞，必要成分是主詞及一個受詞，bet 是二元動詞（two-place verb）。

例 3 I bet you that the French team would win the World Cup finally.

　　我跟你賭法國隊最後會贏得世界杯。

　　→ bet 表示跟誰賭什麼事情，打賭的對象與內容都是受詞，必要成分是主詞及二個受詞，bet 是三元動詞（three-place verb）。

例 4 I bet you a steak that the school team will win the semifinal.

　　我跟你賭一客牛排，校隊會贏得準決賽。

　　→ 賭的人、跟誰賭、賭資、賭的事情都是必要成分，必要成分是主詞及三個受詞，這時 bet 是四元動詞（four-place verb）。

◆ 看似複雜，但就是將 bet 的語意表達完整罷了。sell 也有類似的陣仗，例如：

例 5 I sold Tom my used camera for 20,000 dollars.

　　我把我的二手相機以 20,000 元賣給湯姆。

　　→ I 是主詞，Tom 是間接受詞，my used camera 是直接受詞，for 20,000 dollars 是補語，sell 也是四元動詞（four-place verb）。

◆ 五大句型就是五種動詞必要成分的類型，學習上，只要了解動詞的語意，主詞、受詞、補語等必要成分便呼之欲出，句型也就因應而生。因此，與其忽略動詞語意而背誦句型，不如逆向操作，從動詞語意著手，推測必要成分，順利輸出正確的句式。事實上，有些語法學家主張副詞若是語意上的必要成分，應該也是一種句型。

例 6 Your seat is over there.

你的座位在那裡。

例 7 The Government's Emergency Committee for COVID-19 Prevention meets every two days.

政府的新冠病毒防治緊急委員會成員每兩天召開會議。

→ 例 6 及例 7 的副詞都是語意必要成分，S-V-A 句型。

例 8 She set a vase of flowers on the table.

她把插了花的花瓶放在桌上。

例 9 The waiter laid the tray down on the table.

那名服務生把托盤放在桌子上。

→ 語意上，受詞位置的副詞是動詞的必要成分，屬於 S-V-O-A 句型。

Q05. "The chef is tasting the soup." 的 taste 是連綴動詞嗎?

原來
如此 不是,**taste** 是及物動詞,意思是「嚐一嚐」。

◆ 動詞語意決定主詞、受詞、補語等句子的必要成分,呈現不同的句式,這是語意主導句式,句式呈現語意的英語特性,例如 give 的幾種必要成分的類型都是呼應不同的語意:

例 1 The woman is eager to give freely to those who are in hardship.

那位婦人熱切地慷慨捐贈給困境中的人。

→ give 的意思是捐贈,不及物性質,不需受詞。

例 2 The couple gave a party at a beach restaurant last Friday.

那對夫婦上周五在海灘餐廳舉行一場派對。

→ give 的意思是舉行,搭配活動做為受詞。

例 3 He gave peace to the troubled and he gave power to the weak.

Siftings Herald

他把和平給了遭受磨難的人,能力給了軟弱的人。

→ give 的意思是給予,搭配二個受詞。

◆ 以 taste 而言,不同的語意呈現不同的句式,例如:

例 4 The steak tastes like rubber.

這牛排嚐起來像橡膠。

→ taste 的意思是嚐起來,連綴動詞,搭配補語以說明人對描述主詞 (Described Subject) steak 的感知反應,反應立即完成,不以進行式呈現。

例 5 The chef is tasting the soup.

主廚正嚐著這道湯。

→ taste 的意思是嚐著、嚐一嚐,主詞是經驗者,意志掌控動作的開始、停止,若是持續進行則搭配進行式。

◆ 一些狀態的改變是持續進行,這時連綴動詞搭配進行式,例如:

例 6 The earth is becoming warmer and warmer.

地球變得越來越熱。

例 7 The leaves are turning yellow.

這些葉子逐漸轉黃。

例 8 The weather is getting cold.

天氣漸漸變冷。

Q06. 句子 "I am fond of drawing." 中的介係詞片語 "of drawing" 為什麼是必要成分？

原來如此 補述用法的 **fond** 表示喜愛，交代喜愛的內容才能使語意完整。

◆ 形容詞 fond 置於修飾的名詞後面（補述用法），意思是「喜愛」，交代喜愛的內容，fond 的語意才是完整，如同動詞 like 加接受詞一樣，交代喜歡什麼，語意才算完整。

◆ fond 是形容詞，不加接名詞片語當作受詞，而是以介係詞 of 引介喜愛的內容，of 無特定語意。of 介係詞片語是 fond 的必要成分，補語的角色，二者形成 fond 為中心詞的形容詞片語，例如：

例1 My niece is fond of rock music.
    我的姪女喜愛搖滾音樂。

例2 Mr. Lin is fond of pointing out my mistakes.
    林先生喜歡指出我的錯誤。

◆ fond 置於修飾的名詞前面時，不表示喜歡的，因為「喜歡的」不是人或事物的特質，無法描述名詞。fond 前位修飾名詞，意思是 "happy" 或 "loving" ，例如：

例3 These pictures reminded me of fond memories of my childhood.
    這些照片讓我想起我童年的快樂時光。

Q07. 為什麼過去式動詞要加 -ed？

 原來如此 字尾綴詞 **–ed** 標記事件的時間在過去。

◆ 句子陳述事件，動詞語意投射的主詞、受詞、補語等必要成分必須完整，尤其主詞位置不可留空。此外，句子交代所述事件的時間，這是溝通的重要訊息。動作是事件的核心，時間標記在動詞，標記時間的動詞是時態動詞，時態動詞限定主詞的人稱及數目，又稱為限定動詞。標記時間的方式是動詞黏接屈折詞綴 **-s**、**-ed**，例如以下句子的 work、works 都是時態動詞：

例1 They work every day.

　　他們每天工作。（第三人稱，複數）

例2 He works three days a week.

　　他一週工作三天。（第三人稱，單數）

◆ 動作若是發生在過去，動詞黏接屈折詞綴 **-ed**，形成過去簡單式，例如：

例3 Tom walked to school this morning.

　　湯姆今天早上走路去上學。

例4 They played basketball after school today.

　　他們今天放學後打籃球。

◆ 不是黏接 **-ed** 的過去式動詞是不規則過去式動詞，與動詞原形同源，拼字、唸音相似。不規則過去式動詞是歷史的遺跡，單音節或是雙音節，例如單音節的 put、put，run、ran，do、did，雙音節的 begin、began，become、became，forget、forgot 等。

◆ 英文有八個屈折詞綴，黏接於名詞、動詞、形容詞、副詞等實詞。

單字	屈折詞綴	文法功用	溝通意涵
名詞	s	複數名詞	人、物是複數
	`s	所有格	所有者
動詞	s	現在簡單式	目前存在的事實或仍重複的動作
	ed	過去簡單式	過去發生的動作或存在的狀態
	ing	動名詞 / 現在分詞	存在、持續、進行、主動
	en	過去分詞	完成、被動
形容詞 副詞	er	比較級	形容詞修飾對象的程度較高
	est	最高級	形容詞修飾對象的程度最高

Q08. 為什麼比較級形容詞要加 -er，最高級要加 -est ？

原來如此 形容詞黏接字尾 **-er**，**-est**，標記比較或最高級以使訊息明確。

◆ 英文有一種標記的模式，就是一般的、常用的溝通訊息的語詞不須標記，就是無標—unmarked；若是特殊的、罕用的語詞則須標記，就是有標—marked。無標與有標宛如生物學中的隱性、顯性，有助於描述訊息的屬性與特徵。

陽性與陰性的名詞，陽性通常無標，陰性則是有標一字尾 ess，princess、lioness、tigress 等都是標記陰性的名詞。woman 由 wife 及 man 二詞素構成，標記女人是為人妻的人類，但是 man 卻不標記為人夫的人類。但是，相較於寡婦 widow，鰥夫 widower 卻以 er 標記。

以形容詞而言，未涉及程度差別時是無標，否則就是有標，例如：

例 1 Tom is tall.

　　湯姆是高的。

例 2 Tom is as tall as Mark.

　　湯姆如同馬克一樣高。

例 3 Tom is taller than Jack.

　　湯姆較傑克高。

　　→ er 標記修飾對象的形容詞程度較高，搭配 than。

例 4 Tom is the taller of the two.

　　湯姆是二者中較高的。

　　→ 主詞是二者中形容詞程度較高者，形容詞黏接 er 作為標記，the 限定主詞是一特定對象。

例 5 Tom's smartphone is less expensive than mine.

　　湯姆的手機不比我的手機昂貴。

　　→ less 具有比較意涵，形容詞不重複標記。另外，less 搭配多音節形容詞，標記的字形份量小於形容詞。

例 6 Tom is the tallest in the class.

　　湯姆是班上最高的。

　　→ est 標記修飾對象的形容詞程度最高，the 標記團體中形容詞程度最高的特定對象。

◆ 一、二音節形容詞幾乎都黏接 er、est，多音節形容詞都是搭配 more、most，因為少音節字黏接 er、est，音節數相近，易於辨識，若是多音節字則不易辨識。多音節形容詞分別以語意相稱的 more、most 標記比較級與最高級，標記於前，清楚明確，例如：

cheaper

more expensive

◆ 至於 less，新聞英文中則常見 less 加接單音節形容詞的單字，例如：

例 7 This 10.5%-yielder has a 5.2% discount to NAV, making it less cheap than the other CEFs I've mentioned.

（Forbes, 2018/7/1）

這個 10.5% 的收益工具對淨資產值有 5.2% 的折扣，這使其比我提過的其他 CEF 基金划算得多。

例 8 Fall and spring are less cheap but still better than summer when fares are highest.

（USA Today, 2017/08/15）

秋季及春季較不便宜，但仍較費用最高的夏季好。

◆ 值得一提的是，表示修飾對象的不同特質之間的比較時，搭配 more，例如：

例 9 Tom is more diligent than intelligent.

與其說湯姆聰明，不如說他勤奮。

Q09. 為什麼助動詞 do、does、did 搭配的是原形動詞？

 句子所述事件的時間已標記在助動詞 do、does、 did ，動詞不須重複標記。

◆ 時間標記是英文句子的必要成分，方式是動詞黏接屈折綴詞 -s 或 -ed。

◆ 動詞若是搭配文法功能的助動詞 do，時間標記在 do，動詞不重複標示。

◆ 以現在簡單式或過去簡單式而言，助動詞 do 是解決否定、疑問或強調句型的最後方式，若是不加入 do，這些語意將無法呈現。Do 也可視為這些句型時態的棲身之處，就像標兵一樣，舉著時態的旗幟，隨著句型的變化而移動，例如否定句就佇立在 not 的前面，疑問句移防到塞外—句子的主詞前面，就是句子的外部，強調動作時便留駐在動詞前面，例如：

例 1 A couple of participants do not speak English.

二三位參與者不說英語。

例 2 The security guard did not witness the accident.

守衛沒有目睹那起意外。

例 3 Do you go to the dentist regularly?

你定期去看牙醫嗎？

例 4 Did you call the police?

你有報警嗎？

例 5 We do need some more information.

我們真的需要多一些訊息。

例 6 They did reject the proposal.

他們確實駁回該提案。

◆ 主詞若是第三人稱單數，do 必須黏接字尾綴詞 -es，以 does 另行標記，達到主詞與動詞在人稱及數目上的一致，例如：

例 7 The patient doesn't have dementia.

那名病患未罹患失智症。

例 8 Does your dog love to eat fruit?

你的狗狗喜愛吃水果嗎？

Q10. 為什麼 "The child can play the piano well." 的 play 是原形動詞？

原來如此 can 透露作說者對動作的評論，不是描述發生的動作，沒有對應的時間，不須標記時態。

◆ 情態助動詞表示作說者對於狀態或動作的評論，例如：

例 1 The child can play the piano well.

那孩子能夠彈出一手好琴。

→ 作說者評論孩子彈鋼琴的能力。

例 2 The consultant should attend the review meeting.

顧問應該出席這場檢討會議。

→ 作說者認為顧問出席檢討會議是義務。

例 3 We must get someone to fix that faucet.

我們必須找個人來修理水龍頭。

→ 作說者—we 認為找人來修理水龍頭是必須的。

例 4 One must not drink and drive.

任何人都不許酒駕。

→ 作說者評論酒駕是禁止的行為。

例 5 Jessie will give me a lift to the station this afternoon.

潔西今天下午要順道送我到車站。

→ 說話者說明潔西將進行動作，而動作尚未發生。

◆ 搭配情態助動詞的動作是一個談論的話題，不是描述存在的動作，沒有對應的時間軸，無法標記時態，而且在時態的運作中，動詞沒有取得時態標記，因此保留動詞原形。那麼，句子的時態標記在哪裡呢？就在情態助動詞，例如：

例 6 The guest asked if the computer could access the Internet.

該名房客詢問這台電腦能否上網。

→ could 標記詢問的時間在過去。

例 7 Tom said he would visit the client tomorrow.

湯姆說他明天要去拜訪那名客戶。

→ would 標記是過去要進行的動作。

◆ 例 2 中，should 雖是過去式，但表示的是「現在的義務或責任」，與過去時間無關。若要針對過去的事件提出評論，標記的形式是「should have 過去分詞」，should 標示過去時間，have 是助動詞，過去分詞則是主動詞，說明動作的內容，例如：

例 8 The consultant should have attended the review meeting yesterday.

昨天顧問原本應該出席這場檢討會。

◆ 情態助動詞搭配完成式動作都是指涉過去的時間軸，例如：

例 9 When you got lost in the forest, you must have been very frightened.

你在樹林走丟時，一定很驚恐吧。

→ 「must have 過去分詞」表示推測過去的狀況。

例 10 The athlete could have won the race, but she didn't try hard enough.

該名運動員能夠贏得比賽，但她不夠努力。

例 11 I could have stayed up late last night, but I decided to go to bed early.

昨夜我可能得熬夜到很晚，但我決定早早就寢。

例 12 Tom couldn't have arrived any earlier because there was a terrible traffic jam.

湯姆不可能提早到達，因為塞車嚴重。

→ 「could have 過去分詞」表示過去有能力做到，但未做到，如例 10，或是過去可能發生，如例 11，否定式則表示過去不可能做到，即使已嘗試去做，如例 12。

◆ 「might have 過去分詞」表示臆測過去的狀況，例如：

例 13 Jack was late. He might have forgotten that we were meeting this afternoon.

傑克遲到，他可能忘了我們今天下午要碰面。

Q11. 現在完成式與現在完成進行式有什麼差別？

 原來如此 現在完成式表示直到說話當下已完成或經驗，現在完成進行式強調仍存在或將持續。

◆ 完成式描述直到參考時間已完成的動作或經驗，參考時間若是説話當下，就是現在完成式，動詞是「have 過去分詞」，have 標記時間，限定動詞，但無語意，過去分詞是主要動詞，有語意：

have　　過去分詞
↓　　　　↓
限定動詞　　主動詞

(1) 表示與現在有關且完成的動作：

例 1 I can't go swimming because I have broken my arm.
我不能去游泳，因為我手臂斷掉。

比較：

例 2 We know that Confucius travelled to a lot of countries.
我們都知道孔子周遊列國。
→ **過去的事實**

誤 We know that Confucius has travelled to a lot of countries.
→ **與現在無關，不用現在完成式。**

例 3 Have you done all the chores?
你雜務都做好了嗎？

例 4 The well-known reporter has died.
= The well-known reporter died.
那位知名記者已死亡。
→ 尤其是新聞報導，瞬間動作 die 若是最近的事件，搭配現在完成式，等同於過去式。

(2) 表示截至目前的經驗或重複發生：

例 5 I have never seen an armadillo.
我從未見過犰狳。

例 6 Hank has been to London twice.
漢克去過倫敦二次。

例 7 We've sometimes thought of moving to Canada.

我們偶爾會想要搬去加拿大。

(3) 表示至目前已持續一段時間：

例 8 The foreigner has lived in Hualien for two years.

那名外國人在花蓮住了二年。

例 9 I've known the lawyer for years.

我認識那名律師好幾年了。

◆ 現在完成進行式表示直到説話時已持續一段時間，而且仍然存在或持續的動作，強調持續或未間斷，動詞是「have been 現在分詞」，have 是限定動詞，been 是助動詞，二者都無語意，現在分詞是主要動詞，有語意：

have	been	現在分詞
↓	↓	↓
限定動詞	助動詞	主動詞

(1) 說話時仍然存在：

例 10 The price of oil has been rising.

油價一直上揚。

例 11 Gina has been working in the company since she got married.

吉娜婚後就一直在公司工作。

(2) 強調動作將持續：

例 12 The government has been making pension reforms.

政府持續進行年金改革。

例 13 The President has been attacking the media.

總統持續攻擊媒體。

◆ 進行式通常用於描述暫時的動作或狀態，持續較久的動作或狀態則多搭配現在完成式，例如：

例 12 My father hasn't been working very well recently.

我父親最近工作不順遂。

例 13 He hasn't worked for years.

他幾年沒工作了。

Q12. "We had done the most difficult part." 正確嗎？

原來 如此 不，過去完成式必須伴隨過去時間參考點，不可獨立存在。

◆ 英文描述一個動作，除了標示發生時間是過去、現在或未來，還要說明動作的樣貌。基本上，簡單表示事實，進行表示持續，完成表示經驗，完成進行表示仍要持續，因此英文共有 12 個時態，例如：

例1 過去簡單式

Tom did the work two days ago.

湯姆二天前完成這工作。

例2 過去進行式

Tom was doing the work then.

那時候湯姆正在做這工作。

例3 過去完成式

Tom had done the work for two hours when I called him.

我打電話給湯姆時，這工作他已做了二小時。

例4 過去完成進行式

Tom had been doing the work for two hours when I called him.

我打電話給湯姆時，這工作他一直做了二小時。

例5 現在簡單式

Tom does the work every morning.

湯姆每天早上做工作。

例6 現在進行式

Tom is doing the work now.

湯姆現在正做這工作。

例7 現在完成式

Tom has done the work already.

湯姆已經完成這工作。

例8 現在完成進行式

Tom has been doing the work for two hours.

這工作湯姆已經做了二小時。

例 9 未來簡單式

Tom will do the work tomorrow.

湯姆明天將做這工作。

例 10 未來進行式

Tom will be doing the work tomorrow morning.

明天早上湯姆會在這做工作。

例 11 未來完成式

Tom will have done the work for two hours by the shift time.

交班之前，這工作湯姆將做了二小時。

例 12 未來完成進行式

Tom will have been doing the work for two hours by the shift time.

交班之前，這工作湯姆將持續做了二小時。

◆ 以過去完成式而言，英文沒有表示過去某時之前的時態，若要描述過去二動作的先後順序，我們以過去完成式表示過去較早發生的動作，過去式表示較晚發生的動作，請看以下圖示：

◆ 若是沒有過去時間參考點，直接以說話當下，即現在時間的觀點看動作，過去完成式便成了現在完成式，例如圖示：

◆ 以例 13 而言，句子沒有過去時間參考點，動作對應說話時間，搭配現在完成式，而例 14、15 有過去時間參考點，搭配過去完成式。

例 13 We have done the most difficult part.

我們完成了最困難的部分。

例 14 We had done the most difficult part that everyone told us we couldn't do.

我們完成了最困難的部分，就是每個人都告訴我們那是我們無法做到的。

→ 以事件表示過去時間參考點

例 15 We had done the most difficult part by the end of last quarter.

上一季結束之前，我們完成了最困難的部分。

→ 以具體時間表示過去時間參考點

Q13. "since two months ago."這片語對嗎？

 原來如此 不對，介係詞 since 不可加接 ago 副詞片語。

◆ ago 是副詞詞性，置於時間語詞右側，形成時間副詞，指涉明確的過去時間，搭配過去式，不搭配現在完成式，例如：

例1 I moved to this town two months ago.

　　two months age = two months before now

　　我二個月前搬到這個小鎮。

例2 The customer checked in just a little while ago.

　　那名顧客才在一會兒前報到。

例3 A : Where's Cindy?

　　B : She was doing the laundry outside ten minutes ago.

　　A：辛蒂在哪裡？

　　B：她十分鐘前在外面洗衣服。

◆ before 置於時間語詞右側，指涉過去參考點之前的時間，搭配過去完成式，例如：

例4 I met Mr. Lin two months ago. I had worked with him three years before.

　　我二個月前遇到林先生。三年前我與他共事過。

three years before	two months ago	now

◆ since 可以表示 "from a particular time in the past until a later time, or until now" (*Cambridge Dictionary*)，since 若是連接詞，引導的句子搭配過去簡單式或現在完成式，若是介係詞，加接表示明確過去時間的名詞片語。另外，since 的主子句子搭配現在完成式，例如：

例5 John's been back to the office a few times since he retired.

例6 John's been back to the office a few times since he has retired.

　　約翰自從退休後幾次回到辦公室。

◆ "since two months ago" 為什麼不對？

以過去時間點作為 since 的起點，當然可以，例如 since last week、since last Friday。

◆ "since two months ago" 不對的原因是，since 是介係詞，two months ago 是副詞性質，介係詞不可加接副詞性質的語詞。因此，若將 "two months ago" 改為對應的日期，以名詞片語作為 since 的受詞就對了，例如 since March。

Q14. "There is a book on the table."和"A book is on the table."一樣意思嗎？

 不一樣，前者是引介句，必有下文，後者定格情景。

◆ There is"是引介句，引介下文，猶如開場白，啟動故事情節，常見於童話故事，例如：

例 1 Once upon a time, there were three little pigs. One pig built a house of straw while the second pig built a house with sticks.

很久以前，有三隻小豬。一隻用麥稈蓋房子，而第二隻用枝條蓋房子。

◆ 引介句揭開場景，看官與舞台角色初次見面，主詞是不特定對象，搭配不定冠詞，例如：

例 2 There is a book on the table.

桌上有一本書。

◆ 例 3 定格情景，前無上文，後無下文，作說者明確指出「一本書在桌上」，a 雖是不定冠詞，但表示特定，意思是數量的一本。

例 3 A book is on the table.

一本書在桌上。

例 4 的主詞 "a book of yours" 是不特定，而例 5 的主詞是特定：

例 4 There is a book of yours on the table.

桌上有一本你的書。

例 5 One of your books is on the table.

你的一本書在桌上。

◆ 雖然只是一張桌子、一本書，但是，場景、角色及劇本都不同，若硬說這齣等於那齣，這就是外行人看熱鬧了！

Q15. "There are no books on the table."等於 "There are not any books on the table." 嗎？

原來如此 相較於 "not …any…"，"no" 的否定意味較強烈。

◆ not 是副詞，置於片語或子句前面，例如：

例 1 Wheat is not a vegetable.

小麥不是一種蔬菜。

→ not 置於名詞片語 "a vegetable" 前面。

例 2 It is not because they are refugees.

不是因為他們是難民。

→ not 置於 because 引導的副詞子句前面。

◆ no、any 都是數量詞，no 表示否定，any 表示不確定，都是限定詞，置於名詞前面，例如：

例 3 There are no books on the table.

桌子上沒有書。

→ no 與 books 構成名詞片語。

例 4 There are not any books on the table.

桌子上沒有任何書。

→ any 與 books 構成名詞片語。

◆ 肯定句式表達否定語意，語氣直接而明確，因此，相較於 "not…any"，"no" 的否定語氣較為直接而強烈，句重音也常落在 no，例如：

例 5-1 My niece is not very often eloquent.

我姪女不常滔滔不絕地說話。

例 5-2 My niece is usually shy.

我姪女經常害羞。

→ usually shy 的語氣較 not very often eloquent 直接。

例 6-1 Tom didn't pay any attention to what his coach was saying.

湯姆一點也不注意他的教練在說什麼。

例 6-2 Tom paid no attention to what his coach was saying.

湯姆不注意他的教練在說什麼。

例 6-3 Tom ignored what his coach was saying.

湯姆對他的教練說的話充耳不聞 。

例 7-1 Jack didn't remember to turn off the lights.

傑克不記得要關燈。

例 7-2 Jack forgot to turn off the lights.

傑克忘記要關燈。

例 8-1 I think the pattern is unsuitable.

我認為這圖案不合適。

→ "I think" 是肯定語氣，較確定。

例 8-2 I don't think the pattern is suitable.

我不認為這圖案合適。

→ "I don't think" 是否定語氣，較不確定。

◆ 就著修辭而言，先否定而後肯定則力道十足，例如莎翁的名言：

例 9 Not that I loved Caesar less, but that I loved Rome more.

William Shakespeare
Julius Caesar

不是我不愛凱薩，但我更愛羅馬。

◆ 值得注意的是，名詞若無程度之分，是就是，不是就不是，我們只用 "not a"，"a" 可視為類別，如例 10；若可分程度，可用 "no" 或 "not a"，如例 11：

例 10 A potato is not a fruit.

馬鈴薯不是一種水果。

例 11 It is no / not a surprise that children dislike wearing braces.

孩子不喜歡戴牙套一點也不驚訝。

Q16. "It seems that Tom is not the right person for this job."是名詞子句移位的結果嗎？

原來如此 不是，語意上，seem 不需主詞，名詞子句不移至主詞位置，不能還原就不是移位。

◆ 溝通主題必須明確，句子主詞位置不可留空，即使語意上不需要主詞，也必須填補，這是英文句子結構的要求，也是 there is／are 句型的原因。以 seem 來說，語意上，seem 不需主詞，直接加接名詞子句，表達似乎的事件，但這違反句子主詞位置不可留空的規定，因此以 it 填補，例如：

例1 It seems that Tom is not the right person for this job.
湯姆似乎不是這工作的適合人選。

◆ seem 也可以引介非限定子句，就是不定詞構成的事件，例如：

例2 --- seems Jack to be the right person for this job.

→ Jack 是描述對象，the right person for this job 是針對 Jack 的描述，符合句子的邏輯─句子必須包含描述對象及描述內容，但動詞是不定詞，也就是不標記時態的非限定動詞，因此 "Jack to be the right person for this job" 是非限定子句。

◆ 限定動詞才能賦予前面名詞主格格位，使其扮演主詞角色，因此，置於不定詞前面的 Jack 未取得主格格位而得以移至 seem 前面，化身為限定子句的主詞，例如：

例3 Jack seems to be the right person for this job.

◆ 相對的，例 1 不可改寫為例 4 的寫法，因為 Tom 置於限定動詞 is 前面，限定動詞賦予主格格位以扮演主詞角色，身份明確，不可移出句子。

誤 Tom seems that he is not the right person for this job.

◆ seem 引介的非限定子句可以縮減為名詞或形容詞片語，例如：

例4 Jack seems the right person for this job.

例5 Jack seems competent.
傑克似乎很有才幹。

◆ appear 的句式結構與 seem 類似，但是，seem 描述主觀的認知或感想，appear 描述客觀的事實或印象，用法比較正式，例如：

例 6 It appears that Mark might be right.

看來馬克或許是對的。

例 7 The manager does not appear to be at the briefing room now.

現在經理似乎不在簡報室。

例 8 The CEO appears unaffected by the report.

執行長顯出一副不受報告影響的樣子。

Chapter 2.
標示主從

語意或結構有必要成分及非必要成分,這是主從之分。主從之分可擴大為階層之別,標記主從,辨識階層差異,對於語意、解題、寫作皆相當有益。

Q01. "We paid her in cash so that she left contented."的 so that 子句表示目的嗎？

原來如此 不，**so that** 子句表示結果。

◆ "so that" 引導目的副詞子句，說明因前述動作而產生的想望，搭配 can、could、 will、 would 等情態助動詞，例如：

例 1 I took medicine so that I would get well soon.

= I took medicine so as to get well soon.

我服藥，以便快點復原。

例 2 Stand with us so that we can overcome these hurdles we are facing.

Cape Times

與我們站在一起，我們便能克服我們所面對的這些難題。

例 3 Some supplies of water must be treated so that they can be used.

= Some supplies of water must be treated so as to be used.

A Dictionary of Answers to Common Questions in English

一些水源必須處理，這樣才能使用。

◆ 非正式用法中，**so that** 的 **that** 可省略，例如：

例 4 Switch the flashlight on so we can see what it is.

打開手電筒，我們就看得到那是什麼。

◆ 除了想望，**so that** 也表示結果，結果是事實，不是想望，不搭配情態助動詞，例如：

例 5 It has been raining heavily so that the area flooded.

豪雨一直狂炸，結果整個地區都淹水了。

例 6 We paid her in cash so that she left contented.

我們付她現金，所以她滿意地離去。

◆ 比較例 6，表示想望，搭配情態助動詞：

例 7 We paid her in cash, so (that) she would leave contented.

我們付她現金，好讓她滿意地離去。

◆ **so that** 引導的是副詞句子，但能置於主要子句右側。同樣，**so** 是對等連接詞，引導的子句只置於句子右側，例如：

例 8 Jack missed the bus so he will take a taxi to the gallery.

傑克錯過公車，所以他要搭計程車去美術館。

◆ "so…that" 強調因 so 而產生令人驚奇的結果，例如：

例 9 The speaker spoke so fast that the interpreter could hardly follow.

講者講太快，口譯員幾乎跟不上。

例 10 Tom studied so hard that he easily passed the test.

湯姆非常用功，輕鬆通過考試。

Q02. "Look at the way how those monkeys clean each other." 這句子對嗎？

原來如此 不對。the way 就是 how 的意思，二者不重複出現。

◆ the way 是名詞片語，充當關係副詞，連接說明方式、樣貌的子句，與 how 的語意及功用相同，因此 the way 不與 how 連用。

例1 Look at the way those monkeys clean each other.

Look at how those monkeys clean each other.

看看這些猴子互相清理身體的樣子。

例2 This is the way I quickly memorized a large number of vocabulary words.

This is how I quickly memorized a large number of vocabulary words.

這是我記憶大量單字的方式。

◆ the way 搭配 that 而形成 the way that，用法與 the way 一致。

以英美人士的用法而言，the way 遠較 how 普遍，但是為了結構及語意更清楚，他們傾向以更簡單的句式表達，例如：

例3 Look at those moneys' way of cleaning each other.

看看這些猴子為彼此清潔的方式。

◆ 強調 the way 引介一段說明或目的時，the way 搭配 in which，the way 是名詞片語，in which 引導的是形容詞子句，關係代名詞 which 指涉 the way，而介係詞 in 似乎將焦點置於 which，透露形容詞子句的訊息份量。the way in which 聽起來難免生硬，屬於正式語體，不用於一般的溝通，例如：

例4 We should look at the way in which people are on a pathway to citizenship.

我們應該正視民眾取得公民資格的途徑是如何。

Peter Dutton

例5 The way in which international trade is being approached by the Trump administration simply cannot work.

正受川普政府操弄的國際貿易的手法完全不可行。

Edward Lane

◆ 值得一提的是，the way 提及比照意涵的子句時，不可代換為 how。

例6 Take apart the device on your own, the way the mechanic does.

自己拆開這器具，像技術員那樣作。

Q03. "The next time you want to borrow something, ask me first, please." 這句話正確嗎？

原來如此 正確。 "The next time" 是連接詞，引導時間副詞子句。

◆ 「結構、詞性、功用」是理解句中語詞的三個脈絡，例如 "to V" 結構是不定詞，具有名詞、形容詞、副詞等詞性，扮演這些詞性的角色。

例1 It was fun to go on the roller coaster.

坐雲霄飛車是好玩的。

→ "to go on the roller coaster" 是不定詞，名詞，主詞角色。

◆ next time 的中心詞是名詞，名詞片語，詞性是副詞或片語連接詞，也就是片語結構的連接詞。

以副詞而言， "next time" 不須搭配 the，例如：

例2 See you next time.

下次見。

例3 Next time, ask me first, please.

下次，麻煩先問我一下。

◆ 提及星期、月份、季節、年份或假日等未來時間，next 搭配相關時間名稱，但不搭配 the 或介係詞，因為所指的未來時間為唯一，不須限定：

例4 I have an appointment with the dentist next Wednesday morning.

我下周三早上跟牙醫師約診。

例5 We're going to take a trip to England next summer.

明年夏天我們將到英格蘭旅行。

例6 Next year will be our tenth wedding anniversary.

明年將是我們結婚十周年。

◆ 提及未來某一段時間，特定，搭配 the：

例7 I'll complete the project in the next few days. You can pay me then.

我將於往後幾天內完成這份計畫，那時候你可以付我錢。

例8 The CEO will stay at the headquarters for the next two weeks.

執行長將於往後二周待在總部。

◆ 指涉過去或未來時間，標記 the，但非正式用法中，過去時間常省略 the 以使訊息緊湊，例如：

例 9 The next day we headed north for the town.
　　第二天，我們往北前往那小鎮。

例 10 We're going to spend the first night in the island, and the next day we'll fly south to Manila.
　　我們將在這島上度過第一個晚上，然後第二天飛往馬尼拉。

◆ "next time" 引導副詞子句時，"the next time that" 的縮減，that 省略，the 也可省略，例如：

例 11 (The) next time (that) you want to borrow something, ask me first, please.
　　下次你要借東西，請先問我一下。

例 12 (The) next time (that) we meet the team, we will play even better.
　　下次遇見那支隊伍時，我們會打得更好。

◆ next time 若與從屬連接詞 when 共現將因累贅而貽誤。雖然部分英語母語人士認為 "next time when" 不 OK，若干媒體也常見 "next time when"，但是，當代字典都不見此一用法。語詞用法常有改變，但二從屬連接詞相鄰共現，明顯錯誤，例如：

例 13 Next time when you are in Paris, don't forget to visit this friendly store.

國中基測試題

下次你在巴黎時，別忘了造訪這家友善的商店。

Q04. "Get up now, or you will miss the school bus." 的 "Get up now" 是命令句嗎？

原來如此 不是，"Get up now" 是 if 條件句。

◆ 祈使句搭配 and 引導的對等子句表示肯定結果，搭配 or 引導的對等子句表示否定結果。

例1 Do not judge, and you will not be judged.
　　不要論斷人，這樣你就不會被論斷。

例2 Get up now, or you will miss the school bus.
　　馬上起床，否則你會錯過校車。

◆ 例 2 訊息焦點是對等子句傳達的結果，祈使句表示條件，語意等同於 if 子句，非典型的祈使句。例 1 及例 2 可分別改寫為例 3 及例 4：

例3 If you do not judge, you will not be judged.
　　如果你不論斷人，你就不會被論斷。

例4 If you don't get up now, you will miss the school bus.
　　如果你不馬上起床，你就會錯過校車。

◆ suppose 引導非典型的祈使句，同樣表示條件，意思是 "what would happen if"。

例5 Suppose if we miss the shuttle bus, what will we do then?
　　萬一我們錯過接駁公車，那我們要怎麼辦？

◆ 表示讓步的 "let alone" 及 "believe it or not"，原形動詞起首，同樣是非典型的祈使句。

例6 You couldn't trust her to look after your dog, let alone your baby.
　　你不能信任她來照顧你的狗狗，更別說你的嬰兒。

例7 Believe it or not, I will drop out of school this summer.
　　信不信由你，今年夏天我會休學。

Q05. "If you will invite me, I will join you." 這句話對嗎？

原來
如此 對的。**if** 子句表達主詞的意願時，搭配情態助動詞 **will**。

◆ if 引導的條件子句提及主詞的意願時，搭配情態助動詞 will，例如：

例1 If you will invite me, I will join you.

如果你願意邀請我，我就會加入你。

例2 If you will vote for me, I will work for you.

Gazette Newspapers

如果你們願意投票支持我，我就為你們打拚。

◆ 若是搭配 would，語氣較為婉轉，例如：

例3 If you would invite me, I will join you.

如果你有邀請我，我就會加入你。

◆ if 引導的子句也可表示結果，例如：

例4 Take a sedative, if it will help you to fall asleep.

服一顆鎮定劑，那有助於你的睡眠。

例5 Turn on the air-conditioner, if it will cool the room temperature.

打開空調，這樣室內溫度會變涼爽。

◆ will 也可表示堅持，常重讀，例如：

例6 If you will drink so much, it is not surprising you get drunken.

如果你要喝這麼多，酒醉一點也不意外。

◆ if 子句搭配現在簡單式表示條件，因為條件尚未成真，沒有對應的時間，因此搭配表示泛時的習慣式，也就是現在簡單式，而不是以現在式代替未來式。

Q06. "It was Columbus who discovered America in 1492." 的結構怎麼是這樣？

 強調語詞置於主要子句，非強調語詞置於從屬子句，語意與結構的主從層次明確。

◆ 分裂句是語意與結構相互搭配的標本，充分表現「語意主導句構，句構呈現語意」的句子特性，就是將一個句子分裂為主要子句與從屬子句，強調的語詞置於主要子句，其他語詞置於從屬子句，藉由結構達到強調訊息的目的，例如：

例 1 Columbus discovered America in 1492.

　　哥倫布於 1492 年發現美洲大陸。

　　→ 直接陳述事件，未強調任何語詞。

例 2 It was Columbus who discovered America in 1492.

　　　　主要子句　　　　　　　　從屬子句

　　1492 年發現美洲大陸的是哥倫布。

◆ 強調 Columbus，Columbus 置於主要子句，虛主詞 it 引介，達到聚焦效果，其他成份置於從屬子句，詞序不變。從屬子句提供強調語詞的訊息，但不是形容詞子句，強調語詞若是人，連接詞多用 who 或 whom，以示尊重。

　　強調其他訊息時，that 引導從屬子句，例如：

例 3 It was America that Columbus discovered in 1492.

　　哥倫布於 1492 年發現的是美洲大陸。

例 4 It was in 1492 that Columbus discovered America.

　　哥倫布是於 1492 年發現美洲大陸。

◆ 分裂句不強調標記時態的限定動詞，因為限定動詞若前移至主要子句，從屬子句將缺少限定動詞而違反句子必須包含限定動詞的原則。另外，限定動詞若前移至主要子句，便與 be 動詞連接，造成結構上的混淆。

誤 It was discovered that Columbus --- America in 1492.

Q07. "The Great Wall, which is famous all over the world, is located in the northern part of China." 與 "The Great Wall, located in the northern part of China, is famous all over the world." 二句子有什麼差別？

原來如此　前一句著重長城的位置，後一句著重長城聞名世界。

◆ 形意搭配是英文句式的一大特色，語詞的搭配、形式、位置都呈現句子的結構與語意一體兩面，相互輝映的鋪陳，例如：

例1 The assistant has sent a parcel to the client.

助理已將包裹寄給客戶。

→ to 搭配接收者

例2 The government has avoided making directly negative comments on the issue.

政府一直避免針對該議題直接提出負面評論。

→ avoid 搭配動名詞。

例3 Open the door.

把門打開。

→ 省略主詞，原形動詞置於句首，強調動作。

例4 It sounds as if you had completed everything then.

聽起來你那時候每件事都已完成了。

→ 動詞形式顯示過去事實。

例5 Never did he imagine he'd become a millionaire.

他未曾想像自己會成為百萬富翁。

→ 否定詞 never 移至句首表示強調。

例6 It was the young guy who found out the clue to the mystery.

是那名年輕人發現這謎團的線索。

→ 強調語詞置於主要子句。

◆ 例 6 是分裂句，強調訊息置於主要子句，其他訊息置於從屬子句，例 7、例 8 也是語詞的位置顯示訊息的份量：

例 7 The Great Wall of China, which is famous all over the world, is located in the northern part of China.

    舉世聞名的萬里長城位於中國北方。

    → 著重長城的位置

例 8 The Great Wall, located in the northern part of China, is famous all over the world."

    位於中國北方的萬里長城舉世聞名。

    → 著重長城聞名世界

◆ 語詞結構依序為單詞、片語、句子，基於經濟原則，除非必要，修飾語詞儘量以單詞或片語呈現，達到語詞結構與訊息份量相稱。例 9 的形容詞子句只提到 functional，訊息份量不足，搭配片語即可，而例 10 的修飾訊息繁重，搭配形容詞子句：

例 9 I ordered a camera that is functional.

    I ordered a functional camera.

    我訂一部功能不錯的照相機。

例 10 I ordered a camera that is particularly useful for mountain bikers.

    我訂一部對於山區單車騎士尤其好用的照相機。

例 11 The lid must fit in a perfect manner on the pot.

    蓋子必須與鍋子完全合身。

    → 片語 "in a perfect manner" 可縮減為單詞 "perfectly"：

    The lid must fit perfectly on the pot.

例 12 He is a student who comes from a low-income family.

    他是一位來自低收入家庭的學生。

    → 形容詞子句可改為介係詞片語：

    He is a student from a low-income family.

例 13 A short hike will be included, if the weather permits.

    若是天氣許可，會包括一段短途健行。

    → 副詞子句可縮減為保留主詞的獨立分詞構句：

    A short hike will be included, weather permitting.

◆ 片語或子句結構繁雜，學習不易，若是熟練，寫作時總想多加運用，以展現實力。但是，遣詞用字重在輕重有致，脈絡分明，字裡行間方能表達合宜。因此，語詞的調兵遣將端視語意走向而定，該輕則輕，該重則重，一廂情願乃是運筆大忌。

Q08 為什麼 "Mom made me help Tom do his work." 中，只有 made 標記時態？

原來如此 時態動詞與其發展出的動作或狀態視為一個事件，一個時態動詞即可。

◆ 句子陳述事件，除了說明主題及關於主題的敘述，還要標記時間，就是時態，例如：

例1 Tom finished his job two days ago.

湯姆二天前完成工作。

→ 主題是 Tom，"finished his job two days ago" 敘述 Tom，finished 標記過去時間。

◆ 時態動詞發展出多個相關的動作時，這些動作可視為與時態動詞同一事件，不須另行標記時態，只要以正確的形式呈現即可，例如：

例2 Mom made me help Tom do his work.

媽媽要我協助湯姆完成他的工作。

(1) Mom made me / help Tom do his work.

→ 媽媽要我進行一個動作

(2) me help Tom / do his work

→ 我幫忙湯姆做某事，made 使 help 呈現原形。

(3) Tom do his work

→ 湯姆完成他的工作，help 使 do 呈現原形。

◆ 這些動作的連動有如撞球一樣，球桿（made）打第一顆球（help），第一顆球撞擊第二顆球（do），而一、二球都是一個桿子打出來的。不論是球桿或球，都是一個撞球檯（事件）上的碰撞連動。

當然，有些文法學家認為不論是否標記時態，一個動作就是一個事件，因此例 1 是一個事件，例 2 是三個事件。這是另一種句子分析，有興趣探究的讀者，可參閱功能語法的相關論述。

Q09. 形容詞的順序要背嗎？

 原來如此 不要背，知曉名詞片語的結構，形容詞的順序不是問題。

◆ 形容詞修飾名詞，學習形容詞的順序，先要了解名詞片語的結構。
我們以名詞片語 "a cozy white wool sweater" 來說明名詞片語的四個成份。

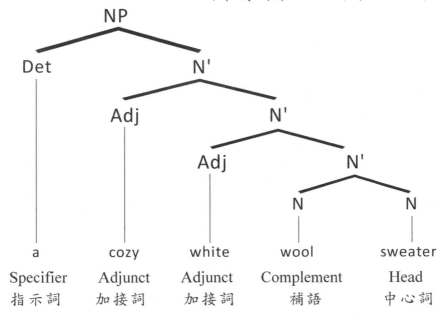

尚未構成片語–NP的部分以N'標記

(1) **中心詞（Head）── sweater**：名詞是名詞片語的中心詞，不可缺項，通常置於片語的最右側。

(2) **補語（Complement）── wool**：表示中心詞的身份、材料、性質、功用的語詞，與中心詞語意關係密切，位置相鄰，宛如姊妹關係。名詞片語的補語只有一個，但可缺項，例如：

例 1 computers 電腦

　　→ 補語缺項

例 2 an English teacher 一位英文老師

　　→ English 是補語，teacher 的身份。

例 3 leather jackets 皮革夾克

　　→ leather 是補語， jackets 的材料。

例 4 a compound restaurant 一家複合式餐廳

　　→ compound 是補語， restaurant 的性質。

例 5 a sleeping bag 一個睡袋

　　→ sleeping 是補語， bag 的功用。

(3) 加接詞（Adjunct）—cozy、white：中心詞的修飾語，形容詞性質，與中心詞宛如女兒關係。修飾語可以缺項，也可以數個連接，例如：

例 6 books 書

　　→ 名詞片語只有中心詞，補語及加接詞都缺項。

例 7 a picture book 一本繪本

　　→ 加接詞缺項，picture 是補語。

例 8 a tall baseball player 一位高個的棒球選手

　　→ tall 是加接詞，baseball 是補語。

例 9 a tall dark-skinned baseball player

　　一位高大且皮膚黝黑的棒球選手

　　→ tall 與 dark-skinned 都是加接詞。

例 10 a nice Australian English teacher

　　一位很棒的澳洲籍英文老師

　　→ nice 及 Australian 都是加接詞。

例 11 a student of law with a very rich academic experience

　　= a student who majors in law and who has a very rich academic experience

　　一位具有豐富學術經驗的法學學生。

　　→ of law 是補語，with a very rich academic experience 是加接詞。

◆ 相較於加接詞，補語與中心詞的語意關聯密切且位置相鄰，這是語意主導詞序。下列名詞片語的加接詞與補語的詞序有誤：

誤 a student with a very rich academic experience of law

誤 a book with blue cover on Linguistics

(4) 指示詞（Specifier）— a，指示詞標示名詞片語的起點，提供中心詞的指涉或數量的訊息，由限定詞扮演。中心詞若是複數或不可數，指示詞可省略，若是可數單數，指示詞必須出現，因為提及單數可數名詞時，必須表明所指為何，例如：

例 12 toxic gas 毒氣

　　→ 中心詞是不可數名詞，指示詞省略。

例 13 desks and chairs 桌子和椅子
→ 中心詞是複數名詞，指示詞可以省略。

誤 used computer
→ 中心詞是單數可數名詞，指示詞不可省略。

例 14 my new racing car 我的新跑車
→ 所有格是限定詞，名詞片語的指示詞。

例 15 these new members 這些新成員
→ these 是限定詞，名詞片語的指示詞。

例 16 those two bottles 這二個瓶子
→ 限定詞 those、two 都是名詞片語的指示詞。

例 17 the first two cards 前二張卡片
→ 限定詞 the、first、two 都是名詞片語的指示詞。

◆ 名詞片語的組成成份如下：

指示詞　修飾語　補語　中心詞

關於名詞片語的組成成分的位置，我們提出以下考量：

(1) 指示詞是名詞片語的標竿，置於最左側，不須記憶。

(2) 補語必須與中心詞相鄰，不須費神。

(3) 最後是作為加接詞的形容詞，順序可以從數目及語意來考量：

(3.1) 為避免訊息複雜，形容詞至多三個，若要增加，通常會予以分類而分布於不同句子，例如：

例 18 two expensive modern road bikes
二部高價的摩登公路腳踏車
→ expensive、modern 是形容詞

例 19 The Lin family is living in a new elegant and luxurious condominium.
林家住在一棟全新雅致又奢華的電梯華廈。
→ new、elegant、luxurious 都是形容詞，分為客觀事實及主觀認定，並將句子拆解如下：

例 20 The Lin family is living in a new condominium. It is elegant and luxurious.
林家住在一棟全新的電梯華廈，雅致又奢華。

例 21 Mom bought me an expensive striped light chic wool sweater.
媽媽買給我一件高價的斜紋輕便時尚羊毛衣。
→ expensive、striped、light、chic 都是形容詞，分類並以二句子呈現：

例 22 Mom bought me a light striped wool sweater. It was chic and expensive.

媽媽買給我一件輕便斜紋的時尚羊毛衣，時尚又昂貴。

(3.2) 二、三個形容詞同時出現時，主觀認定在前，客觀事實在後，而後銜接補語，逐漸呈現名詞的樣貌，例如：

例 23 a big red balloon 一粒大紅色氣球

誤 a red big balloon

→ 相較於大小，顏色的認定不會因人而異，客觀程度高。

例 24 a small diamond-shaped playground 一座小面積的菱形遊樂場

→ 形狀的客觀程度高，置於右側。

例 25 Taiwan is a beautiful tropical island.

台灣是一座美麗的熱帶島嶼。

→ beautiful 是主觀認定，順序在前。

例 26 a nice, young blonde lady 一位優雅又年輕的金髮女子

→ 客觀程度依序是 nice、young、blonde。

例 27 a famous British singer 一名知名的英國歌手

→ 國籍是客觀事實，接近中心詞。

Q10. "red brick" 與 "brick red" 有什麼差別？

 原來如此 red brick 表示一種 brick，顏色是 red；brick red 表示一種紅色，像 brick 的顏色。

◆ 英文字詞有一「右側起始 --Right-Hand-Head」構詞原則，就是數個字形成一個詞時，中心詞置於右側，修飾詞置於左側，整個詞從右而左展開，例如：

例1 an apple pie，a kind of pie made of apples

蘋果派

→ pie 是中心詞，apple 是修飾詞。

例2 a washing machine，a machine used for washing or cleaning laundry

洗衣機

→ machine 是中心詞，washing 是修飾詞。

例3 red brick

紅色磚頭

→ brick 是中心詞，red 是修飾詞。

例4 brick red

→ 磚紅色，red 是中心詞，brick 是修飾詞。

◆ 複合形容詞也符合 "Right-Hand-Head" 的構詞原則，字重音落於最右側的中心詞，例如：

例5 ten-year-old

十歲大的

例6 part-time

兼職的

例7 water-proof

防水的

◆ 複合形容詞若是包含動詞，動詞是中心詞，置於右側，以分詞形式呈現，左側是動詞的受詞、補語、副詞、工具等，例如：

例8 heart-warming

暖心的

→ heart 是 warm 的受詞。

例 9 sweet-smelling

聞起來芳香的

→ sweet 是 smell 的補語。

例 10 hand-made

手工的

→ hand 是 made 的工具，made by hand。

例 11 fast-growing

成長快速地

→ fast 是 grow 的副詞修飾語

例 12 above-mentioned

上述的

→ above 是 mention 的副詞修飾語

◆ 複合形容詞與修飾的名詞可重新分析為形容詞子句與先行詞的關係，修飾的名詞是先行詞，也就是形容詞子句的主詞，而複合形容詞是形容詞子句的動詞部分。

複合形容詞 ＋ 名詞

=> 先行詞　　 ＋ 形容詞子句

例 13 a heart-warming story

a story which warms people's heart

暖心的故事

→ story 是先行詞，warming 是形容詞子句的動詞，heart 是受詞。

例 14 a sweet-smelling rose

a rose which smells sweet

聞起來芳香的玫瑰

→ rose 是先行詞，smell 是形容詞子句的動詞， sweet 是補語。

例 15 a fast-growing development

a development which grows fast

成長快速的住宅區

→ development 是先行詞，grow 是形容詞子句的動詞，fast 是副詞修飾語。

例 16 a hand-made cake

a cake which was made by hand

手工蛋糕

→ cake 是先行詞，made 在形容詞子句中表示被動，hand 是工具，以介係詞片語 by hand 表示。

例 17 the above-mentioned statement

the statement which is mentioned above

上述的陳述

→ statement 是先行詞，mention 在形容詞子句中表示被動，above 是副詞修飾語。

◆ 一些複合形容詞的右側是「名詞 + ed」，ed 是形容詞字尾，黏接名詞，例如：

例 18 baby-faced

娃娃臉的

例 19 old-fashioned

舊式的

例 20 one-legged

一隻腳的

例 21 three-headed

三顆頭的

◆ 分詞及形容詞構成的複合形容詞中，形容詞是中心詞，分詞修飾形容詞，副詞性質，置於左側，符合 "Right-Hand-Head" 的原則，例如：

例 22 a biting cold weather system

一個刺骨寒冷的天氣系統

例 23 a freezing cold winter day

寒冬極冷的一天

Q11. "The cat was lying on the wall, with its tail hanging down."中的 with 介係詞片語怎麼有現在分詞？

原來如此 with 引導非限定子句或小句子，說明附帶狀況。

◆ 單詞或片語表示附帶訊息是結構及語意相稱的特徵，也是理解句子或解析題目的重要脈絡，更是寫作時應當遵循的筆頭功夫。

◆ "with／without 引導非限定子句或小句子"是典型的修飾結構，說明主要子句的附帶狀況、條件或原因。介係詞 with 有「伴隨」的意思，與介係詞片語的訊息相符，但可省略成獨立分詞構句。另外，with 片語的主詞與主要子句的主詞不一致，必須保留，例如：

例 1 Send these files to your outside translators now, with other files to be sent to me before you leave the office.

現在寄這些檔案給委外譯者，其他的檔案你下班前傳給我。

→ 不定詞意味未完成，表示將要進行。

例 2 With winter coming on, some people are getting anxious.

隨著冬天的到來，有些人逐漸感到憂鬱。

→ 現在分詞表示持續，意味存在或即將成真。

例 3 The cat was lying on the wall, with its tail hanging down.

那隻貓躺在牆上，尾巴往下垂。

→ 現在分詞也表示主動。

例 4 Mr. Lin left the meeting room, without a word spoken.

林先生離開會議室，一個字也沒說。

→ 過去分詞 spoken 表示被動。

例 5 The celebrity was born with a silver spoon in his mouth.

這位名人含著金湯匙出生。

◆ with 引介狀況，不含動詞，這種結構稱為小句子—small clause。邏輯上，句子包含描述對象及描述內容，而描述內容除了動作之外，也包括狀態，金湯匙在口中—"A silver spoon was in his mouth." 描述金湯匙的狀態，小句子是 "a silver spoon in his mouth"，搭配 with，形成介係詞片語 "with a silver spoon in his mouth"。

例 6 I noticed a woman staring at me, with her mouth wide open.

我注意到一名女子瞪著我看，她的嘴巴張得大大的。

→ with 引介狀況，小句子。

Q12. "For there to be life, there needs to be liquid water." 句子中的 "there to be life" 是什麼結構？

原來如此 非限定子句，介係詞 for 的受詞。

◆ for 具有介係詞及連接詞二詞性，連接詞表示因為，説明理由，非常正式的用法，對等連接詞，置於主要子句右側，例如：

例1 The government minister resigned for he was involved in the scandal.

那名政府官員辭職，原因是捲入醜聞。

◆ 介係詞 for 可以表示為了、因為、一段時間或距離，加接名詞詞性的語詞作為受詞，例如：

例2 This system is for the use of authorized users only.

這套系統僅供授權的使用者使用。

例3

My wife doesn't eat meat for various reasons.

因著各種理由，我太太不吃肉。

例4 The supervisor is out of the office for a few days next week.

下星期督導會有幾天不在辦公室。

例5 They hiked for miles.

他們健行了幾英哩。

◆ 非限定子句是不定詞、動名詞、分詞或原形動詞等非限定動詞構成的句子，名詞性質，扮演主詞、受詞、補語等角色，例如：

(1) 主詞

例6 Playing online games is interesting.

玩線上遊戲很有趣。

→ "Playing online games" 是動名詞，主詞角色，泛指不特定對象。

(2) 直接受詞

例7 I practiced playing the Ukulele with some guitar players

我跟一些吉他手一起練習彈奏烏克麗麗。

(3) 受詞補語

例8 My boss made me work overtime again.

我的老闆要我再次加班。

例 9 I saw a man lying unconscious on the sidewalk.

我看到一名男子無意識地躺在人行道上。

(4) 介係詞的受詞

例 10 The wolf ran away with its tail rolled up.

野狼捲起尾巴跑走。

→ with 引導非限定子句，its tail 是主詞，過去分詞 rolled up 表示被動狀態。

◆ there 引導存在句也有不定詞、動名詞、分詞等非限定形式。

(1) there to be：不定詞有未完成的意涵，常搭配想望的動詞。

例 11 I don't expect there to be a price collapse.

我不預期會有價格崩跌的情況發生。

例 12 I would like there to be more opportunities for students.

我希望有更多給學生的機會。

例 13 It is common for there to be problems of communication between parents and their children.

親子之間有溝通問題是普遍的。

例 14 It is strange for there to be this much rain in November.

十一月份這麼多雨蠻奇怪的。

例 15 For there to be life, there needs to be liquid water.

要有生命，就要有液態的水。

(2) there being：動名詞有泛時、存在等意涵，扮演主詞、受詞等角色。

(2.1) 主詞

例 16 There being no electricity is a big problem.

沒電是一大問題。

例 17 There being an MRT station nearby is a great advantage.

附近有一捷運站是一大優勢。

(2.2) 受詞

例 18 The dean admitted there being no objection to their admission.

院長承認他們的入學未遭反對。

例 19 The director has denied there being staff changes in the foundation.

該名董事否認基金會有員工更動的情況。

(2.2.1) there being 搭配 for 以外的一些介係詞，例如：

例 20 We are so excited about there being a chance of snow tonight.

今晚有機會下雪，我們好興奮。

例 21 The manager was bored with there being no assistant to help him.

沒有助理協助，經理感到煩躁。

(3) there being 構成句子修飾語，獨立分詞構句，例如：

例 22 There being no one to help out, I had to work on the project alone.

沒有人幫忙，我得獨自趕工。

例 23 There being nothing else to do, we left the office earlier than usual.

沒有其他事情要做，我們提早下班。

Q13. "The project, it turns out, has been more difficult than we expected."中的 "it turns out"是什麼句型?

原來如此 "it turns out" 是插入句,與句子結構無關,也不影響句中語詞的順序。

◆ 插入語是補充句子語意、陳述作說者意念或者銜接句子的語詞,置於句首、句中或句尾,與句子結構無關,附加或省略都不影響句子結構。常見的插入語結構如下:

(1) 名詞片語

例1 The suspect, an illegal immigrant, was arrested this morning.
一名非法移民的嫌犯今天清晨遭到逮補。

(2) 不定詞

例2 To sum up, we need to concentrate on in-service training.
總之,我們必須專注於在職訓練。

例3 To make matters worse, there will be a power shortage this summer.
更糟的是,今年夏天將有電力短缺。

(3) 獨立分詞構句

例4 These base stations are, strictly speaking, illegal.
嚴格來說,這些基地台都違法。

例5 Generally speaking, childbirth is a long process with lots of waiting around.
一般而言,分娩是一個長時等待的冗長過程。

(4) 形容詞片語

例6 Strange to say, no one voted for the candidate.
說來奇怪,沒人投票給這名候選人。

例7 Most important of all, you have to keep these rules in mind.
最重要的是,你必須牢記這些規定在心裡。

(5) 副詞片語

例8 The lamp needs a new bulb, but otherwise it's in good condition.
這盞燈需要一個顆燈泡,不然其他狀況都很好。

例 9 It is indeed a special privilege to welcome you on behalf of the
foundation.

代表基金會歡迎您們真是一項殊榮。

(6) 介係詞片語

例 10 The University of Oxford, for example, is a research university.

例如，牛津大學是一所研究型大學。

例 11 The man was, in fact, near death by the time the rescue team
reached him.

事實上，救援隊伍找到他之前，那名男子已生命垂危。

句子：

**(7) 除了一些慣用的插入句，名詞子句、補述用法形容詞子句或副詞子句
都可視為插入句。**

例 12 Believe it or not, they're getting married soon.

信不信由你，他們很快就要結婚了。

例 13 That is, drinking and driving is the most serious traffic offence.

也就是說，酒駕是最嚴重的交通犯行。

例 14 The project, it turns out, has been more difficult than we
expected.

結果證明，這計劃比我們預期的困難多了。

例 15 The news that Tom will be the starting pitcher in Friday's game
is not true.

湯姆將於周五比賽擔任先發投手的消息不是真的。

例 16 We will, if we have to, deal with the situation on our own.

如果有必要，我們將親自出手處理這個狀況。

例 17 The protest, which started last Sunday, has been widely
criticized by rival parties.

上週日開始的抗議行動飽受反對陣營撻伐。

◆ 例 18 的 "do you think" 不是插入句，而是主要子句，句子結構分析如下：

例 18 What do you think I should do first?

　　　你認為我該先做什麼？

(1) 疑問詞 what 是及物動詞 do 的受詞：

　　　I should do what first.

　　　我應該先做……

(2) what 移至句首，形成間接問句：

　　　what I should do --- first

(3) 加入 you think，what I should do first 是受詞

　　　You think what I should do --- first

(4) 形成疑問句，插入助動詞 do，what 移至句首：

　　　What do you think I should do --- first?

　　　你認為我該先做什麼？

◆ 例 19、20 中的 "do you think" 才是插入句：

例 19 What, do you think, should I do --- first?

　　　我該先做什麼，你認為呢？

例 20 What should I do ---, do you think?

Q14. "Two hairs were found at the scene." 這句話對嗎?

 原來如此 指個別幾根頭髮時,hair 是可數性質。

◆ 名詞常以能否個體化作為可數或不可數的依據,可以個體化的是可數名詞,例如 dog、warthog、armadillo 等,不可個體化的是不可數名詞,例如 air、iron、water 等。

幾乎都視為整體,鮮少視為個體的名詞是不可數名詞,而一些不可數名詞提及個體時仍可呈現單複數,例如 hair,指整頭的頭髮時是不可數名詞,如例 1、2,指幾根頭髮時,hair 就要標示單複數,如例 3、4:

例1 My cousin is growing his hair long.
我表弟在留長頭髮。

例2 Tom had his hair cut short yesterday.
湯姆昨天去把他的頭髮剪短。

例3 I got a white hair.
我有一根白頭髮。

例4 Two hairs were found at the scene.
現場發現二根毛髮。

◆ rain 不分雨滴大小或雨勢程度時,不可數名詞,例如:

例5 We had a lot of rain this afternoon.
今天下午雨下好大。

◆ 描述毛毛雨,單數表示一陣,提及連續大雨,複數呈現磅礴雨勢,例如:

例6 There was a light rain early this morning.
今天清晨下了一陣毛毛雨。

例7 Heavy rains brought severe flooding last week.
上星期豪大雨造成嚴重淹水。

◆ wind 與 rain 的用法相似,不分風勢強弱時,不可數名詞,例如:

例8 There isn't enough wind to fly a kite.
風不夠大,無法放風箏。

◆ 描述輕微、強勁風勢時，分別搭配 a ／ an 或複數形，借助文字形式鋪陳情境、勾勒畫面，例如：

例 9 There was a light wind blowing.

微風輕拂。

例 10 Strong winds made the crossing very choppy.

（Cambridge Dictionary）

強風使橫度非常不舒服。

◆ literature 泛指一般的文學時，不可數名詞，表示多種文學時，可數名詞，例如：

例 11 a brief history of English literature

英國文學簡史

例 12 Department of English Literatures and Cultures

英國文學與文化學系

◆ 物質名詞常因語意而呈現可數性質，例如以下 coffee 都是可數性質：

(1) 特指某一種類

例 13 The hostess served the guests a nice coffee after the meal.

女主人在餐後端給客人一杯很棒的咖啡。

例 14 The food store sells many kinds of organic coffees.

這家食品店賣許多種類的有機咖啡。

(2) 強調不同種類

例 15 The compound restaurant serves coffees.

這家複合式餐廳供應各式咖啡。

(3) 表示份數

例 16 I ordered two coffees with sugar but no milk.

我點了二杯加糖但不加牛奶的咖啡。

(4) 搭配計量單位

例 17 two cups of coffee

二杯咖啡

◆ 值得一提的是，一些物質或抽象名詞常因語意演變而具有可數的性質，
  例如：

  work 工作；works 作品，工廠

  celebrity 名聲；a celebrity 名人

  time 時間；a time, times 時代

Chapter 3.
形意搭配

英文句式有一特徵,就是語意主導句式,句
式呈現語意,語意搭配句式,達成溝通目的。

Q01. 為什麼事實相反的假設句要用早一時間的時態？

原來如此 早一時間的時態表示不可逆轉，無法成真，因此是事實相反的假設。

◆ 一般的溝通是傳達確切的訊息，採用直述語氣，搭配基本句式，例如：

例 1 I am a doctor now.

我現在是一名醫師。

→ 現在的事實

例 2 I was working in a hospital.

我在一家醫院工作。

→ 過去的事實

◆ 若是提及事實相反的訊息，為了凸顯所述非真，我們便運用假設語氣，以特殊句式標記不同於直述語氣的內容。

◆ 以現在事實相反而言，if 子句傳達不可成真的條件，搭配過去時態，時間軸在過去，表示現在不存在，未來不會成真。if 子句陳述不可成真的條件，主要子句則表達事實相反的結果，語意是「就會……」、「就能……」，對應過去式情態助動詞 "would"、"could"，加接原形動詞，呼應 if 子句的過去時態，例如：

例 3 If I were a doctor now, I would work in a hospital.

　　　現在事實相反的假設　　　　　　現在不可實現的結果

如果我現在是一名醫師，我就會在醫院工作。

例 4 If I were good at Japanese, I could talk to that client.

　　　現在事實相反的假設　　　　　　不可實現的結果

如果我精通日文，我就能與那名客戶交談。

◆ 現在事實相反條件句的 be 動詞不分主詞的人稱或數目都是 were，但在流行文化中，常用 was，例如：

例 5 If I was your boyfriend, I'd never let you go.

Boyfriend

如果我是妳的男朋友，我就絕不放手。

◆ 再來看過去事實相反的假設。if 子句傳達過去無法成真的條件，動詞為過去完成式，位於過去之前的時間點，表示過去不存在，達到過去非真假設的目的。主要子句表達過去非真的結果，語意也是「就會……」、「就能……」，以情態助動詞搭配「have 過去分詞」表示，呼應 if 子句的過去完成時態，例如：

例 6 If the manager had accepted the offer, it could have been a
　　　　　　過去事實相反的假設　　　　　　　　　　　　　不可實現的結果

different story.

如果經理接受那個提議，整個狀況就會不一樣。

例 7 If the government had accepted these recommendations, there

would have been many fewer disappointed patients this year.

The Jerusalem

政府如果接受這些建議，今年感到失望的病患就會少很多。

◆ 若是述及過去非真的條件與現在不存在的事實，我們就以過去完成式標記過去非真的條件，過去式情態助動詞搭配原形動詞標記現在不存在的事實，句式呈現語意，各說分明，例如：

例 8 If I had studied medicine in my youth, I would work in a hospital

now.

我年輕時如果研讀醫學，現在就會在醫院工作。

Q02. 假設句中的 but that 為什麼接的是直說語氣？

 原來如此 but 表示轉折，事實相反假設的轉折是直說語氣。

◆ but 是對等連接詞，引導與前面不同或與預期相違的敘述，連接訊息焦點，是一鮮明的轉折記號，例如：

例 1 The lady is not only a writer but also a painter.

那名女子不僅是一位作者，也是一位畫家。

例 2 The assistant is diligent but not imaginative.

助理很勤奮，但沒有想像力。

例 3 A policeman ran after the guy, but he escaped.

一名警察追著那人，但他逃跑了。

◆ but that 是從屬連接詞，but、that 二字構成，又稱為片語從屬連接詞，其他如 if as（宛如）、now that（既然）、as long as（只要）等也是片語從屬連接詞，引導副詞子句。

搭配 but that 子句的是事實相反假設，表示結果；but that 子句以直說語氣陳述事實，意思是「若非」、「要不是」，對應假設語氣的主要子句，例如：

例 4 But that there is water, there would be no fish.

要不是有水，魚就不存在。

◆ 副詞子句若是置於主要子句後面，則是強調條件：

例 5 There would be no fish, but that there is water.

→ (1) but that 子句以直說語氣陳述事實，意思是「要不是有水」。

(2) "there would be no fish" 說明事實相反的結果，"would" 對應中文的「就」，表示不存在的結果。

(3) 若以假設語氣表示條件，就得以 if 引導：

例 6 If there were no water, there would be no fish.

　　　　條件　　　　　　　　　　　　　結果

→ 事實上，這句話要表達的是：

例 7 There is water, and therefore there is fish.

有水，因此有魚。

◆ but 搭配表示原因的介係詞 for，形成片語介係詞 but for，可代換為 without，意思也是「若非」、「要不是」，表示事實，搭配假設語氣 的句子。以上例句可改寫為：

例 8 But for water, there would be no fish.

例 9 Without water, there would be no fish.

　　若非有水，魚就不存在。

Q03. "Not until after midnight did they arrive at the destination."的意思為什麼是「他們直到午夜過後才抵達目的地。」？

原來如此 這是強調時間參考點的倒裝句型。

◆ until 的意思是 "up to the time that"，表示直到那個時候或某事發生時，標記時間參考點。

例1 Tom slept until 10 a.m.

湯姆睡到上午十點。

→ 中文與英文詞序與語意相符。「直到」意味持續一段時間而終止，搭配持續動詞。

例2 Tom didn't go to bed until 10 a.m.

湯姆直到上午十點才上床睡覺。

→ 英文聚焦時間參考點之前的狀態，中文對應的是時間參考點之後的事實。

◆ not until 表示 not before a particular time or event，強調不於某一時間或事件之前發生。

例3 A: Can I use the computer now?

B: Not until you've done your homework.

A: 我現在可以使用電腦嗎？

B: 你做完功課才行。

→ 英文強調「使用電腦」不能於「做完功課」之前發生，中文則是講做完功課之後才行。B 的回應等同於句 4：

例4 You cannot use the computer until you've done your homework.

→ not until 是否定詞，移至句首強調時間參考點，例如句 4 可改寫成句 5。當然，強調句型的主要子句句首搭配助動詞。

例5 Not until you've done your homework can you use the computer.

◆ 分裂句式可以強調時間參考點。

例6 It is not until you've done your homework that you can use the computer.

→ 強調 not until 引導的時間參考點，"It is not until you've done your homework" 是主要子句，乘載強調的訊息，that you can use the computer 是從屬子句，未強調的部分。

Q04. "Tom was being polite while talking to the principal." 為什麼用 being ？

 being 凸顯當下的狀況。

◆ 英文時態包括時式－過去、現在、未來等時間範疇，態貌－簡單、進行、完成、完成進行等，時式與態貌共同呈現一個動作，例如：

例1 The trainee has done the best job.

那名實習生已做到最好了。

→ **現在時式，完成態貌，現在完成式。**

◆ 現在分詞表示進行、持續、主動，動作必然存在，而且對應明確的時間範疇，例如：

例2 Tom is talking on the phone now.

湯姆正在講手機。

例3 Judy was reading a novel then.

裘蒂那時候在看小說。

例4 They will be playing again this Sunday.

本周日他們會再次出賽。

→ **未來進行式可表示預定發生。**

例5 Leo was being polite when talking to the principal.

里歐與校長談話時很有禮貌。

例6 The boy was being quiet while on the bus with us.

那位男孩跟我們一起搭公車時蠻安靜的。

◆ 現在分詞 being 有如特寫鏡頭，將閱聽者的目光聚焦當下。當然，若是收起 being，只是少了聚焦當下的特寫鏡頭，平鋪直敘一個場景罷了。

◆ 特寫鏡頭 being 也使被動語態增添聚焦當下的效果而形成被動語態進行式，也就是說被動語態進行式只是在被動語態簡單式加上 being 而賦予當下的語意，二者隨著 being 的收放而切換，例如：

例7 The house was being painted yellow this morning.

今天早上這棟房子正被漆成黃色。

例8 I felt as if I was being watched.

我感覺好像一直被盯著看。

◆ 若未標記當下，呈現的是被動結果狀態：

例 9 The house was painted yellow this morning.

　　今天早上這棟房子被漆成黃色。

例 10 I felt as if I was watched.

　　我感覺好像被監視。

◆ 另外，being 也用來捕捉受事者當下被動狀態的特寫鏡頭，增添閱聽者身歷其境的感受。

例 11 I saw the dog being kept in a small cage.

　　我看見那隻狗一直被關在一個小籠子裡。

例 12 I noticed the car being driven past me while I was running away.

　　我跑開時，我注意到那部車正好從我旁邊開過去。

Q05. "the late president"表示校長遲到了嗎？

 原來如此 不是，"the late president" 是指已故的校長。

◆ 語詞在句中的分布位置不僅標示訊息份量，更是可能影響其功用及語意。形容詞置於修飾的名詞前面，限定該名詞，稱為限定用法，置於後面，描述該名詞，稱為補述用法。

例1 They are all illegal workers.

他們都是非法勞工。

These workers are all illegal.

這些勞工都是違法的。

◆ 有些形容詞的限定及補述用法的語意不同，限定用法偏向暫時或長時，補述用法則是暫時的狀態，但是二者有時不易區分，例如：

例2 the late president

已故的校長。

→ 長時的狀態。

The president was late to the meeting this morning.

今天早上校長開會遲到。

→ 一時的狀態。

例3 She is an ill kid.

她是個生病的孩子。

→ ill 表示生病的，一時生病或是長期臥病。

例4 The drug has caused an ill effect.

該藥品已引起不良效應。

→ ill 可代換為 bad，一時或是長時的狀態。

例5 I am feeling ill.

我感到不舒服。

→ ill 可代換為 sick，一時的狀態。

◆ 字首 a- 有 upon、intensive 的意思，黏接動詞而衍生形容詞，表示變成或處於某一動作的狀態，搭配補述用法，例如：

例4 The snake is still alive.

這條蛇還活著。

例5 I couldn't fall asleep.

我無法入眠。

例 6 I find it not easy to stay awake during literature lessons.

我發現上文學課要保持清醒不容易。

例 7 Tom was ashamed to admit his mistake.

湯姆羞於承認錯誤。

◆ 有些形容詞的限定及補述用法只是語意不同，沒有暫時或泛時的差別，例如：

例 8 my present address

我現在的地址

例 9 the present mayor

現任市長

例 10 Not all the members were present.

不是所有的會員都出席。

例 11 a certain amount of money

一筆某金額的錢

例 12 I feel certain that you're doing the right thing.

我確定你在做對的事。

例 13 a fond memory

一段愉悅的回憶

例 14 I am fond of music.

我喜愛音樂。

例 15 She is a responsible assistant

她是位認真負責的助理。

例 16 I called the person responsible.

我打電話給負有責任的人。

Q06. "*Please turn on it."為什麼不對？

 相較於代名詞 it，介副詞 on 是新訊息，置於句尾訊息焦點位置，取得句重音，以聲音標示訊息份量。

◆ 英文有「舊訊息引介新訊息」的趨勢，舊訊息詞序在前，新訊息詞序在後，且常置於句尾一訊息焦點位置，搭配句重音，以聲音標示訊息份量，例如：

例1 There is a fan beside the bookshelf. Please turn it on.

書櫃旁邊有一支電扇，請打開它。

→ 代名詞 it 指涉前句的 "a fan"，舊訊息，介副詞 on 說明動作，新訊息，置於 it 的右側句尾位置。

◆ "turn on" 的受詞若是名詞片語，表示首次提及的新訊息，置於 on 的左側或是右側，例如：

例2 Please turn the fan on.

例3 Please turn on the fan.

請打開那支電扇。

◆ 就著尾重原則一結構大的語詞置於句尾的修辭原則，相較於介副詞 on，名詞片語的結構較大，置於 on 的右側。名詞片語若加入修飾語，結構擴大，置於 on 的右側更是符合尾重原則。

例4 Turn off the new fan.

關掉那支新電扇。

例5 Turn off the new fan on the left.

關掉左邊的新電扇。

例6 Turn on the exhaust fan in the bathroom when you are taking a bath or shower, and turn on the range hood in the kitchen whenever you are cooking.

泡澡或是淋浴時，打開浴室裡的抽風電扇；每當做菜時，打開廚房的抽油煙機。

Q07. 如何快速學會可分開與不可分開片語動詞？

 搭配介副詞，受詞為名詞片語，可分開；搭配介係詞，不可分開。

◆ 片語動詞主要是動詞搭配介係詞或介副詞所構成，語意如同單詞動詞一樣不可切割，例如：

例 1 look at 注視

例 2 put off 延期

例 3 give up 放棄

例 4 take care of 照顧

◆ 及物性質的片語動詞加接受詞，形成動詞片語，例如：

例 5 The boy is looking at his smartphone.

男孩正看著他的手機。

例 6 The manager decided to put off the meeting.

經理決定將會議延後。

例 7 The government must give up the plan.

政府必須放棄這項計畫。

例 8 I have to take care of my little brother tonight.

今晚我必須照顧我弟弟。

◆ 若是知曉介係詞或介副詞的意涵，便可意會到分辨可分開或不可分開的片語動詞其實是一假議題。

介係詞引介二者關係，語意與名詞有關，並且賦予名詞受格格位以扮演其受詞角色，同時與受語構成介係詞片語。介係詞的受詞不論是名詞片語或是代名詞，都不移出介係詞片語。

搭配介係詞的片語動詞辨識要點如下：

(1) 語意與名詞有關。

(2) 受詞不論是名詞或代名詞都不可移位。

(3) 搭配介係詞的是不可分開的片語動詞。

◆ **介副詞**是與介係詞同形的副詞，修飾動作，語意與動詞相關。及物性質的片語動詞其受詞若是名詞片語，介副詞置於名詞片語的左側或右側，但是基於訊息與結構尾重原則，名詞片語置於介副詞的右側，代名詞則置於介副詞的左側。以例 6 為例，受詞若是代名詞，應改寫如下：

例 9 The manager decided to put it off for now.

→ 介副詞不加接受詞，若出現受詞，那是片語動詞的語意所產生的，如例6。

搭配介副詞的片語動詞辨識要點如下：

(1) 語意與動作相關的是介副詞。

(2) 受詞若是名詞片語，介副詞可置於其左側或右側。

(3) 受詞若是代名詞，基於尾重原則，幾乎都置於介副詞左側。

(4) 搭配介副詞的是可分開的片語動詞。

◆ 片語動詞是可分開或不可分開端視搭配的是介係詞或介副詞，不須考量整個片語動詞。另外，閱讀文本時，片語動詞呈現正確詞序，讀者無須費神分析可否分開；寫作時，無論是介係詞或介副詞，名詞片語都可置於右側，至於代名詞，就是「介係詞右側，介副詞左側」的原則。考試選項若是違反詞序原則，例如 "turn on it "，則是不符測驗與評量原則，不在本文討論範圍。

◢ 圖一：含介係詞的片語動詞樹狀圖例示。

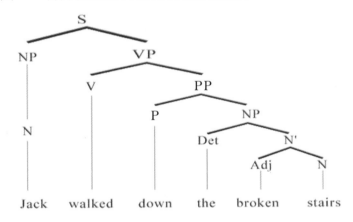

◢ 圖二：含介副詞的片語動詞樹狀圖例示。

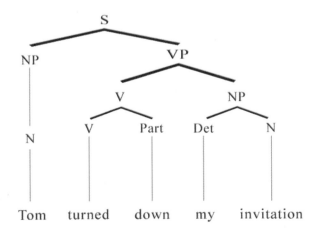

Q08. "A thief was arrested by the police at the station." 被動句型為什麼是「be 過去分詞」？

原來如此 被動式描述受事者的被動結果狀態，**be** 動詞表示狀態，過去分詞表示被動結果。

◆ 主動式陳述蓄意產生動作的主事者對於受事者的影響，主事者是主題，扮演句子主詞，受事者是受詞，句型如下：

主詞　　　及物動詞　　受詞
主事者　　　　　　　　受事者

例1 The police arrested a thief at the station.
　　警方在車站逮捕一名竊賊。

◆ 被動句描述受事者受到影響，主題是受事者，扮演主詞角色，稱為受事者主詞。另外，被動句是 be 動詞搭配過去分詞，表示受事者主詞的被動結果狀態，句型如下：

受事者主詞　　be 動詞　　過去分詞
　主題　　　　狀態　　　被動結果

例2 A thief was arrested by the police at the station.
　　　主題　　　　被動結果

　　一名竊賊在車站遭警方逮捕。

◆ 被動式若不提及主事者，便是聚焦受事者的被動狀態，若是提起，則是有意強調主事者而使其成為訊息焦點：

例3 A jumbo jet was forced to land at one of New York's tiniest airports.
　　一架廣體噴射機被迫降落在紐約一處最小的機場。
　　→ 受事者主詞是 "a jumbo jet"，未提及迫使降落的原因，句子聚焦在迫降這一結果。

例4 The professor's talk was frequently interrupted by his children while being interviewed live.
　　現場訪問時，教授的談話頻頻受到他孩子的打岔。
　　→ 受事者主詞是 "The professor's talk"，"his children" 是主事者，句子的訊息焦點。

◆ 值得注意的是，一些教學常提及主動語態與被動語態互換，並以受詞與主詞位置變換作為句型互換的特徵。事實上，主動語態強調主事者產生動作，被動語態描述受事者受動作的影響，不同觀點的敘述不可互換。另外，主詞與受詞是句子結構的成分，只有位置的挪移，沒有結構的替換，因此，若是以主事者或受事者描述，似乎較為具體真實，並能擺脫句子結構的框架。

Q09. "Tom was made to work hard." 句中的 "to work" 為什麼是不定詞？

 原來如此 過去分詞不加接動詞原形。

◆ 使役動詞 make 掌控受事者，驅使其意志完成指令，搭配動詞原形，主事者、使役動作、受事者、原形動詞形成完整的事件，例如：

例 1 Mom made me do the dishes after dinner.
媽媽要我晚餐後洗碗。

例 2 The janitor made the man clean up after his dog.
管理員要該名男子收拾他的狗屎。

◆ 被動語態中，過去分詞表示受事者主詞受到使役的狀態，不定詞說明使役的結果，就是受事者主詞要進行的動作，例如：

例 3 I was made to do the dishes after dinner.

例 4 The man was made to clean up after his dog by the janitor.

◆ 英語語詞加接時，似乎有過去分詞與原形動詞不相鄰的傾向，因此，使役動詞的被動句式中，受詞補語還原省略的 to 而以不定詞呈現。二黏接 ing 字尾的語詞也不相鄰，例如進行式的 begin 搭配不定詞而不搭配動名詞。

例 5 He was beginning to lose his sense of self.
他逐漸開始失去自我。

Q10. " Your video had me laughing hysterically." 這句話用 laughing 是否正確?

 正確,表示主事者驅使受事者持續進行動作。

◆ 使役動詞 have 搭配原形動詞當受詞補語,表示主事者驅使受事者進行動作的事實,例如:

例 1 The instructor had me sign my name on the card.

指導員要我在卡片上簽名。

例 2 My supervisor had me come back to the office soon.

我的主管要我儘快回到辦公室。

◆ 受詞補語若是現在分詞,表示主事者造成受事者持續進行動作,呈現持續的樣貌,例如:

例 3 Your video had me laughing hysterically.

你的影片讓我不停笑翻。

例 4 The message had me feeling that my heart was going to burst.

那訊息讓我一直覺得心臟就要迸開來。

◆ 受詞補語若是過去分詞,主事者已對受事者造成影響,例如:

例 5 I had my hair cut at a new barbershop this morning.

我今天早上在一家新理髮院剪頭髮。

例 6 I had my hair dyed black at the beauty salon.

我在美容院將頭髮染成黑色。

Q11. "The machine needs repairing." 為什麼可用動名詞 repairing？

原來如此　動名詞具有「存在」的意涵，強調機器需要維修的事實或狀態。

◆ 不定詞具有「未完成」的意涵，強調動作，與未來時間有關。need、want、require 等動詞搭配被動式不定詞，強調主詞「需要被怎樣」的動作，例如：

例4 The machine needs to be repaired.

那部機器需要維修。

例5 The guy wants to be put in jail with some gangsters.

那人要跟一些幫派份子一起入監服刑。

例6 Not all ingredients in cosmetics are required to be disclosed.

不是所有的化妝品成分都要公布。

◆ 動名詞具有「存在」的意涵，說明一個狀態、事實或是習慣，與未來時間無關。因此，need、want、require 等搭配動名詞時，強調主詞「需要被怎樣」的事實或狀態，被動意涵，如例 7～9，但中譯與例 4～6 一致：

例7 The machine needs repairing.

例8 The guy wants putting in jail with some gangsters.

→ want 搭配動名詞，要求、需要的意思。

例9 Not all ingredients in cosmetics require disclosing.

→ 主動式 require 的主詞是受事者，搭配動名詞表示被動，但不可只接不定詞，因此下列句子是錯誤的，而例 10 是正確的句子。

誤 Drivers require to wear seat belts.

例10 Drivers are required by law to wear seat belts.

法律要求駕駛人繫上安全帶。

◆ deserve 的意思是「應該受到」，被動意涵明顯，訊息焦點是動作，因此，較常以被動式不定詞表示主詞應該受到的被動動作，例如：

例11 War veterans deserved to be treated with respect.

退伍軍人應當受到禮遇。

◆ to blame, to let（出租）作為主詞補語，且無修飾語時，常以主動形式表示被動，例如：

例 12 The student is to blame.

= The student is to be blamed.

該名學生該受責備。

例 13 The apartment is to let.

= The apartment is to be let.

這套公寓要出租。

Q12. decide 為什麼要接不定詞當受詞？

 原來如此 decide 表示決定去做某事，**to** 有動作發展的意涵，二者語意呼應，因此 **decide** 搭配不定詞。

◆ 字源上，to 有 "in the direction of"、"for the purpose of "、"further" 等語意，"in the direction of " 表示空間移動的方向，介係詞詞性，例如：

例 1 Tom went to the station by bus.

湯姆搭公車到車站。

→ to 表示 the station 是空間移動的方向，從空間移動的方向衍伸為時間、話題、感官反應的方向。

例 2 The meeting will be postponed to next week.

會議將延至下星期。

例 3 When it comes to the issue, I totally agree with you.

一提到這議題，我完全同意你。

例 4 I am looking forward to seeing you again.

期待再次見到您。

◆ to 譬喻為想望、規劃的方向，搭配相關語意的動詞，這時 to 是不定詞的標記，引介動詞，說明想望、規劃、未完成的內容，例如：

(1) 想望

例 5 They hope to visit us next year.

他們希望明年拜訪我們。

例 6 I wish to make a complaint.

我要申訴。

→ wish: to want to do something

例 7 Peter decided to go abroad for further study next year.

彼得決定明年出國深造。

例 8 My cousin wanted to go swimming this afternoon.

我表弟今天下午要去游泳。

例 9 The bad guy intended to escape.

那名歹徒企圖逃跑。

例 10 Did you remember to pay the bill?

你記得要去付帳單嗎？

例 11 We expect to be landing at London Heathrow in an hour's time.
我們預期一小時之內降落倫敦希斯洛機場。

例 12 He promised faithfully to quit smoking.
他信誓旦旦保證要戒菸。

(2) 規劃

例 13 They planned to go on a vacation next week.
他們計畫下周去度假。

例 14 They arranged to have dinner this weekend.
他們約好在這周末一起晚餐。

例 15 We were busy preparing to go on holiday.
我們正忙著準備度假。

(3) 未完成

例 16 She failed to reach the Wimbledon Final this year.
她今年未能打入溫布登網球決賽。

例 17 If you need anything, don't hesitate to call me.
你如果需要什麼，馬上打給我。

例 18 Were you just pretending to be interested?
你只是假裝有興趣嗎？

Q13. "The clerk to work overtime still didn't complete the task."這句話對嗎？

 原來如此 不對，已發生的動作應以 ing 標示。

◆ 不定詞的標記 to 源自介係詞 to，表達未完成或將進行，有時也表示事實。現在分詞表示進行或持續，與表示存在或完成的動名詞是近親。不定詞與現在分詞都可後位修飾名詞，但使用時機及語意不同。

　　誤 The clerk to work overtime still didn't complete the task.

　　　→ didn't complete 表示過去，"work overtime"已發生，應搭配現
　　　　在分詞。

　　例1 The clerk working overtime still didn't complete the task.

　　　= The clerk who worked overtime still didn't complete the task.

　　　加班的員工仍未完成這項工作。

◆ 完成式現在分詞不用於後位修飾名詞，例 2 中的形容詞子句不縮減為
例 3：

　　例2 The clerk who had worked overtime finally completed the task.

　　　加班的員工終於完成這項工作。

　　誤 The clerk having worked overtime finally completed the task.

◆ 第一句（誤）例句若改為未來的事件，搭配 to work overtime，如例3，
而例 3 是例 4 的縮減：

　　例3 The clerk to work overtime will complete the task.

　　　要來加班的員工將完成這項工作。

　　例4 The clerk who is to work overtime will complete the task.

◆ 例 7 ～ 9 的不定詞表示已完成的事實：

　　例5 It is the first film to win an Oscar with a transgender lead.

　　　它是第一部跨性別者主演而贏得奧斯卡獎的影片。

　　例6 The movie was the first animation to win the award.

　　　這部電影是第一部獲獎的動畫片。

　　例7 John was the first one to come to the office.

　　　約翰是第一位到辦公室的人。

Q14. 為什麼"Mr. Lee asked me to erase the board."的受詞補語是不定詞？

 原來如此 **ask** 驅使受事者進行動作，不定詞表示進行的動作。

◆ ask 表示主事者要求受事者進行動作，搭配不定詞，是否完成從言談中知曉，不同於 make、have、let 等使役動詞的受詞補語不含 to，透露動作已完成，例如：

例1 Mr. Lee asked me to erase the board, and I did it.

　　李老師要我擦黑板，我擦了。

　　→ 主事者要求，受事者完成動作。

例2 Miss Chen asked me to take out the trash, but I didn't.

　　陳老師要我倒垃圾，但我沒做。

　　→ 主事者要求，受事者未完成動作。

◆ 我們可以將受詞及受詞補語視為一個事件，表示 ask 要求的內容，受詞是事件的主題，受詞補語是敘述部分：

例3 Mr. Lee asked / me to erase the board, and I did it.

　　→ "me to erase the board" 是 Mr. Lee 要求的事件，主題是 me，"to erase the board" 是要進行的動作。

例4 Miss Chen asked / me to take out the trash, but I didn't.

　　→ 主題是 me，"to take out the trash" 是要進行的動作。

◆ 將受詞與受詞補語視為一個事件，受詞是主題，受詞補語是敘述部分，合乎句子的構成邏輯—句子應包含描述對象及描述內容。受詞補語是不定詞，非限定動詞，因此受詞與受詞補語構成的事件是「非限定子句」—非限定動詞構成的句子。

Q15. 為什麼 see、hear 不搭配不定詞當受詞補語？

原來如此 **see、hear** 是對存在的現象產生的感官反應，無法驅使受詞進行動作，不搭配表示不存在的不定詞。

◆ see、hear 是主詞對受詞的動作或狀態所產生的感官反應，而感官反應不是意志所能驅使，主詞不是感官動作的產生者，而是經驗者（experiencer）─獲得視覺或聽覺感官經驗者，例如：

例 1 I saw a stranger in the hall.

我在走廊看見一名陌生人。

例 2 I heard the noise.

我聽見噪音。

→ 意志無法掌控感官反應，但是 "a stranger"、"the noise" 是感官投射的對象，非典型的受事者。

◆ 我們可以描述感官接收到的受詞的動作或狀態，例如：

例 3 I saw a stranger wandering in the hall.

我看見一名陌生人在走廊上晃來晃去。

例 4 She heard someone making noise in her backyard.

她聽見有人在她的後院發出噪音。

→ 現在分詞標記動作進行時的感官經驗，似乎是將過程錄影起來，呈現身歷其境的經驗。

例 5 I saw two policemen enter the convenience store. .

我看見二名警察進入便利商店。

例 6 I heard someone call my namejust now.

剛才我聽見有人叫我的名字。

→ 不含 to 的不定詞標記事實，記錄全部過程，意味全程目睹、聽見。相對於錄影，動詞原形宛如一張照片，交代感官經驗的事實。

◆ 表達感官接收的是受詞的被動狀態時，搭配過去分詞，當然，若要呈現當下的特寫鏡頭，我們以現在分詞 being 標記，例如：

例 7 I saw a cat thrown from the back of a van.

我看見一隻貓被從一部廂型車後面丟出來。

例 8 I saw a dog being hit by a car.

我看見一條狗被汽車撞到。

Q16. "The man was seen to enter the office." 這句話正確嗎？

 正確，不定詞表示事實，表示對於整個動作的感官經驗。

◆ 我們以感官投射對象作為主詞，描述其被動狀態，現在分詞呈現當下進行或反覆的動作，例如：

例 1 A man was seen entering the anteroom.

　　一名男子被看見進入接待室。

例 2 The machine was heard starting up.

　　那部機器被聽見啟動了。

◆ 感官動詞被動語態中，若要呈現感官接收的動作事實，我們便將主動語態省略的 to 還原，也就是以動詞原形表示感官經驗。

◆ 為什麼要將 to 還原？

因為英文句式避免過去分詞與原形動詞相鄰，猶如被動語態 make、have、let 等使役動詞不加接動詞原形，同樣將 to 還原。這些是英文語詞共現上的講究。

例 3 The man was seen to come out of the house.

　　那名男子被看見從房子出來。

例 4 Tom was never heard to use harsh words of language with others.

　　湯姆從未被聽到使用犀利言詞對別人。

Q17. 為什麼"*I hope you to join us."句子不對？

 原來如此 hope 表示想望，未驅使受詞 you 進行動作。

◆ hope 的意思是希望，表示主詞希望去做某事或某事能夠成真，例如：

例 1 I hope to join you later.

我希望等一下加入你們。

→ 不定詞表示主詞希望去做的動作，動作產生者就是句子的主詞。

◆ 連接詞 that 引導的名詞子句說明主詞希望的事件，that 常省略。

例 2 I hope (that) I can join you later.

我希望等一下能夠加入你們。

例 3 I had hoped that my daughter would study music, but she didn't want to.

我曾希望我女兒攻讀音樂，但她不要。

→ "had hoped" 表示希望的事未成真。

◆ 談話中，說話者常以代詞 so 表示 hope 所指的事件，例如：

例 4 A: Tom will come back soon.

B: I hope so.

A：湯姆很快會回來。

B：希望如此。

◆ 希望是心理活動，不會影響或驅使他人進行動作，因此 hope 不加接受詞及不定詞當受詞補語，這與 see、hear 等感官動詞不搭配不定詞當受詞補語是一樣的。

誤 I hope you to join us.

◆ 若希望的是依賴或急切需要的，常以進行式凸顯此一念茲在茲的想望，例如：

例 5 I am hoping your dog is OK.

我希望你的狗狗沒事。

例 6 I am hoping my cellphone will be fixed as soon as possible.

我非常希望我的手機儘快修好。

例 7 I'm really hoping it doesn't rain again this weekend.

我真希望這周末不會再下雨。

例 8 The injured man was hoping for an offer of compensation.

受傷男子希望能夠得到賠償金。

◆ hope 也常搭配進行式表達委婉或禮貌，尤其是不確定對方的回應時。
當然，若搭配過去進行式，則是以非當下凸顯委婉，例如：

例 9 I was hoping you will give me some advice.

希望你能給我一些建議。

例 10 I was hoping you could tide me over.

希望你能幫助我度過難關。

Q18. I was wondering what happened to him." 是指過去的想法嗎?

原來
如此 **不是,這是委婉的表達,與過去時間無關。**

◆ 口語溝通時,若以現在式提出想法或徵詢意見,時空聚焦於當下,語氣直接,一般視為非正式用法。若以過去式表達,意念置於過去,語氣間接,較為禮貌,若是搭配強調當下的進行式,則更加委婉,較為正式,例如:

例1 I wonder whether you could pass me the power bank.

能不能把行動電源遞給我?

→ 現在式的語氣直接,一般視為非正式用法。

◆ 相較於過去簡單式,過去進行式較為委婉,例如:

例2 I wondered if you agreed with that.

不知道你是否贊同那件事。

例3 We were wondering whether you'd like to have dinner with us today.

不知道你今天是否要與我們一起吃晚餐。

例4 I was wondering what happened to him.

我不知道他怎麼了。

◆ 相較於過去簡單式或過去進行式,現在進行式的語氣直接多了,例如:

例5 I am wondering whether to stay for another hour or just start off right away.

我不知道是要多待一小時或是馬上出發?

◆ 委婉語氣透露想望,不奢求實現,猶如假設語氣,常搭配過去式或過去式情態助動詞,例如:

例6 What were you wanting?

你想要什麼?

例7 Did you want to take this one?

你要買這一件嗎?

例8 Could I speak to Mr. Lin, please?

我可以和林先生講話嗎?

例9 Would you mind closing the door for me?

你介意幫我關上門嗎?

Q19. 為什麼 finish 接的是動名詞？

 動名詞有存在或完成的意涵，與 finish 的語意相符。

◆ 英文中，每一個語詞都有內蘊的含意，主導其句式表現，就像生物的 DNA，不同的 DNA 展現不同的生命樣貌。因此，解碼語詞的 DNA，便能理解，甚至預測其搭配、詞序、語氣等表現，例如不定詞表示事件的發展，搭配想望、計畫語意的動詞。

例 1 I decided to sign up for the workshop.

我決定報名參加這場研討會。

例 2 Tom planned to buy a house in this area.

湯姆打算在這地區買一棟房子。

例 3 The man intended to break into the villa.

該名男子企圖闖入這棟別墅。

◆ 動名詞也有蘊含的語意，也就是 DNA。

動名詞的構詞是動詞黏接 -ing，名詞性質，既是名詞，就像物品一樣是存在的，既是存在，當然就是完成且是泛時。因此，動名詞的 DNA 是「存在」或「完成」，搭配語意相稱的語詞，例如：

例 4 I have finished reading that paper.

我看完那篇論文了。

例 5 Jack has enjoyed playing music since junior high school.

傑克自從國中就一直喜愛彈奏音樂。

→ 存在的事物才能引人進入 joy 的感覺。

例 6 Leo stopped using the computer and left.

里歐停止使用電腦，然後離開。

→ 停止當下的動作，才會進行下一動作。

例 7 I forgot turning off the lights when I left the office.

我忘了下班時有把燈關掉。

→ 忘記完成的動作，表示做過。

◆ practice—練習，持續、重複的意涵，與存在相關，搭配動名詞，例如：

例 8 We practiced speaking English in groups today.

我們今天分組練習講英文。

◆ accuse一控告是針對已發生的犯行，若是未發生，則無從控告，因此搭配動名詞，介係詞 of 引介控告的內容。

例 9 The woman was accused of stealing shoes from the showroom.

那名婦人被控從展示廳竊取鞋子。

◆ 帶有心理因素或主觀意念的動詞常搭配動名詞，陳述存在的動作，例如：

例 10 The trainee admitted making a mistake.

該名實習生承認犯了一個錯誤。

例 11 The boy denied breaking the window.

那名男孩否認打破窗戶。

例 12 I have always regretted not having studied harder in college.

我一直懊悔大學時期沒好好用功。

例 13 Many members suggested putting the matter to the discipline committee.

許多會員提議將該起事件送交紀律委員會。

Q20. "The government spent a lot of money to fight against air pollution." 這句話正確嗎？

原來
如此　表示 **spend** 的目的或結果，搭配不定詞。

◆ spend 表示花費金錢或時間，常以介係詞片語說明用途，介係詞的受詞若是名詞片語，介係詞保留，以免造成結構及語意上的混淆。

例1 The secretary spends too much money on clothes.

祕書花太多錢買衣服了。

例2 The house owner spent a lot of money for decoration and all equipment.

屋主花很多錢在裝潢及所有的設備上。

例3 Jack is planning to spend some time at home with his family.

傑克打算花一些時間在家陪伴家人。

例4 The President hasn't spent much time on foreign affairs so far.

目前為止，總統還沒花很多時間在外交事務上。

◆ 介係詞搭配持續動作的動名詞，表示 spend 的內容或過程，介係詞可以省略。

例5 Hank spent a lot of money entertaining his relatives.

漢克花很多錢款待他的親戚。

例6 John spent much time revising his composition.

約翰花了一些時間校訂他的文章。

例7 The government spent a lot of money fighting against air pollution.

政府花費大筆金錢在防制空氣汙染。

◆ 提到 spend 的目的或結果時，搭配不定詞，持續或瞬間動作端視語意而定。

例8 The government spent a lot of money to fight against air pollution.

政府花費大筆金錢防制空氣汙染。

→ 目的或結果

◆ J. Reb Materi 的一句話明確顯示 spend 搭配動名詞或不定詞的語意差異：

例 9 Many people spend their health gaining wealth, and then have to spend their wealth to regain their health.

許多人花費他們的健康在獲取錢財上，然後他們必須花費在自身的健康上。

◆ spend 表示停止或耗弱時，及物性質，主詞是事物，受詞不是時間或金錢。

例 10 The woman's anger soon spent itself.

那名婦人的怒氣很快就煙消雲散了。

→ spend 表示 stop，煙消雲散。

例 11 The hurricane will probably have spent most of its force by the time it reaches the northern parts of the country.

Cambridge Dictionary

颶風抵達該國家北部地區之前，將可能已耗弱大半力道了。

→ spend 表示耗弱。

Q21. "It was awful, but I couldn't help laughing."句中的 help 為什麼加接 laughing ?

原來
如此　**help 是 stop—停止的意思，加接動名詞 laughing 表示存在的動作。**

◆ 例 1 中的 help 是 stop—停止的意思，"couldn't help"表示無法停止某一動作的發生，對應中文「不禁」、「忍不住」、「不得不」。言談之間，laughing 已經發生，而不是「要發生」，搭配存在意涵的動名詞—laughing。

例 1 It was awful, but I couldn't help laughing.

這真是糟糕，但我還是忍不住大笑起來。

例 2 A: Stop giggling!

B: I can't help it!

A: 停止傻笑！

B: 我忍不住！

→ "it" 是指 "giggling"，存在的動作。

例 3 Cindy burst into tears—she couldn't help herself.

辛蒂突然哭了出來，無法克制自己。

→ couldn't help 搭配反身代名詞，表示無法克制自己。

◆ "cannot help but" 加接原形動詞，因為 help 是原形動詞，平行結構是原形動詞，連接詞 but 表示「而是、只好」，引介並強調無法避免的動作，語氣上較 "cannot help" 強烈，例如：

例 4 I cannot help but do so.

我不得不這麼做。

Q22. "living room"的 living 是現在分詞或是動名詞？

 動名詞，表示功用。

◆ 動名詞常與名詞形成複合名詞，詞重音在前面的動名詞。語意上，動名詞通常表示名詞的功用，例如：

例 1 the 'living room

= the room for living

起居室

例 2 'drinking water

= water for drinking

飲用水

例 3 a 'washing machine

= a machine used for washing

一部洗衣機

◆ 分詞為形容詞性質，與名詞構成名詞片語，詞重音在名詞一片語的中心詞，例如：

(1) 現在分詞

例 4 a crying 'baby

一個哭著的嬰兒

例 5 flying 'birds

飛著的鳥

例 6 the dancing 'girl

那位正在跳舞的女孩

(2) 過去分詞

例 7 canned 'food

罐頭食品

例 8 iced 'coffee

冰咖啡

例 9 computerized 'lottery

電腦彩券

◆ 例 6 的詞重音在 girl，若在 dancing，dancing 便是動名詞，意思是「舞者」，以舞蹈為業的人。複合名詞與名詞片語的唸音不同，若是構詞一致，詞重音位置便成了分辨語意的依據，例如：

例 10 an 'English teacher

　　　一位英文老師。

　　　→ English teacher 是複合詞。

　　　an English 'teacher

　　　一名英格蘭籍的老師。

　　　→ an English teacher 只指英格蘭籍的老師，不含蘇格蘭、威爾斯或北愛爾蘭等大英國協其他地區，因此，若要表示來自英格蘭的老師，較清楚的寫法是 "a teacher from England"。

例 11 a 'greenhouse

　　　一間溫室。

　　　→ 複合名詞

　　　a green 'house

　　　一棟綠色的房子。

　　　→ 名詞片語

Q23. "The dean called a teacher from Kaohsiung."有幾種解釋？

 原來如此 二種解釋，一是院長打電話給一位來自高雄的老師，一是院長從高雄打電話給一位老師。

◆ 英文有四種歧義來源，也就是雙關語的類型：

(1) 語意歧義，通常是同形異義字所造成的歧義，例如：

例1 Insurance salesmen are frightening people.

① 保險銷售員都是令人害怕的人。

② 保險銷售員在嚇人。

例2 When a lawyer dies, he lies still.

① 律師死的時候，就躺著不動。

② 律師死的時候，仍然要説謊。

(2) 結構歧義，不同的語詞結構所造成的歧義，例如：

例3 The dean called a teacher from Kaohsiung.

① 介係詞片語 "from Kaohsiung" 修飾 "a teacher" ，形容詞性質，二者形成名詞片語 "a teacher from Kaohsiung" ，意思是「一位來自高雄的老師」。（如樹狀圖 -1）

② "from Kaohsiung" 修飾 "called a teacher" ，副詞性質，二者形成動詞片語 "called a teacher from Kaohsiung" ，意思是「從高雄打電話給一位老師」。（如樹狀圖 -2）

(3) 變形歧義，省略或挪移所造成的歧義，例如：

例4 Miss Lin loves Gina as much as Mandy.

① Miss Lin loves Gina as much as Miss Lin loves Mandy.

林老師如同喜愛吉娜一樣地喜愛曼蒂。

→ 從屬子句省略 Miss Lin loves。

② Miss Lin loves Gina as much as Mandy loves Gina.

林老師如同曼蒂一樣地喜愛吉娜。

→ 從屬子句省略 loves Gina。

(4) 語用歧義，言談情境賦予不同於字面的語意，例如：

例5 I'm good.

① 我很好。

② 沒關係，我不用。

例 6 I'm still up in the air.
　　① 我還沒決定呢！
　　② 我還在學飛行呢！

◆ 以例 3 而言，我們看到一個語詞在句中的結構、詞性、功用等方面的表現，結構是既定的，例如 "from Kaohsiung" 就是一個介係詞片語，詞性與功用是相對的，形容詞修飾名詞，副詞修飾動詞。

樹狀圖 -1

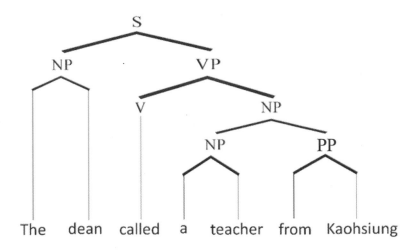

樹狀圖 -2

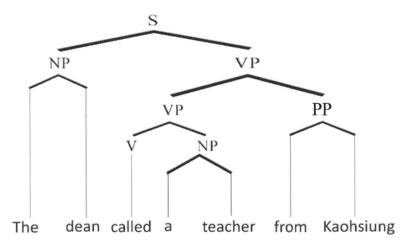

◆ 請依照樹狀圖，將片語標記 S, NP, N, VP, PP, P, Det 等填入正確的號碼上，並想想句子的語意。

圖 1

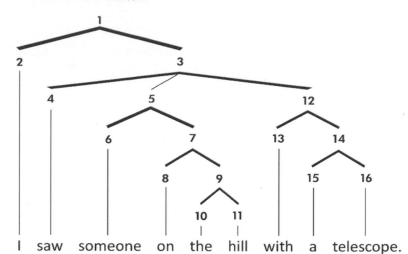

圖 2

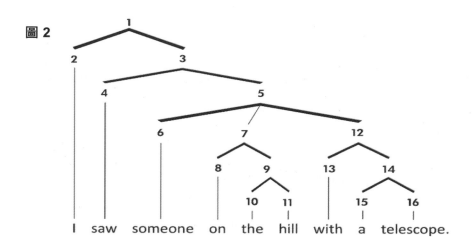

解答：（圖 1.2 答案一樣）
1. S 2. NP 3. VP 4. V 5. NP 6. N 7. PP 8. P 9. NP 10. Det 11. N 12. PP 13. P 14. NP 15. Det 16. N
中譯：
圖 1 我用望遠鏡看見某個山丘上的人。
圖 2 我看見某個山丘上帶著望遠鏡的人。

Q24. "I don't think it will rain tomorrow." 及 "I think it won't rain tomorrow." 有什麼差別？

原來
如此 前句表示主詞的意念較弱，後句則較強。

◆ 表達否定看法時，"I don't think" 表示意念較弱且不確定，態度較為委婉，如例 1；not 若在名詞子句，表示意念較強，態度較為直接，如例 2。至於中譯，「不」直接對應否定詞 not 即可。

例1 I don't think it will rain tomorrow.

我不認為明天會下雨。

→ "I don't think" 透露不確定的意念。

例2 I think it won't rain tomorrow.

我認為明天不會下雨。

→ "I think" 透露確定的意念。

◆ 為使語氣婉轉，英美人士常以否定傳達個人的看法，而不以肯定直接論斷，因此，一般認為 "I don't think" 較常用。事實上，若要凸顯個人看法，仍應使用 "I think"，例如：

例3 I think he won't continue to express those opinions.

我認為他不會繼續表達那些意見。

例4 I think it won't be that easy.

我認為不會那麼簡單。

◆ 對於存在的事件，語氣不須婉轉，直接陳述想法及事實，例如：

例5 I thought he had a cold.

我是認為他感冒了。

例6 I thought we played really well.

我認為我們打得很棒。

例7 I didn't think we would run that fast.

沒料到我們會跑這麼快。

例8 He didn't think I needed to stop playing football.

他沒料到我得放棄打橄欖球。

例9 We didn't think they were going to do anything else.

我們沒料到他們要去做別的。

Q25. "Tom went to bed until his parents got back home."這句話正確嗎？

 原來如此 不正確。"went to bed" 不會持續至 "his parents got back home"。

◆ 依照是否能夠持續，動作分為持續動作及瞬間動作。持續動作是持續一段時間才完成的動作，搭配進行式表示過程，完成式表示完成，例如：

例 1 Tom is playing oboe.
湯姆正在吹黑管。

例 2 The chef has cooked for three hours.
主廚已經煮了三小時。

例 3 Hank has been doing the work for two days.
那工作漢克一直做了兩天。

◆ 瞬間動作是一旦發生便立即完成，不搭配進行式或完成式，例如：

例 4 My grandfather died of liver cancer.
我祖父死於肝癌。

例 5 The manager joined the company five years ago.
經理在五年前加入這家公司。

例 6 I borrowed this book from the library.
我從圖書館借到這本書。

例 7 The tourists arrived at the hotel as scheduled.
這批觀光客按照行程抵達飯店。

◆ until 的意思是直到，表示結束，若搭配持續動詞，表示持續一段時間的動作要結束，例如：

例 8 Jack slept until 11 o'clock this morning.
傑克今天早上睡到十一點。

例 9 They stayed at the meeting point until I arrived.
他們在會面處一直待到我抵達。

例 10 They waited until the rain had stopped.
他們一直等到雨停。

◆ 若是表示「直到某時才開始」，由於動作尚未開始，更是尚未持續，搭配否定式的瞬間動作，例如：

例 11 Tom didn't go to bed until his parents got back home.

湯姆直到他父母返家才去睡覺。

例 12 I didn't fall asleep until after 5 o'clock this morning.

我直到清晨五點才睡著。

Chapter 4.
鄰近原則

為了形成語意字群，或是指涉明確，相關的
語詞會相鄰排列，這是相鄰原則。

Q01. "*With ponytail hair style, I met a cute boy." 這句子正確嗎？

原來如此 不正確，修飾名詞的介係詞片語不可移出名詞片語而置於句首。

◆ 強調語詞常前移至句首以達到聚焦訊息的效果，這是前移的修辭手法。語詞前移，原來位置不填補而留下挪移的痕跡。主詞、受詞、補語或修飾語詞都常移至句首。

(1) 主詞

例 1 Those bigwigs were talking and laughing in the lobby.

Those bigwigs, they were talking and laughing in the lobby.

是那些大咖在大廳裡大談闊論，開懷大笑。

→ 逗號將主詞與句子隔開，主詞位置以代名詞填補，造成主詞前移的效果。

(2) 受詞

例 2 The woman has rescued a number of stray dogs these years.

A number of stray dogs, the woman has rescued these years.

那位婦人這幾年救了不少流浪狗。

例 3 You couldn't pay me to see that show.

That show you couldn't pay me to see.

即使你招待，我也不去看那場表演。

例 4 My landlady made a chocolate cake for me.

A chocolate cake my landlady made for me.

我的女房東做一個巧克力蛋糕招待我。

(3) 補語

例 5 The man eventually became rich and famous.

Rich and famous, the man eventually became.

最後那名男子功成名就。

(4) 副詞修飾語

例 6 I guess the thief is hiding somewhere inside the building.

Somewhere inside the building, I guess the thief is hiding.

我猜想那名小偷就躲在建築物裡面的某個地方。

例 7　We will make no further comment on this sensitive issue.

On this sensitive issue, we will make no further comment.

我們不針對這敏感議題進一步評論。

◆ 感嘆句也是語詞前移的結果。

例 8　What a nice day it is!

好棒的一天！

例 9　How sweet those words are!

那些話好窩心！

例 10　How beautifully the candle is burning!

這蠟燭燒得好美！

◆ 英文的溝通模式是重點在前，修飾在後，主要子句在前而從屬子句在後易為閱聽者接受，這種句子稱為鬆散句。從屬子句前移，重點掉尾，這種句子稱為掉尾句，從屬子句後面常見逗號，例如：

例 11　鬆散句：We canceled our picnic because it was raining all day.

我們取消了我們的野餐活動，因為下一整天的雨。

掉尾句：Because it was raining all day, we canceled our picnic.

因為下一整天的雨，我們取消了我們的野餐活動。

◆ 修飾名詞的介係詞片語不可前移至句首，若是挪移，介係詞片語將成為副詞詞性，修飾動作，因此，名詞與介係詞片語必須維持鄰近關係。

誤　With ponytail hair style, I met a cute boy.

例 12　I met a cute boy with ponytail hair style.

我遇見一位綁馬尾的俏男孩。

◆ 副詞詞性的介係詞片語可以前移：

例 13　I met two of my previous colleagues in the party.

In the party, I met two of my previous colleagues.

派對中我遇到我的二位前同事。

Q02. " I saw a mouse running out from under the sofa. "句中的介係詞 from 為什麼接介係詞片語？

原來如此 介係詞片語可當另一介係詞的受詞，共同構成一個介係詞片語。

◆ 依照構詞型態，介係詞可分為單詞介係詞及片語介係詞，單詞介係詞就是單詞構成的介係詞，例如 at、on、in、from 等，片語介係詞是介係詞與其他幾個字共同構成的介係詞，例如 because of、in front of、on account of 等片語，最右側一定是介係詞。單詞或是片語介係詞的語意都不可分割，例如 in front of 的意思就是「在……前面」。

◆ 介係詞加接受詞以形成介係詞片語，例如：

(1) 單詞介係詞

例 1 at the corner

在角落

例 2 in the bottle

在瓶子裏面

(2) 片語介係詞

例 3 because of the thick fog

由於濃霧

例 4 in spite of his injury

儘管負傷

◆ 介係詞片語除了修飾功用，還可當句子的主詞，例如：

例 5 From 10 to 12 would be fine with me.

10 點到 12 點我可以。

例 6 Around 9 p.m. is OK.

晚上九點左右可以。

◆ 介係詞片語可做為另一介係詞的受詞，構成一個有關空間的介係詞片語，例如：

例 7 I saw a mouse running out from under the sofa.

我看見一隻老鼠從沙發底下跑出來。

例 8 The man managed to hide cocaine in between his teeth.

該名男子設法將古柯鹼藏在牙縫中。

例 9 The police broke the door and dragged him from under the bed.

警方破門，然後將他從床底下拖出來。

Q03. 為什麼 "What made you change your mind?" 句中 made 的受詞補語是原形？

原來如此 make 是使役動詞，受詞補語以原形動詞標記其對事件的掌控程度。

◆ 使役動詞 make、have、let 的主事者以意志驅使受事者進行動作，搭配原形動詞作為受詞補語，例如：

例1 What made you change your mind?

什麼使你改變心意？

例2 I'll have someone collect your luggage.

我會要人去領取你的行李。

例3 My sister decided to let her hair grow long.

我妹妹決定讓她的頭髮留長。

◆ 動詞原形的受詞補語標示 have、make、let 對於受詞的強烈操控，略去不定詞標記 to 使使役動詞與受詞補語之間的句構距離縮短，凸顯要求達成使命的力度。

◆ 另外，若要表示主事者驅使受事者開始或持續進行動作，make、have 搭配現在分詞當受詞補語，例如：

例4 This song made me crying.

這首歌讓我哭個不停。

例5 This anime really made me laughing a lot.

這部動畫真的令我笑個不停。

例6 The janitor will have the pump working soon.

管理員很快就會使抽水機開始運作。

Q04. "Don't get him talking about political issues." 這句話用 talking 正確嗎？

 原來如此 正確。**get** 搭配現在分詞當受詞補語，表示主詞驅使受詞開始進行動作。

◆ get 常搭配受詞及受詞補語，受詞補語表示受事者受影響而改變的狀況，幾種結構如下：

(1) 形容詞

例1 Mrs. Lin had to get her son ready for school.
林太太得幫她的兒子預備好去上學。

(2) 不定詞，受事者受驅使或說服而進行動作，例如：

例2 I can't get my laptop to work!
我無法讓我的筆電運作！

例3 I can't get my dog to calm down quickly.
我無法快速讓我的狗平靜下來。

例4 Get the janitor to help out if possible.
可能的話，讓管理員來幫一下忙。

例5 Why don't you get her to eat out with us?
何不勸她跟我們一起出去吃飯？

(3) 現在分詞，受事者開始進行動作。

例6 Don't get him talking about political issues, or he will never stop.
不要讓他打開政治議題的話匣子，否則他會滔滔不絕。

例7 The office was very hot until we got the air conditioner working.
辦公室直到冷氣開始運轉才不熱。

(4) 過去分詞，受事者的被動結果狀態或是經驗。

例8 I'm going to get my hair dyed red tomorrow.
我明天要去把頭髮染紅。

例9 I got my son dressed before breakfast.
早餐前我就幫我兒子穿好衣服。

例10 I always get the twins confused.
我總是將那對雙胞胎給搞混了。

Q05. "The car was stolen which the man had rented yesterday."這句話對嗎？

 英美人士不接受，名詞片語應保持完整，名詞的修飾語詞，無論是介係詞片語或形容詞子句，都不應移出名詞片語。

◆ 句子中語意緊密的成分應該相鄰，以使訊息連貫而完整，例如：

例1 I saw an armadillo on the side of the road.

我在路邊看到一隻犰狳。

→ 及物動詞 saw 與受詞 an armadillo

例2 The boy comes from Australia.

那位男孩來自澳洲。

→ 主詞 The boy 與動詞 comes

例3 I met my previous boss in the shopping mall.

我在購物賣場遇見我的前老闆。

→ 動詞片語 met my previous boss 與修飾語 in the shopping mall

◆ 語意關聯的語詞常因一些原因而分離，例如：

(1) 形成疑問句

例4 What did you see --- on the side of the road?

你在路邊看到什麼？

→ 及物動詞 see 與受詞分離。

(2) 強調

例5 In the shopping mall, I met my previous boss.

在購物賣場，我遇見我的前老闆。

→ 副詞性質的介係詞片語因強調而前移至句首。

(3) 插入修飾語詞

例6 The boy in blue jacket comes from Australia.

穿藍色牛仔褲的那位男孩來自澳洲。

◆ 訊息單位應保持完整，組成成分不應挪移而造成語意不連貫，如下面例句不為英美人士所接受，如例 7 則是適當的寫法：

誤 The car was stolen which the man had rented yesterday.

→ 形容詞子句與先行詞分離

例 7 The car which the man had rented yesterday was stolen.

　→ 考量語意明確，形容詞子句與先行詞相鄰。

◆ 關係代名詞指涉介係詞的受詞，介係詞與關係代名詞也應相鄰，以使介係詞片語結構完整，語意連貫，例如：

例 8 The couple adored the hostel at which they stayed.

這對夫婦非常喜歡他們入住的民宿。

◆ 例 10 的 where 是指 in the box、on the box、under the box，還是 outside the box，語意不明確，因此，保留介係詞是必要的。保留介係詞，語意明確，常視為正式用法，如例 11。

例 9 Let me show you the box where I found the card.

讓你看我找到卡片的盒子。

例 10 Let me show you the box in / on / under which I found the card.

讓你看我在那裡面 / 上面 / 底下找到卡片的那個盒子。

◆ 分詞構句是否保留連接詞也是語意考量，例如：

例 11 Crossing the finish line, the runner took a selfie.

跨越終點線，那名跑者自拍。

　→ 連接詞省略，語意不明確。

例 12 While/Before/After/ If crossing the finish line, the runner took a selfie.

　→ 連接詞保留，明確表示自拍的時機或條件。

Q06. "I gave Tom a ball." 可代換為 "I gave a ball to Tom." 嗎?

 原來如此 不,訊息焦點不同,不可代換。

◆ give 表示「給誰某物」時,必須提到給誰(間接受詞)及給的物品(直接受詞),間接受詞與直接受詞都是語意完整的必要成分,但是,詞序會影響訊息的份量,例如:

例1 I gave Tom a ball.

我給湯姆一顆球。

◆ 依據尾重原則,例 1 的訊息焦點是 "a ball",對應的問句如例 2:

例2 What did you give Tom?

你給湯姆什麼?

→ "a ball" 回應 "what",答句的訊息焦點。

◆ 例 3 以介係詞 to 引介 "a ball" 的接收者 "Tom",形成介係詞片語,而介係詞片語的結構較名詞片語 "a ball" 大(介係詞片語包含名詞片語),因此, "to Tom" 置於 "a ball" 的右側,Tom 也就成為訊息焦點。例 4 是對應例 3 的問句:

例3 I gave a ball to Tom.

我把一顆球給湯姆。

例4 Whom did you give a ball to?

你把一顆球給誰?

→ "Tom" 回應 "whom",答句的訊息焦點。

◆ 基於尾重原則,無論是直接受詞或是間接受詞,結構複雜或字數多的語詞置於右側,例如:

例5 Castro gave his men a chance to accompany the President abroad.

Philippine Star

卡斯楚給他的人民一個在海外陪伴總統的機會。

→ "a chance to accompany the President abroad" 是直接受詞,包含不定詞,置於間接受詞—his men 的右側。

Q07. "I hurried to the drug store, only to find it closed."中的 only 是什麼意思？

 原來如此 only 搭配表示結果的不定詞，意味著「只有這樣的結果」，負面或不幸的節奏，中文可以對應「不料」。

◆ "only to V" 副詞性質，only 的意思是僅僅，不定詞表示結果，「僅僅這樣的結果」當然是事與願違，一種失望而產生負面或不幸的結果 — with the negative or unfortunate result that (*Oxford Dictionary*)。由於是結果，"only to V" 置於事件之後，例如：

例1 I hurried to the drug store, only to find it closed.
我趕到那間藥局，不料發現打烊了。

例2 The house survived the fire, only to collapse in the earthquake two weeks later.
這棟房子從祝融中存留下來，不料在二周後的地震中倒塌。

例3 The man turned into the car park, only to find his way blocked.
該名男子轉進停車場，不料發現路不通。

◆ 「only to V」可以還原為限定動詞，例1～例3 可以改寫為例4～例6：

例4 I hurried to the drugstore, and only found it closed.

例5 The house survived the fire, and only collapsed in the earthquake two weeks later.

例6 The man turned into the car park, and only found his way blocked.

◆ only 修飾 "have to"，強調為了目的而必須做，意思是只要、只需，例如：

例7 If you need any help, you have only to ask.
= If you need any help, all you have to do is to ask.
如果需要任何協助，儘管開口。

例8 You have only to do what you were told.
= All you have to do is to do what you were told.
你只要做人家吩咐你的事就好。

◆ "only too…to" 中的 "only too" 是 "very" 的意思，例如：

例 9 We are only too willing to accept the proposal.
　　我們非常樂意接受該提議。

例 10 I am only too delighted to accept your kind invitation.
　　我非常高興接受你親切的邀請。

Q08. "Tom never smokes or drinks."的"or" 是什麼意思？

原來
如此　"or" 的意思是 "and not"。

◆ 否定二者時，常以否定詞搭配對等連接詞 or，這時 or 表示 and not，例如：

例1 Tom never smokes or drinks.

= Tom never smokes and never drinks.

湯姆從不抽菸喝酒。

例2 Helen couldn't see or hear.

= Helen couldn't see and couldn't hear.

海倫看不見也聽不到。

◆ 同時或接連發生的二個動作可用 and 連接，視為一個動作，例如：

例3 Don't drink and drive. Don't do it.

酒後不開車。不可這樣做。

→ drink 及 drive 是連貫，甚至同時發生的動作。

例4 Don't eat and talk at the same time.

不要同時吃東西又講話。

→ 同時發生而視為一個動作。

例5 Don't walk and use your smartphone.

不要邊走路邊滑手機。

→ 同時發生而視為一個動作。

Q09. "Don't drink and drive."為什麼就是指喝酒？

 wine 是 drink 最常見的受詞，可以省略。

◆ 從人類的飲料發展歷史來看，除了水之外，最早出現的就是酒，尤其是啤酒及葡萄酒，取自穀物或水果發酵釀製的酒精飲料。酒源自人類的生活需求，進而豐富精神文明，聖經中有水變酒的典故，中國的詩詞歌賦及金庸小說處處可聞酒香。

◆ 就字源而言，喝—drink 若要演變為名詞，當然是飲料，更直接的是酒，因此，drink 又有飲料或酒的意思，一些與酒相關的字都是 drink 的同源字或衍生字，例如 drunk、drunken 都是酒醉，drunkard 是指醉漢。

◆ drink 最容易聯想的受詞是酒，若無特別意涵，通常省略，這和中文的用法一致，例如：

例 1 Don't drink and drive.
不要酒後開車。

例 2 My friends and I were drinking at a bar.
我和朋友們在酒吧喝酒。

例 3 Some people prefer to drink old wine.
一些人偏愛喝老酒。
→ old wine 具有特別意涵，不可省略。

例 4 咱們來喝兩杯。

例 5 老頭子又喝多了。

◆ 省略的受詞在字面上看不到，稱為隱匿受詞，及物動詞變成不及物，sing、eat、smoke、devour 等都有搭配隱匿受詞的用法，例如：

例 6 Cindy was singing (songs) all night with her beautiful voice.
莘蒂整夜以甜美的聲音飆歌。

例 7 My dog is eating (food).
我的狗狗正在吃東西。

例 8 Don't smoke (cigarette) in here.
不要在這裡面抽菸。

例 9 We returned home to devour (a meal).

我們回家大啖一頓。

◆ feed（餵食）的隱匿受詞 food，stoke（添柴火）的隱匿受詞 wood，milk（擠牛奶）的隱匿受詞 milk 都包含在動詞。

例 10 I feed (food) my dog twice a day.

我一天餵我的狗狗二次。

例 11 Don't forget to stoke (wood) the fire, so it doesn't go out.

別忘了添柴火，火就不會熄掉。

例 12 Milking a cow by hand is a skilled process.

用手擠牛奶是一項專門技術的過程。

Q10. 電影片名《玩命關頭》— "Fast and Furious"有什麼語言意涵？

 原來如此 這是平行結構，押頭韻，短音節字在前，長音節字在後。

◆ 平行的語詞常是短音節字在前，多音節字在後，以合乎音韻趨勢，例如電影《玩命關頭》的原名 "Fast and Furious"，二字都是快速的意思，單音節的 fast 在前，多音節的 furious 在後，營造餘音繞樑的效果。另一方面，押頭韻是音節首子音相同的字重複出現而形成的押韻格式，音韻諧和、節奏明快，令人印象深刻，是常見的命名技巧，例如：

> Costco 好市多
>
> → 可能取自 Cost Coin，價美物廉的發想。
>
> Coca cola 可口可樂
>
> Coffee Corner 咖啡角落
>
> Donald Duck 唐老鴨
>
> French Fries 薯條
>
> Samsung 三星
>
> KYMCO 光陽機車
>
> Pride and Prejudice 傲慢與偏見
>
> Sense and Sensibility 理性與感性

◆ 構詞方面，不規則動詞三態變化一起唸音時，字首不論是單子音或是子音群，押頭韻甚是明顯。

do	did	done
run	ran	run
bring	brought	brought
drink	drank	drunk
fly	flew	flown
strike	struck	struck

◆ 一些同源的名詞與不規則動詞也常見押頭韻。

blood	bleed	bled	bled
food	feed	fed	fed
gift	give	gave	given
song	sing	sang	sung

Q11. "Brian as well as his roommates is going to the concert tonight." 這句話對嗎？

原來如此 對，但主詞部分可寫成 "As well as his roommates, Brian is going to the concert tonight."

◆ 主詞與動詞在人稱、單複數，甚至性別一致是許多印歐語系語言的特性，英語尤其強調數目的一致。以對等連接詞而言，除了 and 表示合併之外，"neither… nor"、"either…or" 連結的語詞不可合併，直述句中，動詞與鄰近的名詞單複數一致。

例 1 Brian and his roommates are sophomores.

布萊恩和他的室友都是大二生。

→ 合併：They are sophomores.

例 2 Neither Brian nor his roommates come from Hong Kong.

布萊恩和他的室友都不是來自香港。

例 3 Either Brian or his roommates is going to the baseball game.

不是布萊恩就是他的室友要去看棒球比賽。

◆ "not only…but also" 焦點是後者，動詞與後者數目一致。

例 4 Not only Brian but also his roommates are interested in the new video game.

不僅是布萊恩，他的室友也對這款新電玩感到興趣。

◆ "as well as" 前面的 as 是副詞，後面的 as 是介係詞，也就是說，名詞片語 "A as well as B" 應分析為 A 連接 as 引導的介係詞片語，A 是中心詞，B 是介係詞的受詞，附帶一提的舊訊息。因此，"as well as" 出現在主詞時，A 決定動詞數目，但為避免混淆，"as well as B" 以逗號隔開。

例 5 Brian, as well as his roommates, is going to the concert tonight.

布萊恩連同他的室友今晚要去聽音樂會。

◆ 例 5 的主詞是 Brian，但 "as well as his roommates" 造成主詞與動詞部分不相鄰，結構不連貫，語意也容易混淆，因此常將 "as well as his roommates" 移至句首，這時 "as well as" 等同於 "besides" 或 "in addition to"。

例 6 As well as his roommates, Brian is going to the concert tonight.

= Besides / In addition to his roommates, Brian is going to the concert tonight.

◆ "as well as his roommates" 也常移至句尾，但結構改變。

例 7 Brian is going to the concert, and his roommates are as well.

Q12. "Cindy is too willing to marry Tom."是說 Cindy 不願嫁給 Tom 嗎？

原來 如此 不是，**Cindy 十分願意嫁給 Tom。**

◆ " too…to " 句型可分為二部分，一是 too 與形容詞或副詞所形成的片語，二是表示結果的不定詞。too 的意思是 "more than enough"，too 片語若表示負向的狀況，結果就是負向，意思是「太……而不能……」，這是因果關聯的中文對應。

例 1 The water is too cold to swim in.

水太冷了，無法在裡面游泳。

例 2 Three hours is too long to wait.

三小時太長了，等不下去。

◆ 搭配 not、never 等否定詞，否定負向的原因或結果，句子呈現肯定意涵。

(1) 否定詞在 too 前面

例 3 It's never too late to mend.

亡羊補牢，猶未晚也。

例 4 It's not too late to learn.

活到老，學到老。

例 5 English is never too difficult to learn.

英文絕不會難到學不起來。

(2) 否定詞在不定詞標記 to 的前面，結果正向，原因也是正向，too 是「很、非常」的意思。

例 6 The clerk is too careful not to have noticed it.

這位職員很細心，不會沒注意到。

例 7 The foreign student is too clever not to learn Chinese well.

這位外國學生很聰明，不會學不好中文。

◆ too 片語若不表示負向的原因，不定詞則是肯定的結果。

例 8 My supervisor is too ready to suspect.

我的主管愛起疑心。

例 9 Cindy is too willing to marryTom.

辛蒂十分願意嫁給湯姆。

例 10 Tom was too glad to hear from his uncle again.

湯姆很高興再得到他叔叔的訊息。

例 11 John is too eager to fill in for his partner.

約翰很樂意幫他夥伴代班。

◆ too 搭配 but、only、all 等副詞，加強肯定語氣，but too、only too、all too 都是 very 的意思。

例 12 Jack is but too ready to help out.

傑克非常樂意幫忙。

例 13 I will be only too pleased to meet Mr. Lin again.

我將非常樂於再次見到林先生。

例 14 We are all too satisfied to take your advice.

我們非常樂意接受你的建議。

◆ very 與 too 修飾形容詞的意涵不同，"very" 是增強形容詞的程度，"too" 則是過於所需的程度，例如：

例 15 Leo is very careful, but sometimes, he seems to be too careful.

里歐非常細心，但有時候似乎太過謹慎。

Q13. "We dined in a restaurant last night." 為什麼地方副詞置於時間副詞前面？

 相較於時間訊息，空間訊息與動作的關係較為緊密，句構上較接近動詞。

◆ 語意關聯密切的語詞相互接近，這是詞序上的形意搭配，也是鄰近原則，例如：

(1) 名詞片語，補語較修飾功用的加接詞接近名詞：

> 限定詞　　加接詞　　補語　　名詞

例1 a quality and exquisite silk necktie
一條高級又高雅的絲質領帶

(2) 同位語子句較形容詞子句接近名詞，限定形容詞子句又較補述形容詞子句接近名詞：

> 名詞　　同位語子句　　限定形容詞子句　　補述形容詞子句

例2 the fact that the woman is guilty, which very few people believe
　　　　　　同位語子句　　　　　　　　　補述形容詞子句

那個事實—那名婦人有罪，幾乎沒有人相信

(3) 地方副詞較時間副詞接近動詞：

> 動詞　　地方副詞　　時間副詞

例3 We dined in a restaurant last night.
我們昨晚在一家餐廳用餐。

例4 Van Gogh lived in Paris, from 1886 to 1888.
梵谷自 1886 年至 1888 年住在巴黎。

◆ 為什麼地方副詞比較接近動詞呢？因為地點可當動詞的位置受詞，標示事件的地點，動詞的必要成分。地點也可當動作的目標或來源，補語角色，與動詞的語意關係緊密。時間訊息只有修飾功能，通常置於地方副詞的右側，距離動詞較遠。

(1) 地點作為動詞的受詞：

例 5 We climbed the mountain together.

我們一起爬那座山。

例 6 The delegation will visit these countries.

該代表團將走訪這些國家。

(2) 地點作為動作的目標或來源：

例 7 The cargo has arrived at the destination.

該批貨物已送達目的地。

例 8 Elephants are walking to the river.

大象正往河流走去。

例 9 The family immigrated from Russia.

這戶人家移民自俄羅斯。

◆ 空間對於動作的限制多於時間，一些動作只有在特定的空間才會發生，因此，一些表示場所的單字或複合詞都包含相關的動作，足見地點與動作密切關聯。

> factory 工廠，字根 fact，make — 製造
>
> auditorium 禮堂，字根 au，hear — 聽
>
> dining room 餐廳，dine，吃正餐
>
> living room 客廳，live，生活

(3) 若是強調時間訊息，時間副詞移至句首，例如：

例 10 Last night, a terrible attack occurred downtown.

昨夜，市中心區發生一起可怕的攻擊事件。

例 11 In 2008, a severe earthquake happened in Wenchuan, China.

2008 年，中國汶川發生一起強烈地震。

◆ 精確的地方或時間清楚描述動作，詞序上較為接近動詞，例如：

例 11 The lady took selfies on the balcony in the old house.

那位婦人在老房子的陽台上自拍。

例 12 I woke up around five this morning.

我今天清晨五點左右醒來。

Q14. 為什麼情態副詞總是置於地方或時間副詞前面？

 原來如此 情態副詞顯示動作的樣貌，與動詞的語意關聯密切，比較接近動詞。

◆ 地方副詞說明動作的空間訊息，時間副詞提供時間訊息，而情態副詞描述動作的樣貌，呈現動作的本質，語意關聯密切，因此與動詞相鄰：

動詞　　情態副詞　　地方副詞　　時間副詞

例 1 Engineers were working hard in the laboratory all night.
工程師整夜都在實驗室努力工作。
→ hard 是情態副詞，in the laboratory 是介係詞片語結構的地方副詞，all night 是名詞片語結構的時間副詞。

例 2 The security guard has been standing still at the door for one hour.
警衛一直在門口站著不動一小時了。
→ still 是情態副詞，at the door 是介係詞片語結構的地方副詞，for one hour 是介係詞片語結構的時間副詞。

◆ 動詞加接受詞，情態副詞置於受詞右側，受詞是動詞的必要成分，二者不可置入其他語詞。

例 3 The man closed the door quietly.
那名男子靜靜地把門關上。
→ closed 和 the door 之間不可置入語詞。

例 4 The chef fixed the meal cheerfully.
主廚愉悅地調理菜餚。
→ fixed 和 the meal 之間不可置入語詞。

◆ 句子若包含數個動詞組，情態副詞與所修飾的動詞組相鄰，這是語意對應詞序的相鄰原則。

例 5 The instructor asked Tom quietly to leave the classroom.
指導員靜靜地要求湯姆離開教室。
→ quietly 修飾 askedTom。

例 6 The instructor quietly asked Tom to leave the classroom.

指導員靜靜地要求湯姆離開教室。

→ quietly 也是修飾 asked Tom，情態副詞置於動詞組前，具有強調意味。

例 7 The instructor asked Tom to leave the classroom quietly.

指導員要求湯姆安靜離開教室。

→ quietly 修飾 to leave the classroom。

◆ 情態副詞修飾與主詞相鄰的動詞組時，情態副詞可前移至句首，目的
是引發閱聽者的注意或好奇，例 5、6 可改寫為例 8，例 7 若是改寫，
則與修飾的動詞組產生遠距關係而導致語意混淆。

例 8 Quietly, the instructor asked Tom to leave the classroom.

不作聲響地，指導員要求湯姆離開教室。

◆ 一些置於句首的情態副詞是針對句子所述內容的評論。

例 9 Luckily, my brother had some money with him.

幸好我弟弟身上帶些錢。

例 10 Personally, I won't agree with you.

以個人來說，我不贊同你。

例 11 Hopefully, I will win the lottery one day.

但願有一天我能中頭彩。

Q15. "Especiall organic food has incredible health benefits."中的副詞 especially 是修飾整句嗎？

原來如此 不是，**especially** 修飾名詞 **organic food**。

◆ 形容詞與副詞都是修飾功能的詞類，形容詞修飾名詞，副詞修飾動詞、形容詞、其他副詞、句子，甚至名詞。

修飾動詞的副詞描述動作的樣貌，稱為情態副詞，大都是形容詞字幹黏接副詞詞綴 -ly。構詞上，副詞詞綴 -ly 不會黏接其他字尾綴詞，也就是說，-ly 是單詞最右側的詞綴，這個構詞模式與句子底層結構一致──副詞是句子最右側的組成成分。

(1) –ly 是單詞的最右側詞綴：

carefully 小心地

occasionally 偶爾

friendly 友善地

friendliness 友善

godliness 虔誠

→ 形容詞字幹黏接 –ness 而構成名詞。

(2) 副詞是句子最右側的組成成分：

例 1 Tom was driving carelessly.

湯姆那時開車不小心。

例 2 We moved the boxes carefully.

我們小心搬動箱子。

◆ 情態副詞常修飾整個句子，陳述作說者對於句子所述內容的評論，大多置於句首，置於句尾時，語氣較弱，例如：

例 3 Luckily, they came back safe and sound the next day.

幸運地，他們隔天平安歸來。

They came back safe and sound the next day, luckily.

他們隔天平安歸來，還好。

例 4 Personally, I cannot live without music.

以我個人來説，沒有音樂我是活不下去。

I cannot live without music, personally.

沒有音樂我是活不下去，這是就我個人來説。

◆ 副詞修飾形容詞或其他副詞時，說明程度或評論，一些程度副詞同樣是形容詞字幹黏接副詞詞綴 -ly。

程度

例 5 My pet pig is quite smart.

我的寵物豬相當聰明。

例 6 The truck driver drove too slowly.

那位卡車司機開太慢了。

例 7 Those Russian dancers performed extremely well.

那些俄羅斯舞者表演地非常精彩。

例 8 It's a really difficult decision.

它是個非常困難的決定。

例 9 An incredibly loud bang followed the flash.

Cambridge Dictionary

閃電之後跟著一聲震耳欲聾的巨響。

◆ 一些程度副詞搭配心理或情緒狀態的動詞，例如：

例 10 The news surprised me very much.

這消息令我非常驚訝。

◆ 副詞修飾名詞或代名詞時，常是限制或強調修飾對象。

例 11 Especially organic food has incredible health benefits.

尤其是有機食物擁有極佳的健康益處。

→ especially 修飾名詞片語 organic food

例 12 Only a dog accompanied the old woman.

只有一隻狗陪伴那位老人。

→ only 修飾名詞片語 a dog

例 13 Even the chief engineer could not fix the machine.

甚至連總工程師都無法修理這部機器。

→ even 修飾名詞片語 the chief engineer

例 14 The residents there seem to be well taken care of.

那裡的居民似乎受到良好照顧。

→ there 修飾名詞片語 the residents

例 15 You alone should maintain dental hygiene.

你自己要維持牙齒衛生。

→ alone 修飾代名詞 you

Chapter 5.
指涉明確

不像中文誰是誰常語焉不詳，指涉明確是英文句式的重要特徵，也是印歐語系普遍的性質。指涉明確就是明確指出談話中涉及的人、事、物是哪一位？哪一樁？哪一個？知道就知道，不知便不知，清楚交代。

Q01. 為什麼母音為首的名詞搭配的是 an ？

 原來如此 **an** 連接母音為首的單字，形成 **CV** 拼音結構。

◆ 以字源而言，**an** 較早出現，源自古英文的 **one**，黏接字尾 y 構成限定詞 **any**，**other** 黏接 **an** 構成 **another**，「另一個」的意思。**an** 置於母音前面，符合 **CVC** 拼音趨勢，置於子音前面，/n/ 音漸漸脫落而形成 **a**，符合子音與母音相鄰的語音排列。

　　　an + 母音起首的單字

　　　an apple

　　　an eel

　　　an igloo

　　　an octopus

　　　an umbrella

　　　a + 子音起首的單字

　　　a book

　　　a friend

　　　a chair

　　　a yo-yo

◆ 英語是拼音文字，子音與母音相鄰是最好的語音排列及音節構造。因此，音節劃分有一「音節首子音優先」的原則─子音優先劃分在右側母音的音節以形成拼音的組合。

　　　pa-per

　　　tea-cher

　　　Si-mon

◆ 字根黏接字尾綴詞時，若是子音相鄰，我們常插入一母音並增加一字母─填補字母。

　　　cent-i-meter

　　　techn-o-logy

　　　act-u-al

◆ 單數名詞形成複數時，黏接屈折字尾 -s，由於有聲子音與母音都是有聲，數量較無聲子音多，因此字尾 -s 唸有聲子音 /z/，例如：

      dogs

      hands

      pens

      monkeys

      kangaroos

      umbrellas

◆ 字尾是無聲子音的單字黏接複數字尾 -s 時，為了發音順暢，無聲的性質將 /z/ 同化為無聲的 /s/，例如：

      z → s / -C + _____

      maps

      cats

      desks

      thanks

◆ 字尾是與 /z/ 同樣是嘶擦音的 / s、z、ʃ、tʃ、ʒ、dʒ / 時，為了避免嘶擦音相鄰而不易唸音，我們插入響度較小的母音 /ɪ/，並增加填補字母 e 以作為字母對應。

      classes

      buzzes

      dishes

      watches

◆ 單字字尾若是不發音的 e 字母，正好對應母音 /ɪ/，因此不須加上填補字母 e，例如：

      dances

      cheeses

      garages

      oranges

Q02. "two hundred dollars"的 hundred 為什麼不是複數形？

 原來如此 hundred 搭配數詞 two，形成明確的數字，就像 twenty、twenty-five 一樣，不須是複數型。

◆ hundred、thousand、million、dozen 搭配數詞或 a few、several 等不定數量詞時，形成明確的數字，不須標記複數。數詞在名詞片語中是補語，名詞才是中心詞，單複數由中心詞標記。

例 1 one pound

一英鎊

例 2 two hundred dollars

二百元

例 3 a few dozen eggs

幾打蛋

例 4 an audience of several thousand

數千名觀眾

◆ hundred、thousand、million、dozen 表示不明確的數字時，複數語意，標記複數字尾。複數語詞不加接名詞，以 of 介係詞引介，of 表示數量、數目或特定單位。數詞與 of 介係詞片語形成名詞片語，數詞是中心詞，介係詞片語是補語。

例 5 hundreds of residents

數以百計的居民

例 6 thousands of students

數以千計的學生

例 7 several millions of people

數百萬的人

例 8 hundreds of thousands of immigrants

數十萬的移民

Q03. "The orange is not the tangerine."表示全體嗎？

 原來如此 the 多指特定，鮮少表示類別。

◆ 泛指一個群體的總稱時，無須考量特定或不特定，不搭配冠詞，可數名詞以複數形表示。

例1 Oranges are not tangerines.

柳丁不是橘子。

例2 Pencils are not pens.

鉛筆不是鋼筆。

◆ 泛指的物質名詞

例3 I have always preferred tea to coffee.

我一向偏好茶飲甚於咖啡。

例4 Christians believe Jesus turned water into wine.

基督徒相信耶穌把水變為酒。

例5 Children should get close to nature.

孩童應該親近大自然。

◆ 搭配定冠詞 the 指涉特定。

例6 The oranges will be processed into juice.

這些柳丁將加工成果汁。

例7 The pencils were imported from China.

這些鉛筆進口自中國。

◆ 特指的物質名詞

例8 I am not clear where the coffee you ordered comes from.

我不清楚你訂的咖啡來自哪裡。

例9 The wine tastes smooth.

這款酒品嚐起來蠻醇厚的。

例10 I never really understood the nature of the artist's work.

我從未完整理解那位藝術家的作品特質。

◆ 不定冠詞 a、an 標示群體中的分類。

例 11 Citruses are a tangerine.

柑橘是一種橘子。

例 12 A baby zebra can stand soon after it is born.

斑馬幼獸出生不久就能站立。

◆ 不定冠詞 a、an 不可標示群體，以下句子是錯誤的：

誤 Do you like a cat?

誤 A tiger is an endangered species in the wild.

◆ 電影、文件或討論的主題常以單數名詞搭配 the 表示群體。

例 13 The tiger is an endangered species in the wild.

老虎是一種野外的瀕臨絕種動物。

例 14 The pen is mightier than the sword.

文勝於武。

→ "the pen" 是指 "writing 寫作"，特定的意涵，搭配 the。

◆ 我們常用單數名詞搭配 a、an 定義某一群體。

例 15 A dictionary is a book which explains the meanings of words.

字典是一本解釋字義的書。

例 16 An encyclopedia is a book with a collection of information about many subjects.

百科全書是一本包含許多主題的大量訊息的書。

Q04. "A Mr. Lin called you when you were in the meeting. "為什麼專有名詞前面有不定冠詞"a"？

原來如此 不定冠詞 a 標記非共同認知。

◆ 溝通過程提及的人、事、物是否共同認知決定搭配的冠詞，如例 1 至例 8 的 the 標示共同認知， 說話者與聽話者都知道的指涉對象，例 11 ～ 12 以 a 標記非共同認知。另外，the 也表示非共同認知，如例 14 ～例 15：

例1 The Jeddah Tower in Saudi Arabia will be the tallest building in the world.
位於沙烏地阿拉伯的吉達塔將是世界最高建築物。

例2 Do not smoke indoors, including in the teaching building.
不得在室內吸菸，包括教學大樓。

例3 Don't put your coat on the sofa.
不要把你的外套放在沙發上。

例4 Some children are swinging in the park.
一些孩童正在公園裡玩鞦韆。
→ 現在進行式對應明確時間，the park 表示共同認知。

例5 Girard has been called the Einstein of the social sciences.
吉哈一直被譽為社會科學的愛因斯坦。
→ the 標記共同認知的 Einstein，不是某一位 Einstein。

例6 The earth moves around the sun.
地球繞著太陽運行。

◆ 除了共同認知，特定情境的 sun 也搭配 the，非特定情境搭配 a。

例7 Today, the setting sun above the horizon made a beautiful scene.
今天，地平線上的落日構成一幅美麗景致。

例8 In my mind, a rising sun looks bigger than a setting sun.
在我看來，上升的太陽看起來比下沉的太陽來得大。

◆ 泛指一般或當下的 sky，搭配 the，某一情境下的天空搭配 a。

例9 Look at the cloudless sky.
看看這無雲的天空。

例 10 The forecast was for a clear sky this morning.

= The forecast was for clear skies this morning.

天氣預報顯示今天早上天空晴朗。

例 11 A Mr. Lin called you when you were in the meeting.

一位林先生在您會議時打電話給您。

◆ 不定冠詞 a 標記非共同認知的對象，比較例 12：

例 12 Mr. Lin called you when you were in the meeting.

林先生在您會議時打電話給您。

→ 無標記，共同認知的 Mr. Lin。

例 13 She loves window shopping in the department store.

她喜歡在百貨公司瀏覽櫥窗而不購物。

→ 未特指哪一家百貨公司，the 標示非特指。

例 14 The patient was advised to exercise in the park every morning.

有人建議該名病患每天早上在公園運動。

→ 未特指哪一處公園，the 標示非特指。

Q05. 怎麼分辨 "a number of" 與 "the number of" 的用法？

原來如此   "a number of" 是限定詞，許多的意思； "the number of" 是 "the number" 搭配 "of 介係詞片語" ，表示名詞的數量。

◆   "a number of" 是限定詞，意思是許多，搭配複數名詞以形成名詞片語，中心詞是複數名詞。

例 1   a number of students

    許多學生

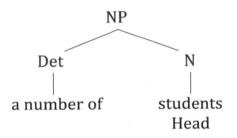

◆   辨識上，a 是不定冠詞， "number" 不是名詞片語的訊息焦點，因此， "a number of" 構成的名詞片語當句子主詞時，搭配複數動詞。

例 2   A number of students are from Hong Kong.

    許多學生來自香港。

◆   "the number of" 是 "the number" 搭配 "of 介係詞片語" 所形成的名詞片語，定冠詞 the 標記 number 是訊息焦點，也是名詞片語的中心詞，of 介係詞片語是 number 的修飾語。

例 3   the number of students

    學生人數

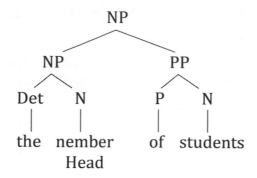

◆ number 表示數目，指涉複數名詞，因此，of 加接複數名詞。 "the number of" 構成的名詞片語當句子主詞時，中心詞是 number，搭配單數動詞。

例 4 The number of members has been reduced to less than 100.

會員人數已減少至不到 100 人。

例 5 The number of the students who failed Physics was 250.

物理學不及格的學生人數是 250 人。

◆ "a number of" 與 "the number of" 的分辨直接從冠詞著手，搭配 "a" 的 number 不是訊息焦點，複數名詞才是中心詞，搭配複數動詞；搭配 "the" 的 number 是訊息焦點，搭配單數動詞。

Q06. "I don't like this kind of film." 的 film 為什麼不加限定詞？

 原來如此 film 說明 kind 的內容，不具指涉意義，不加限定詞。

◆ 情態助動詞或 do 助動詞加接動詞原形，時態標記在助動詞。含 kind 的名詞片語中，kind 是中心詞，搭配限定詞標記指涉性質，of 引介的名詞是修飾語，不須標記指涉，例如：

(1) 可數名詞與 kind 的數目一致以形成對稱：

單數名詞

例1 I don't like this kind of film.
　　我不喜歡這類的影片。

例2 The clerk is not this kind of person.
　　該名職員不是這類的人。

例3 Jogging is a kind of sport.
　　慢跑是一種運動。

複數名詞

例4 Hank likes all kinds of sports.
　　漢克喜歡各種運動。

例5 My mom likes all kinds of fruits.
　　我媽媽喜歡各種水果。

例6 The country now exports all kinds of industrial products.
　　該國目前出口各種工業產品。

(2) 搭配不可數名詞，依語意決定 kind 單複數。

單數 kind

例7 That is a kind of food.
　　那是一種食物。

複數 kinds

例8 Peter enjoys all kinds of music
　　彼得喜愛各種音樂。

◆ "most of the students" 中，of 介係詞片語標示中心詞 most 的範圍，搭配限定詞，因此，"most of students" 是錯誤形式。"most students" 不加定冠詞 the 是因為 most 與 the 都是限定詞，二者具有排他性。

誤 most the students

◆ 部分詞表示名詞的數量單位，例如容器、度量衡或是一般的名詞。包含部分詞的名詞片語中，名詞是訊息焦點，標示名詞片語的重音。部分詞除了真實呈現名詞的計量方式之外，二者也有約定成俗的搭配限制，這與漢語頗為相似，例如：一起車禍、一首曲子、一套房子、一匹馬等。

(1) 容器

a bag of sugar 一袋糖

a can of soda 一罐汽水

a cup of coffee 一杯咖啡

a glass of water 一杯水

a bowl of noodles 一碗麵

(2) 形狀

a cake of soap 一塊肥皂

a belt of trees 一排樹木

two drops of oil 二滴油

a bar of chocolate 一條巧克力

a bundle of bananas 一串香蕉

(3) 群體

a band of stray dogs 一群流浪狗

a flock of birds 一群鳥

a school of fish 一群魚

a herd of cattle 一群牛

a pride of lions 一群獅子

(4) 度量衡

two inches of snow 二英吋積雪

a pound of steak 一磅牛排

an acre of land 一畝土地

two square kilometers 二平方公里

(5) 一般名詞

a piece of wood 一塊木材

a bit of money 一些錢

a group of tourists 一群觀光客

Q07. "Tom is taller than all the students in his class." 這句話對嗎？

 原來如此 不對。個體不能與所在的團體成員比較。

◆ 句子除了結構要正確，語意還要合乎邏輯，就二者比較而言，個體不能與所在的團體成員比較。

誤 Tom is taller than all the students in his class.

例1 Tom is taller than all the other students in his class.
湯姆比他班上所有其他學生高。

例2 Tom is taller than any other student in his class.
湯姆比他班上任何其他學生高。

◆ other 除了限定詞，也有不定代名詞的性質，可數，指其餘全部時搭配定冠詞 the。

例3 There are two pens on the table. One is blue, and the other is red.
桌上有二支筆。一支是藍色的，另一支是紅色的。
→ 二支筆中的第二支是僅剩的一支，單數，搭配 the。

例4 There are four pens on the table. One is blue, and the others are red.
桌上有四支筆。一支是藍色的，其餘都是紅色的。
→ 總數是四支筆，三是所剩全部，複數，搭配 the。

例5 There are ten students in the reading room. Some are 7th graders, and others are 8th graders.
閱覽室裡有十名學生，有些是七年級生，有些是八年級生。
→ 不是群體全部，some 搭配 others，others 不是指其餘全部。

例6 There are twelve students in the reading room. Some of them are 7th graders, and the others are 8th graders.
閱覽室裡有十二名學生，有些是七年級生，其餘的是八年級生。
→ 群體全部，"some of" 搭配 "the others"，the others 表示其餘全部。

◆ an 黏接 other 形成 another，意思是另一個，不定指。

例 7 There are three pens on the table. One is blue, another is red, and the other is green.

桌上有三支筆。一支是藍色的，另一支是紅色的，其餘一支是綠色的。

→ one 是指 a pen，不特定的一支是 another。

例 8 There are many keys to success. One is courage, another is confidence, and still another is perseverance.

成功有許多關鍵因素，一是勇氣，一是信心，還有另一是堅毅。

→ 成功的關鍵因素還有其他，句中所列都是不定指，也不是全部。副詞 still 的意思是「還」，出現在三個或三個以上中最後提及的不定指，單複數不拘。

例 9 There are four pens on the table. One is blue, another is red, still another is green, and the other is purple.

桌上有四支筆。一支是藍色的，另一支是紅色的，還有一支是綠色的，其他一支是紫色的。

→ 總數是四支，前三支都是不定指，green 是最後一不定指，以 still another 表示，purple 是指剩的一支，以 the other 表示。

例 10 Some are blue, others are red, and sill others are green.

一些是藍色的，一些是紅色的，還有一些是綠色的。

→ 三部分都是不定指，第三部分搭配 still。

◆ 強調二者對比時，以 "one…another" 表示。

例 11 It is one thing to say, and another to do.

說是一回事，做是另一回事。

◆ "each other" 及 "one another" 指涉明確，搭配相互動詞，例如 agree、argue、consult、help 等，先行詞在前，因此不會充當主詞，但可形成所有格。

例 12 Both parties decided to sue each other.

雙方都決定控告對方。

例 13 They don't know each other's names.

他們不知道彼此的名字。

例 14 The board members agreed with one another.

董事會成員都彼此認同。

→ 一般認為 "each other" 僅指二者，"one another" 則指三者以上，事實上 "each other" 及 "one another" 都可通用。

Q08. "Reading comic books is fun."是誰在看漫畫書？

 泛指一般大眾，無定指。

◆ 句子結構包含主部及述部，主部是主詞部分，事件的主題，述部是動詞部分，針對主題的描述。主題及其描述構成句子的語意要件，只要合乎這要件的字串都可視為一個句子，因此，句子分為以下三類型：

(1) 限定子句：標記時態，主詞明確。

例1 Mom made a chocolate cake this morning.

　　媽媽今天早上作了一個巧克力蛋糕。

例2 The manager went to the meeting hall by taxi.

　　經理搭計程車去會議廳。

(2) 非限定子句：不標記時態，主詞可能不出現。

(2.1) 不定詞

例3 The lifeguard wanted to hold my hand.

　　那名救生員要抓住我的手。

　　→ "to hold my hand" 是非限定子句，主詞是 the lifeguard，與限定子句的主詞一致，省略。

例4 I want Tom to join us.

　　我要湯姆加入我們。

　　→ "Tom" 與 "to join us" 構成非限定子句，Tom 與限定子句主詞 --I 不一致，保留。

例5 It is so kind of you to say that.

　　你那麼説，人真好。

　　→ "of you to say that" 是非限定子句，主詞是 "you"。

(2.2) 動名詞

例6 Would you mind my opening the window?

　　你介意我打開窗戶嗎？

　　→ "my opening the window" 是非限定子句，主詞是說話者。

例7 A giant panda enjoys playing in the snow.

　　貓熊喜愛在雪堆裡嬉戲。

　　→ "playing in the snow" 的主詞是 "A giant panda"。

例 8 Reading comic books is fun.

讀漫畫書很有趣。

→ "Reading comic books" 是非限定子句，主詞泛指讀漫畫書的人。

(2.3) 分詞

例 9 The course is appropriate for those who is interested in traditional diagnoses.

這課程適合那些對傳統診斷有興趣者。

→ interested in traditional diagnoses 的主詞是關係代名詞 who。

例 10 Don't forget to fill in the form attached to the letter.

別忘了填寫附在信裡的表格。

→ attached to the letter 的受事者主詞是 the form。

(3) 不含動詞的句子：稱為小句子，名詞、形容詞、副詞或介係詞片語等構成的句子。

(3.1) 名詞

例 11 Councilors elected Mr. Lin chairman.

議員選出林先生擔任主席。

→ "Mr. Lin chairman" 是小句子，Mr. Lin 是主詞，chairman 是敘述部分。

例 12 We consider the man an illegal immigrant.

我們認為男子是非法移民。

→ "the man an illegal immigrant" 是小句子，an illegal immigrant 說明主詞 the man 的身分。

(3.2) 形容詞

例 13 We consider the customer dishonest.

我們認為那位客人不誠實。

→ "the customer dishonest" 是小句子，"dishonest" 說明主詞 "the customer" 的狀態。

例 14 Don't let me down.

不要令我沮喪。

→ "me down" 是小句子，"down" 說明主詞 "me" 的狀態。

(3.3) 介係詞片語

例 15 The bus driver expected the man off the bus immediately.

公車司機期待那名男子立即下車。

→ "the man off the bus immediately" 是小句子，"off the bus immediately" 說明主詞 "the man" 的狀態。

例 16 We viewed Dave as a strong candidate for the job.

我們將戴夫視為該職位的強力候選人。

→ "Dave as a strong candidate for the job" 是小句子, "as a strong candidate for the job" 說明主詞 Dave 的身分

補充學習

關於主詞包含動名詞時,時態動詞的單複數的判斷。例如:

例 1 Spelling lessons are difficult for me.

拼字課程對我是困難的。

例 2 Playing video games is lots of fun.

打電玩很好玩。

句法依據

1. 句子主詞應是名詞詞性的結構,例如名詞片語、動名詞等。

2. 名詞片語(NP)的中心詞(Head)是名詞,動詞片語(VP)的中心詞是動詞,受詞是 VP 的補語(Complement)。

結構分析

1. 例 1 的主詞是名詞片語(NP)—拼字課程:

1.1 語意上,lessons 是訊息焦點,也是 NP 的中心詞。

1.2 spelling 是動名詞,表示 lessons 的內容—lessons for spelling。

1.3 spelling 是 NP 的補語,lessons 不是其受詞。

1.4 時態動詞與主詞的中心詞(lessons)的數一致,因此是 are。

2. 例 2 的主題是動名詞 -- 打電玩:

2.1 playing 是動名詞,video games 是受詞(VP 結構上的補語)。

2.2 動名詞表示一個事件,單數,時態動詞是 is。

◆ 另外, "Drinking water is important." 則是二種分析皆成立:

1. 喝水是重要的—drinking water 是動名詞,water 是受詞。

2. 飲用水是重要的—drinking water 是名詞片語,water 是中心詞,drinking 表示 water 的功用。

解題技巧:

名詞若是動詞的受詞,視為一事件,搭配單數動詞,否則就是名詞片語,時態動詞與名詞單複數一致。

Q09. "It is important to me to stay on task." 為什麼用介係詞 to，而不是 for？

 原來如此 "to me" 是指對誰而言，不是不定詞的主詞。

◆ 語意上，例 1 的主詞是不定詞 "to stay on task"，因為結構較補語（important）大，基於修辭考量而移至補語右側。介係詞片語 "to me" 表示對誰而言，to 的意思是 in connection with，與補語的關聯密切，而不是不定詞的主詞，因此，例 1 可分析為 "It is important to me" 及 "to stay on task" 二意群：

例1 It is important to me / to stay on task.

堅持到底對我很重要／某件事情對我很重要，就是堅持到底。

◆ 例 1 的底層結構如例 2，而 "to me" 可前移至句首，表示強調，如例 3：

例2 To stay on task is important to me.

例3 To me, it is important to stay on task.

對我來說，堅持到底很重要。

◆ 提到不定詞的主事者時，以介係詞 for 引介，介係詞片語與不定詞語意關聯密切，表示相較之下對誰而言，二者形成一完整意群，例如：

例4 It is important / for me to stay on task.

我堅持到底很重要。

→ it 是指 for me to stay on task。

◆ for 介係詞片語是副詞性質，可移至句首以表示強調，如例 5，而例 5 的底層結構如例 6：

例5 For me, it is important to stay on task.

對我來說，堅持到底很重要。

例6 For me to stay on task / is important.

◆ 補語表示作說者評論主事者的行為（不定詞）時，以介係詞 of 引介主事者，形成的介係詞片語與補語形成意群，不可移至句首，例如：

例7 It is kind of you to do me a favor.

It is kind of you / to do me a favor.

你真好，幫了我一個忙。

例8 It was mean of you / to mention her weight.

你提到她的體重，真讓人不悅。

◆ 當然，介係詞片語若是缺項，不定詞的主詞或談論的對象便是泛指，也就是無特指對象，例如：

例 9 It is never too late to learn.

活到老，學到老。

例 10 It is difficult to obtain reliable evidence.

要獲得可靠證據不容易。

例 11 It is kind to forget about other people's mistakes.

忘卻他人的錯誤是和善的。

Q10. "Tom usually talks to himself." 為什麼用反身代名詞 "himself"？

 原來如此 受詞指涉主詞，受詞以反身代名詞標示，若不是指涉主詞，以人稱代名詞表示。

◆ 受詞指涉的是主詞時，受詞以反身代名詞標示，受詞不是指涉主詞時，受詞以人稱代名詞表示。

例1 Tom usually talks to himself.

湯姆經常自言自語。

→ himself 標示受詞指的是主詞 Tom。

例2 Tina is usually bored with herself.

緹娜經常覺得自己很煩。

→ herself 表示 Tina 是對自己厭煩，而不是別人。

例3 Tom usually talks to him.

湯姆經常跟他談話。

→ 人稱代名詞 him 表示受詞不是 Tom。

◆ 值得注意的是，語意若是明確，指涉主詞的受詞仍可用人稱代名詞。

例4 You will need to bring some money with you.

你要隨身帶些錢。

例5 Close the door after you.

隨手關上門。

◆ 除了主詞，反身代名詞也標示受詞，甚至所有格。

例6 We are going to tell the boy a story about himself.

我們將告訴那名男孩一個關於他自己的故事。

→ 反身代名詞標示受詞 the boy。

例7 I care about you for yourself, not for your fortune.

我在意的是你自己，不是你的財富。

→ 反身代名詞標示介係詞 about 的受詞 you。

例8 Jack's messages are all about himself.

傑克的訊息都是關於他自己。

→ 反身代名詞標示所有格 Jack's。

◆ 反身代名詞與指涉的主詞一定在同一子句，以句子結構限制指涉對象，符合語意相關，結構相近的鄰近原則。

例 9 Mr. Lin knows Tom usually talks to himself.

林老師知道湯姆經常自言自語。

→ Mr. Lin 與 himself 不在同一子句，himself 不會指涉 Mr. Lin。

例 10 That Tom usually talks to himself has been known to Mr. Lin.

湯姆經常自言自語已經讓林老師知道了。

→ himself 指涉同一子句的主詞 Tom，而不是超越所在子句範圍的 Mr. Lin。

◆ 反身代名詞也有強調詞的功用，強調所指涉的名詞或代名詞，置於名詞、代名詞或動詞片語的右側，這時反身代名詞是副詞性質。

例 11 I myself prefer a light lunch during work hours.

我個人偏好上班時吃清淡的中餐。

例 12 You will save some money if you do it yourself.

如果你自己做的話，你可省下一些錢。

Q11. "Some people say Hawaii is spoiled, but I don't think so.",so 的功用是什麼?

 原來如此 so 是代詞,代替前面所指的內容。

◆ 代詞是虛詞性質,代替前面述及的單詞、片語、子句或句子,避免重複。

例1 Some people say Hawaii is spoiled, but I don't think so.

一些人說夏威夷被糟蹋了,但我不這麼認為。

→ so 代替 "Hawaii is spoiled"

例2 I got my Master's degree in Chicago, and I met my wife there.

我在芝加哥取得碩士學位,而且我在那裡遇見我老婆。

→ there 代替 in Chicago

例3 The earthquake hit around midnight, and I was sleeping then.

地震大約午夜來襲,那時候我正在睡覺。

→ then 代替 around midnight

例4 Mr. Lin really works hard, and his wife does, too.

林先生工作非常辛苦,他老婆也是。

→ does 代替 really works hard

◆ 代詞代替語意完整的組成成分,一般來說,句子的組成成分具有以下特徵:

(1) 可以省略

例5 The woman from Sri Lanka can play on traditional Indian tabla drums very well.

那名來自斯里蘭卡的婦人很會演奏傳統的印度塔布拉鼓。

例6 The woman can play on traditional Indian tabla drums.

那名婦人會演奏傳統的印度塔布拉鼓。

(2) 可以獨立存在

例7 A: What shoe size are you looking for?

B: 42.

A: 你在找幾號鞋子?

B: 42 號鞋子。

(3) 可以插入句中

例 8 The candidate, to my surprise, lost in the election.

令我驚訝的是，該名候選人落選了。

→ to my surprise 是插入句中的組成成分。

(4) 可以並列

例 9 The man jumped into the water, swam to the boy and dragged him to the river bank.

男子跳下水，游向男孩，然後將他拖向河岸。

→ "jumped into the water" 、 "swam to the boy" 、 "dragged him to the river bank" 等動詞片語都是組成成分。

(5) 可以挪移

不定詞

例 10 It is essential to conserve and manage our water resources.

維護並管理我們的水資源是必要的。

例 11 I think it important to look on the bright side of things.

我認為看事情的光明面是重要的。

強調語詞

例 12 In the conference, the facilitator provided an opportunity to each participant to speak.

會議中，主持人提供每一位與會者一次發言機會。

例 13 Only by constant practice can you speak English fluently.

只有藉由持續的練習你才能流利講英語。

◆ 組成成分都有詞性及功用，此為結構、詞性、功用的組成成分解析脈絡。

實詞的結構：

結構	名詞	動詞	形容詞	副詞
單詞	●	●	●	●
片語	●	●	●	●
子句	●		●	●

組成成分的詞性與功用：

功用 結構	成分			修飾				
	主詞	受詞	補語	名詞	動詞	形容詞	副詞	子句
名詞片語	●	●	●	●	●			
形容詞片語			●	●				
副詞片語			●	●	●	●	●	●
不定詞	●	●	●	●				●
動名詞	●	●	●	●				
分詞			●	●	●	●	●	●
介係詞片語	●	●	●	●	●	●	●	●
名詞子句	●	●	●	●		●		
形容詞子句				●				
副詞子句			●		●	●	●	●

◆ 請閱讀以下文章，並分別寫出名詞子句、形容詞子句、副詞子句。

Since the arrival of COVID-19 in December of 2019, the world has seen varying degrees of changes to the lives of citizens in practically every country. The lifestyle changes range from the required wearing of face masks to social distancing to total lockdowns in cities, provinces and countries.

The psychological consequences of these infection prevention measures include daily inconvenience, frustration, social isolation, and depression. With stress levels at unprecedented levels, it is not surprising to see high rates of domestic violence and divorce in affected communities.

The economic consequences include the closure of many companies and the shutdown of entire industries. The travel industry has been hit especially hard, since most international borders have been closed for months. With so many hotels and airlines declaring bankruptcy, holiday travel may never be the same again. In a promising sign, countries that have a low rate of coronavirus infection are discussing resuming airline travel between themselves by October of 2020.

Some say there is a silver lining to every tragedy. If we look for a silver lining to the first half of 2020, we may find some promising developments. Some parts of the economy are doing well, including online services and online shopping. With the drastic reduction of air travel and highway traffic, there has been a noticeable drop in air pollution. The demand for oil and the price of gasoline reached incredibly low prices. Blue skies are more common these days, and people can get a preview of how our world can look without dependence on fossil fuels. Perhaps there will be motivation to do more to reduce carbon emissions.

Finally, I believe that during major emergencies, people can appreciate their relationships and not take so many things for granted. When we can go back to school, restaurants and offices, and when we can comfortably embrace our friends again, the world can feel warmer and brighter.

※ 解答

名詞子句

1. that during major emergencies, people can appreciate their
   relationships and not take so many things for granted
2. there is a silver lining to every tragedy
3. how our world can look without dependence on fossil fuels

形容詞子句

1. that have a low rate of coronavirus infection

副詞子句

1. Since the arrival of COVID-19 in December of 2020
2. since most international borders have been closed for months
3. When we can go back to school, restaurants and offices
4. When we can comfortably embrace our friends again
5. If we look for a silver lining to the first half of 2020

Q12. "The dog looks cute." 是狗狗認為自己看起來 cute 嗎？

 原來 如此 不是，是狗狗刺激人的視覺而產生對狗狗的反應。

◆ look 表示看起來時，連綴動詞，說明人接收外物刺激而產生視覺反應，刺激的來源該為人的感官反應負責。

例 1 The dog looks cute.

那隻狗狗看起來可愛。

→ "The dog" 刺激人的視覺，使人產生狗狗是 "cute" 的感官反應，而加以描述，因此稱為描述主詞。

→ 例 1 未提到感官經驗者，意味著說話者就是感官經驗者，常省略，若要提起，則以介係詞 "to" 引介。

例 2 The dog looks cute to me.

那隻狗對我來說看起來很可愛。

例 3 It sounds strange to some customers.

對一些客人來說，聽起來怪怪的。

◆ 除了以形容詞直接描述，我們常以譬喻來表達感官反應。

例 4 The dog looks like a little tiger.

那隻狗狗看起來像一隻小老虎。

例 5 The dog looks like that it used to stray with other street dogs.

那隻狗狗看起來像以前曾和其他浪浪流浪街頭。

Chapter 6.
結構保留

不論是組成成分或是 wh- 詞的移位，移位的語詞都可還原至原來的位置，這是一種結構保留。若將移位視為句式的變形，變形之前是底層結構，變形之後則是表層結構。了解移位的軌跡，並從格位、詞性、語意等方面檢視 wh- 詞，將有助於掌握句式變化的脈絡，不可免俗的，更有助於解題。

Q01. "*I don't know how to do." 正確嗎？

 不正確，do 是及物動詞，加接名詞性質的 wh- 詞當受詞。

◆ 動詞是句子的核心，動詞的語意投射的主詞、受詞、補語構成句子的必要成分，不同的必要成分構成不同的句型，這是七大句型的由來。至於不定詞、動名詞、分詞、原形動詞等非限定動詞構成的非限定子句雖不標記時態，但是主詞仍然存在，受詞、補語仍須完整。

例 1 I need to complete the task as soon as possible.
我需要儘快完成這工作。
→ "to complete the task as soon as possible" 的主詞是 I，與限定動詞的主詞一致，省略。the task 是動詞 complete 的受詞，as soon as possible 是修飾語。

例 2 Playing video games is fun.
打電玩很好玩。
→ 動名詞構成非限定子句 "Playing video games"，主詞泛指一般的人，games 是動詞 playing 的受詞。

例 3 The secretary is making coffee in the pantry.
祕書正在茶水間泡咖啡。
→ "making coffee in the pantry" 是現在分詞構成的非限定子句，主詞是 "The secretary"，coffee 是 making 的受詞，in the pantry 是 "making coffee" 的修飾語。

例 4 Seen from the hilltop, the village looks like a picture.
從山頂望去，這座村莊看起來好像一幅圖畫。
→ "Seen from the hilltop" 是過去分詞構成的非限定子句，受事者主詞是 the village，與主要子句一致，省略。

◆ 不定詞搭配 wh- 詞的結構稱為名詞片語，與不定詞一樣，扮演句子的主詞、受詞、補語等必要成分。

例 5 Which to choose from entirely depends on your needs.
挑選哪一個完全依照你的需求而定。
→ "Which to choose from" 當主詞。

例 6 The tourist is wondering who to ask.
那名觀光客不知道要問誰。
→ "who to ask" 當受詞。

例 7 The question is how to get tickets.

> → how to get tickets 當補語。

◆ wh- 詞指涉不定詞的受詞或修飾語，詞性與語意必須對應。以例 8 來講，do 是及物性質，受詞是必要成分，名詞詞性，語意上是指事物，無指涉對象或範疇，wh- 詞選用 what。

例 8 I don't know what to do ---.

誤 I don't know how to do ---.

◆ 上句錯誤的句子乍看之下合乎中文的意思「我不知道怎麼辦？」，因為「怎麼」對應 "what" 或 "how" 似乎都可以，但是二者詞性不同，how 是副詞，詢問程度或方式，修飾不及物動詞或已接受詞的動詞片語而不扮演受詞角色。

及物動詞　　　　受詞
不及物動詞　　　副詞

例 9 Tell me how to fix the machine---.

告訴我怎麼修理這部機器。

> → how 修飾及物動詞片語 "to fix the machine"。

例 10 The cub doesn't know how to swim---.

那隻幼獸不知道怎麼游泳。

> → how 修飾不及物動詞 "to swim"。

◆ why 原則上不搭配不定詞，但可形成平行結構。

例 11 Before we can decide what to do, we need to understand why to do it.

◆ wh- 詞取代句中語詞而移至句首（限定或非限定子句），這是 Wh-Movement，疑問句、間接問句、形容詞子句、感嘆句、名詞片語都是 Wh-Movement 的模式。wh- 詞與取代的語詞在詞性及語意上相互對應，易於辨識，也保留了句子的結構完整。

Q02. "Where are you from?"的"Where"為什麼是在句首？而且 are 要移至 you 的前面？

 原來如此 where 是溝通的主題，置於句首；are 移至主詞前是以倒裝詞序表示疑問語氣，要求聽者回答。

◆ 英語句式是主題在前，敘述在後，也就是 SVO 的詞序。

例1 The man signed a contract with Facebook.
那名男子與臉書簽一份合約。

例2 The event has been canceled.
活動已經取消。

◆ 以疑問句來說，詢問的訊息是溝通焦點，也是句子主題，基於主題在前的原則，wh- 詞置於句首。另外，句子的動詞若是 be 動詞，則是移至主詞前面，以不同於直述句的詞序作為標記，要求聽者回答。

例3 Where are you from--- ?

你來自哪裡？

→ 底層結構：You are from ---.
　　　　　　　　Where

◆ 句子若包含情態助動詞，也是移至主詞前面，標記要求聽者回答的溝通訊息。

例4 Should I turn the heating on?
我該打開暖氣機嗎？

→ 底層結構：I should turn the heating on.

例5 What should we be worried about ---?

我們該擔心些什麼？

→ 底層結構：We should be worried about ---.
　　　　　　　　　　　　　　　　　What

◆ 現在或過去簡單式形成疑問句時，因為動詞不可移至句首，我們的解決方式是尋求助動詞 do 的支援（Do Support）─ 主詞前面插入 do 或 did。

例 6 How did you learn to cook --- ?

你是怎麼學會烹飪的？

→ **底層結構**：You learned to cook ---.
　　　　　　　　　　　　　　　　　　How

◆ 中文的疑問語詞未移至句首，留駐直述句的位置，訊息詢問句（information seeking questions）句尾常加上「呢」，確認詢問句（confirmation questions）句尾則常加上「嗎」。

例 7 你來自哪裡呢？

例 8 你功課做完了嗎？

Q03. I don't know what I should do."句子有 what，怎麼不是疑問句式？

 原來如此 間接問可不要求聽者回答，搭配直述句式。

◆ 間接問句不是直接提出問題，而是告知他人的一個問題—a question that is reported to other people，也無意要求聽者回答，主詞與動詞的詞序不變。

◆ 間接問句是 Wh-Movement 的句型，wh- 詞取代句中語詞並前移至間接問句首。

例1 Can someone tell me what happened?

有人告訴我發生什麼事嗎？

→ what 取代主詞。

例2 Would you please let me know whom I can contact ---?

麻煩讓我知道我能跟誰聯繫，好嗎？

→ whom 取代 contact 的受詞。

例3 Consumers want to know how the steak tastes ---.

消費者要知道那份牛排嚐起來怎樣。

→ how 取代連綴動詞的補語。

例4 I was just wondering when we can start selling our products ---.

我只是想知道我們什麼時候可以開始賣我們的產品。

→ when 取代時間副詞。

◆ 間接問句是名詞性質，可當句子的主詞、受詞、補語。

例5 How the Egyptian pyramids were built --- remains a mystery.

埃及金字塔是如何建造的仍是一個謎團。

→ 間接問句 "How the Egyptian pyramids were built" 當主詞。

例6 I have been wondering who will be there to take my place.

我一直想知道誰會在那裏占我的缺。

→ 間接問句 "who will be there to take my place" 當動詞 wonder 的受詞。

例7 The problem is how we should define the protection of the Arctic region ---.

問題是我們該如何定義北極地區的保護。

→ 間接問句 "how we should define the protection of the Arctic region" 當主詞補語。

例8 I don't know what I should do ---.

我不知道我該怎麼辦。

→ what 是代名詞，意思是 the thing that，包含先行詞—the thing 與關係代名詞—that，引導的是名詞子句，例 8 可代換為例 9：

例9 I don't know the thing that I should do ---.

我不知道我該做的事。

◆ 間接問句若是置於疑問句中，針對主要子句作答。

例10 A: Excuse me, would you please show me where the restroom is?

B: Sure. It is in the back left corner.

A: 抱歉，能麻煩您告訴我化妝室在哪裡嗎？

B: 當然，就在左後方角落處。

→ Sure 是針對主要子句 "would you please show me" 的回應。

Q04. "George really likes the green T-shirt, but I like the blue one." 為什麼是用 one？

原來如此 one 代替名詞片語的中心詞，類別的概念，指涉「哪一個」。

◆ one，一個、一位，用於指涉群體或範圍中的一特定對象，也就是溝通中提及的人或物中，藉由限定詞或形容詞標示的，對照名詞片語的結構，one 取代中心詞，而補語、加接詞、指示詞等都是標示 one 是特定對象。

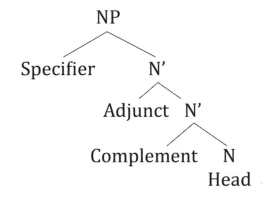

例1 George really likes the green T-shirt, but I like the blue one.
　　喬治很喜歡那件綠色 T 恤，但我喜歡藍色那件。
　　→ 指涉 T-shirt，the、blue 標示 T-shirt 中特定的一件。

例2 The bookstore now sells new books as well as used ones.
　　這家書店現在賣新書，連同二手書也賣。
　　→ 指涉 books，used 標示 books 中的特定範圍。

例3 My helmet looks like a new one.
　　我的安全帽看起來像一頂新的。
　　→ 指涉 helmet，new 標示 helmet 中特定性質的一件。

◆ 限定詞若是缺項，則是指涉不特定的某一個，例如：

例4 I am looking for an apartment. I'd like one with a big balcony.
　　我在找一間公寓，我想要一間有大陽台的公寓。
　　→ one 指涉具有 with a big balcony 特徵的某一公寓。

例 5 If you don't have a car to get around, you'll need to rent one.

如果你沒有車子開著到處逛逛，你就需要租一部。

→ one 指涉任何一部車子。

例 6 I have two bikes, and I can lend one to you.

我有二部單車，我可以借你一部。

→ one 指涉二部單車中不特定的一部。

◆ it 代替的是整個名詞片語，指涉提及的單數或不可數對象，they 指涉的是複數對象。

例 7 I'd like a strong dark-roast coffee, but I don't like it to be bitter.

我要一杯濃烈黑咖啡，但不喜歡讓它變苦澀。

→ it 指涉前面提及的那杯咖啡。

例 8 I received a yellow scarf as my prize, but I don't like it.

我收到一條黃色圍巾作為獎品，但我不喜歡。

→ it 指涉前面提及的那條圍巾。

例 9 Jack bought me two trench coats, but I don't really need them this winter.

傑克買給我二件風衣，但今年冬天我真的穿不到。

→ them 指涉前面提及的那二件風衣。

◆ which 詢問範圍中的哪一個，對應的是名詞片語的中心詞，回答時以 one 搭配冠詞及形容詞標示哪一個。

例 10 A: Which do you like better?

　　 B: The blue one.

　　 A: 你較喜歡哪一個？

　　 B: 藍色那個。

→ which 問句常將選項置於句末，情境更為明確。

例 11 A: Which do you prefer for dinner? Tacos or pizza?

　　 B: Tacos / Pizza.

　　 A：晚餐你比較喜歡吃什麼？玉米餅或披薩？

　　 B：玉米餅／披薩。

◆ **what** 用於詢問訊息，無特定範圍，對應的是整個名詞片語。

例 12 A: What would you like to drink?

B: Orange juice.

A: 你想要喝什麼？

B: 柳橙汁。

例 13 A: What did you receive as your prize?

B: A yellow scarf.

A: 你收到什麼當獎品？

B: 一條黃色圍巾。

Q05. "These are the things which you should bring with you."為什麼用 which ？

 原來如此 which 用於指涉明確，先行詞置於關係代名詞前面並作為關係代名詞的指涉對象，因此，which 是關係代名詞。

◆ which 的指涉對象明確且常出現於句子中。

例1 A: Which would you like to drink, coffee or cola?

B: Coffee, please.

A：你要喝哪一個，咖啡或可樂？

B：咖啡，麻煩妳。

→ coffee、cola 是 which 的指涉對象。

例2 A: Which would you choose to buy?

B: The one made of natural fibers.

A：妳要選購哪一件？

B：天然纖維製成的那一件。

→ which 詢問已知範圍中的哪一個。

◆ 關係代名詞指涉先行詞，先行詞置於關係代名詞前面，標示關係代名詞的指涉對象，明確指涉的性質與疑問句一致，因此 which 是關係代名詞。相較於 which，that 不是 wh- 詞，不具取代語詞並移至句首的功用，因此，that 不是關係代名詞，但是 that 具有引導子句的功用，常用來取代關係代名詞。

例3 These are the things which you should bring --- with you.

這些是妳應該隨身攜帶的物品。

◆ 相較於 which，what 詢問「什麼」，指涉對象不明確，不具關係代名詞功用。

例4 A: What would you like to drink?

B: Coffee, please.

A：你要喝什麼？

B：咖啡，麻煩妳。

例5 These are what you should bring --- with you.

這些是妳應該隨身攜帶的物品。

例6 I don't know what happened to the kids today.

我不知道今天孩子們發生什麼事。

◆ 形容詞子句與間接問句的比較：

(1) 都不是獨立子句。

(2) 都不具疑問功用，主詞與動詞的詞序都不變。

(3) 具關係代名詞功用的 wh- 詞有 who、who、whom、which，關係副詞功用的 wh- 詞有 when、where，但所有 wh- 詞都可用於間接問句。

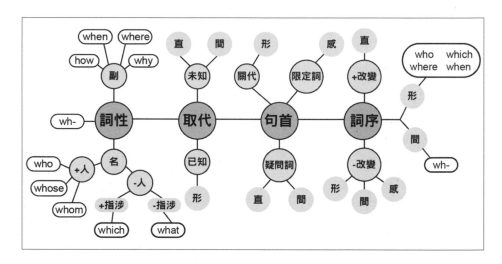

◆ Wh- Movement ◆

* Wh- 詞是指 what、 which、who、whom、whose、when、where、why 及 how 等字詞。

* Wh- 詞的主要特性是**取代語詞，且移至該語詞所在的片語或句子首**，取代的語詞位置留下移位的痕跡─trace，簡稱 t，這個模式稱為 Wh-Movement。

* Wh-Movement 大多出現在直述句詞序是"Ｓ Ｖ Ｏ"的語言，例如英語，相較於英語，中文是"疑問詞原位"的語言，沒有 Wh-Movement。

  比較以下英文與中文意思相同的句子：

  例 1 Where are you coming from？

  　　你剛剛從哪裡過來？

  　　→ 英文句子呈現 Wh-Movement，中文疑問詞留在原來位置。

* where、when、how 取代副詞性質的語詞，what、which、who 取代名詞片語，wh- 詞與取代的語詞詞性與語義必須相稱。

  例 2 I don't know what to do *t*.

  　　我不知道該怎麼辦。

  　　→ what 取代及物動詞 do 的受事者，並移至名詞片語首，即不定詞 to 的前面。

  例 3 I'm not sure whom to ask t for help *t*.

  　　我不確定跟誰求助。

  　　→ whom 取代及物動詞 ask 的受事者，並移至名詞片語首。

  例 4 Tell me how to fix this device *t*.

  　　告訴我怎樣修理這部裝置。

  　　→ how 取代表示方法的副詞，並移至名詞片語首。

  例 5 Where to find your account number *t*.

  　　在哪裡找到你的帳號。

  　　→ where 取代表示位置的副詞，並移至名詞片語首。

◆ why 不搭配不定詞，但可形成平行結構，例如：

例 6 Before we can decide what to do, we need to understand why to do it.

我們能夠決定做什麼之前，我們需要了解為什麼要做。

→ why to do it 與 what to do 是平行結構。

◆ **Wh-Movement 形成的句型**

(1) Wh- Questions

助動詞或 be 動詞移至主詞前面，或是主詞前面加入助動詞是為標記疑問且要求聽者回答的溝通意涵，例如：

例 7 A：How are you doing *t* ?

B：Great.

A：你近來好嗎？

B：很好。

→ how 取代表示狀況的副詞，前移至句首，留下 trace。

→ be 動詞移至主詞前標記疑問且要求聽者回答的溝通意涵。

例 8 What did you buy *t* ?

你買什麼？

→ what 取代動詞 buy 的受事者，前移至疑問句首，留下 trace，同時標記 buy 加接受詞的底層結構。

→ 主詞前面加入助動詞 did 標記疑問且要求聽者回答的溝通意涵。

◆ Wh- 詞 what、who、which、whose 取代主詞或是主詞中的限定詞時，沒有 Wh-Movement，不需搭配助動詞而以直述句的詞序呈現，例如：

例 9 What's wrong with you?

你怎麼啦？

例 10 Who owns this bag?

誰擁有這個袋子？

例 11 Which looks better?

哪一個看起來比較好？

例 12 Whose house was used in the film?

　　誰的房子被用在這部電影中？

　　→ whose 是限定詞，與 house 構成名詞片語 whose house。

(2) 間接問句

間接問句是非常普遍的禮貌用法，常用於與不認識的人的對話，不貿然要求對方回應問題，而是先委婉徵詢對方是否願意回應。由於不是直接要求回答提問，不是直接問句的詞序，這就是間接問句採用直述詞序的原因。間接問句是名詞性質，可以扮演主詞、受詞、補語等角色。

例 13 Could you tell me where the MRT station is？

　　麻煩告訴我捷運站在哪裡，好嗎？

　　→ where 取代地方訊息，前移至間接問句首，成為間接問句的主題。

◆ 間接問句也出現在一般陳述或疑問的句子，提出疑問性質的訊息，同樣不是要求回答疑問的訊息，wh- 詞後面採用直述詞序。

例 14 I am not sure where I lost my wallet .

　　我不確定我在哪裡丟掉我的皮包。

例 15 I have no idea what you are talking about .

　　我不知道你在講什麼？

　　→ what 是代名詞，等同於 the thing which

例 16 Please find out what time the train is due .

　　請查一下火車幾點到站。

(3) 形容詞子句

形容詞子句與間接問句的 Wh-Movement 模式相同，都是取代句中的語詞並前移至句首，Wh- 詞引導的句子是直述詞序。引導形容詞子句的 Wh- 詞是關係代名詞或關係副詞。

◆ 形容詞子句

例 17 This is the man who said hello to me just now.

　　這位是剛才跟我打招呼的先生。

　　→ 主格關係代名詞 who 作為形容詞子句的主詞，形容詞子句是直述句型。

◆ 間接問句

例 18 I don't know who said hello to me just now.

我不知道剛才是誰跟我打招呼。

→ 疑問詞 who 作為間接問句的主詞,間接問句是直述句型。

◆ 形容詞子句

例 19 The man whom I met *t* in the elevator is my boss.

我在電梯遇到的那位先生是我的老闆。

→ 受格關係代名詞 whom 取代 met 的受詞並移至形容詞子句首,形容詞子句是直述句型。

◆ 間接問句

例 20 I don't know whom I met *t* in the elevator.

我不知道我在電梯裡遇到誰。

→ 疑問詞 whom 取代 met 的受詞並移至間接問句首,間接問句是直述句型。

◆ 形容詞子句

例 21 I got my PhD in Edinburgh, where I met my wife *t*.

我在愛丁堡拿到博士學位,我在那裡遇見我妻子。

→ 關係副詞取代 in Edinburgh,引導補述用法的形容詞子句。

◆ 間接問句

例 22 It would be unbelievable if you forgot where you met your wife *t*.

如果你忘了你是在哪裡遇見你老婆的,那就難以置信了。

→ 疑問副詞 where 自動詞片語右側移至間接問句首。

(4) 感嘆句

◆ what 表示多麼,限定詞性質,引導的名詞片語作為感嘆句的訊息焦點,置於感嘆句首。

例 23 What a beautiful day it is!

它是多麼美好的一天啊!

→ what 引導的名詞片語是訊息焦點,感嘆句的主詞及動詞可以省略。

例 24 What a beautiful day!

多麼美好的一天啊!

→ wh- 詞不置於句中,what 詞引導的名詞片語不移至動詞右側。

◆ How 有「多麼」的意思，形成感嘆句，置於感嘆句首，例如：

例 25 How I love the summer holidays!

我好喜愛夏季的假日啊！

→ How 搭配形容詞或副詞，形成感嘆句，例如：

How amazing!

好令人驚奇啊！

例 26 How wonderful it is to see you!

看到你，好棒！

例 27 How beautifully she sang! Everyone was delighted.

她唱得真好，大家都很開心。

◆ 複合關係代名詞 ◆

◆ 關係代名詞指涉先行詞並引導形容詞子句，形容詞子句與先行詞形成名詞片語，例如：

例 1 The river which flows through London is called the Thames.

這條流經倫敦的河流被稱為泰晤士河。

→ 關係代名詞 which 指涉先行詞 the river，引導形容詞子句 which flows through London，形容詞子句與先行詞構成名詞片語。

◆ 複合關係代名詞是兼具先行詞與關係代名詞的語詞，包含先行詞，引導名詞子句，扮演主詞、受詞、補語等角色。複合關係代名詞包括 what、whatever、whoever、whomever、whichever 等，字尾 ever 有強調的意思。

◆ what，the thing which 那一個、the things which 那一些

例 2 The thing which I wanted to find out first was how long it was going to take.

What I wanted to find out first was how long it was going to take.

我首先想要知道的是要花多長時間。

→ what 引導的名詞子句當主詞

例 3 We can see the things which appear to be bats.

We can see what appear to be bats.

我們能看到的似乎是蝙蝠。

→ what else 是其他什麼的意思，else 其他的、另外的

例 4 What else did Tom tell you?

湯姆還告訴了你什麼？

◆ whatever，anything which，任何……的事物

例 5 Whatever he did was right.

任何他做的都是對的。

例 6 I'll say whatever comes to my mind.

我想到什麼，就說什麼。

◆ whoever，any person that 任何人

例 7 Whoever comes will be welcome.

誰來都會受到歡迎。

例 8 Whoever else said that?

還有誰那樣說？

◆ whoever 還有 the person who 的意思，用於身分不重要或不知道的人。

例 9 We wrote a letter of thanks to whoever had supported us.

我們寫一封感謝信給支持過我們的人。

◆ whoever 也有究竟是誰，表示驚訝的意思。

例 10 Whoever told you that?

到底是誰告訴你的？

例 11 Whoever could that be calling so late?

這麼晚了到底是誰打電話來呢？

◆ whomever 是非常正式用法，一般都是 whoever 作為受詞。

例 12 She was free to marry whomever she chose.

她選擇嫁給誰就能嫁給誰。

◆ 子句雖然是受詞功能，但是 whoever 或是 whomever 是由子句的角色決定，例如：

例 13 Send the sample to whoever is in charge of sales.

誰負責行銷，就將樣品寄給誰。

→ whoever 在子句中是主詞，主格。

例 14 Give it to whoever you see in the office.

你在辦公室看見誰，就把它給誰。

→ whoever 取代 whomever。

◆ whichever，anyone that、anything that、either one which，指涉人或物。另外，不同於 what、whatever、whoever 等，which、whichever 不搭配 else，因為 which、whichever 指涉不確定的對象。

例 15 Whichever of you gets to the museum first should start queuing for tickets.

你們之中誰先抵達博物館，誰就應該開始排隊買票。

例 16 Take whichever of these chocolates you like.

你喜歡這些巧克力中的哪一個，就拿。

◆ 除了名詞子句之外，whoever、whatever、whichever 等複合關係代名詞引導的句子還有副詞性質，形成副詞子句。複合關係代名詞在子句中可以扮演主詞、受詞、補語等角色。

◆ whatever，no matter what 無論什麼、regardless of what 不管什麼

例 17 We won't cancel the party, whatever the weather.

無論天氣怎樣，我們都不會取消派對。

→ whatever the weather 的意思是 no matter what the weather is like

例 18 Whatever happens, don't let go of my hands.

無論發生什麼事，不要放開我的手。

例 19 Whatever else may be said of you, you should be calm.

不論別人還說了你什麼，你都該冷靜。

* whichever，no matter which 無論哪一個、regardless of which 不管哪一些

    例 20 You can either have the set menu or a la carte, whichever you want.

    你們可以套餐或是合菜，你們要哪一種餐都可以。

    例 21 A：Do you want tea or coffee?

    B：I don't mind. Whichever you're making?

    A：你要茶或咖啡？

    B：我不介意，你在沖泡什麼都好。

* whoever，no matter who 無論是誰、regardless of which 不管是誰

    例 22 Whoever you ask, you will get the same answer.

    No matter who you ask, you will get the same answer.

    無論你問誰，你都會得到相同的答案。

* when、where、how 也可搭配 ever 而形成 whenever、wherever、however。

    例 23 Call in whenever you like. I'm always in the office.

    你喜歡的時間就打電話進來，我都在辦公室。

    → whenever you like 是 at any time at all that you like 的意思。

    例 24 Wherever you are, you'll find people are phubbing.

    不論你在哪裡，你都會發現人們在滑手機。

    → Wherever you are 是 No matter where you are 的意思。

    例 25 However you try to explain this question, I still can't understand it.

    不論你怎麼努力說明這個問題，我還是無法理解。

    → However you try to explain this question 是 No matter how you try to explain this question 的意思。

◆ whether ◆

◆ whether 是否，字源的語意是 which of the two，二者中的哪一個，標示二個選擇或是可能，語意衍伸為「無論二者怎樣都不重要或結果都是一樣」。whether 雖是 wh 字母起首，但不具取代語詞而移至句首的性質，不是 wh-words。另外，whether 的語法功能是形成間接問句或副詞子句。

例 1 I doubt whether it'll work.

我懷疑這是否有用。

例 2 Tom asked me whether I was interested in working for him.

湯姆問我是否有興趣為他工作。

例 3 I can't decide whether to paint the wall green or yellow.

我無法決定要把牆壁漆成綠色或是黃色。

→ whether 搭配 or 表示二者選擇。

例 4 I'm wondering whether to have the fish or the beef.

我不知道要吃魚還是吃牛肉。

→ whether 搭配不定詞。

例 5 I don't know whether the exam is on Monday or Tuesday.

我不知道考試是在周一或者周二？（可能性）

I don't know if the exam is on Monday or Tuesday.

→ if 子句表示除了周一及周二，還有其他可能的日期。

例 6 Tom doesn't know whether Cindy is in Taiwan or whether she's gone to China.

湯姆不知道莘蒂是在台灣或是前往大陸了。（可能性）

例 7 It all depends on whether or not he has the time.

這完全取決於他是否有時間。

→ whether 搭配 or not，凸顯肯定或否定二種可能性。

◆ whether……or 還可表示無論怎樣都不影響結果，例如：

例 8 The ticket will cost the same, whether we buy it now or wait till later.

無論我們現在買票或是等到稍後再買，票價都是相同。

例 9 Let's face it - you're going to be late whether you go by bus or train.

我們面對吧，不論搭公車還是火車，你都會遲到的。

例 10 The demonstration will go ahead whether it rains or not.

示威遊行將繼續前進，無論會不會下雨。

例 11 Whether or not we're successful, we can be sure that we did our best.

不論我們是否成功，我們都能確定我們盡力了。

◆ if 引導間接問句，加接 ask 詢問、know 知道、wonder 不知道、find out 發現等動詞時，表示二或更多可能性，這時 if 與 whether 同義，而且可以搭配 or not，以下是 Oxford Dictionary 的例句：

例 12 Do you know if he's married?

你知道他結婚了嗎？（結婚或尚未結婚二種可能）。

例 13 He couldn't tell if she was laughing or crying.

他分辨不出她是在笑還是在哭。（笑或是哭二種可能。）

例 14 I wonder if I should wear a coat or not.

我不知道我是否該穿上一件外套。

→ if 間接問句搭配 or not。

◆ Cambridge 字典也有 if 搭配 or not 的例句：

例 15 I don't care if he likes it or not - I'm coming!

我不在乎他喜不喜歡，我反正要來！

◆ 英國著名文法學者 R. Quirk 曾舉過以下例句：

例 16 I don't care if your car breaks down or not.

我不在乎你的車子是否拋錨。

◆ 以下 if 搭配 or not 的例句都引自美國的文法著作：

例 17 I don't care if you come or not.

(Understanding Grammar, New York, 1954, p.28)

我不在乎你來不來。

例 18 She asked me if I was going to the store (or not).

(Grammar for Use, p. 138)

她問我是否要去那家店。

- if 除了是否之外，還有如果、雖然、每當等語意，為了避免混淆，if 引導的間接問句有一些用法限制。以下幾種 whether 的用法不可代換為 if。

- whether 子句作為主詞，or not 可以省略。

  例 19 Whether we'll go camping tomorrow depends on the weather.

  我們明天是否去露營要看天氣而定。

- if 子句可以當移位的主詞，例如：

  例 20 It is not clear to me if she likes the present.

  我不清楚她是否喜歡這禮物。

- 通常是 whether 子句作為補語。

  例 21 The question is whether or not his leg is fully recovered.

  問題是他的腿是否完全復原。

- whether 子句作為介係詞的受詞，or not 可以省略。

  例 22 Tom is worrying about whether he hurt Cindy's feeling.

  湯姆擔心是否傷了辛蒂的感情。

  例 23 There was a big argument about whether the factory should be relocated to Vietnam.

  有一個很大的爭論，就是關於工廠是否要遷到越南。

- whether 搭配不定詞，不定詞與限定子句的主詞一致。

  例 24 Tom seemed undecided whether to go or stay.

  湯姆對是否要去或留下來似乎舉棋不定。

  例 25 They debate whether to accept the government's offer.

  他們爭論是否接受政府的建議。

- whether 子句作為同位語。

  例 26 The question whether there is water on Mars remains open.

  火星是否有水的問題還沒有答案。

- whether / if 引導的間接問句不以現在式表示未來。

  例 27 I'm not sure whether I'll see him tomorrow.

  我不確定我明天是否會看到他。

◆ whether / if 引導的副詞子句以現在式表示未來。

例 28 Whether we go by bus or train, it'll take at least four hours.

不論我們是搭巴士或火車，至少都要花四小時。

例 29 I'm very sorry if I've offended you.

如果我冒犯了你的話，我很抱歉。

Q06. "As is often the case, Tom was late again." 的 "As is often the case" 是什麼結構？

原來如此 形容詞子句，**as** 是準關係代名詞，先行詞是主要子句。

◆ 與構詞上的功能轉換詞一樣，英語的一些語詞常因用法擴增而改變詞性或句型結構，例如：

例 1 The CEO will chair the meeting tomorrow.

明天執行長將主持檢討會議。

→ chair 從椅子轉換為主持會議，動詞。

例 2 The committee will OK our proposal.

委員會將批准我們的提案。

→ OK 從形容詞轉換為批准，動詞。

例 3 I can't find the book that I got from the library.

我找不到從圖書館借來的那本書。

→ 補語連詞 that 取代關係代名詞。

◆ 為了結構簡潔，語意搭配，連接詞 as, but, than 不是 wh-words，但是搭配一些語詞時充當關係代名詞，因此稱為準關係代名詞。

as

◆ 連接詞性質的 as 有如同的意思，充當準關係代名詞時，先行詞搭配 as、such、the same 等語詞。

as…as

例 4 I have studied as many papers, as Prof. Lin recommended.

林教授推薦的論文有多少篇，我就已經讀了多少篇。

→ as many papers 是先行詞，搭配副詞 as，修飾形容詞 many，像…這麼多的意思。as Prof. Lin recommended 是形容詞子句，準關係代名詞 as 是 recommended 的受詞。

例 5 He is as great a musician as has ever lived.

他是有史以來最偉大的音樂家。

→ as great a musician 是先行詞，搭配副詞 as，very 的意思，修飾形容詞 great。

◆ **as has ever lived** 是形容詞子句，準關係代名詞 **as** 是主詞，**ever** 表示強調。

例 5 可改寫為例 6 及例 7：

例 6 He is the greatest musician that has ever lived.

例 7 He is as great a musician as any other musician that has ever lived.

◆ **such…as**

例 8 It is preferable to use any such material as can be easily cleaned.

用可以輕易清理的材料比較好。

→ as can be easily cleaned 是形容詞子句，準關係代名詞 as 是主詞，any such material 是先行詞，搭配限定詞 such。

◆ **the same…as** 表示同一個或是相似的一個。

例 9 Tom went to the same school as I did.

Tom 跟我上同一所學校。

例 10 This is the same bag as I lost last week.

這個袋子和我上一週弄丟的那個袋子相似。

◆ **the same…that** 表示同一個。

例 11 Tom sat in the same row that/as we did.

湯姆跟我們坐在同一排。

◆ **as** 常以主要子句作為先行詞，「如……的」的意思，**as** 形容詞子句搭配 **be** 或是 **seem**，補述用法，可以置於句首、句中或是句尾。

例 12 As was expected, the candidate won the election.

例 13 The candidate won the election, as was expected.

如同大家期待的，該名候選人贏得選舉。

◆ **as** 搭配形容詞或是分詞，**be** 動詞可以省略。

例 14 As expected, the candidate won the election.

◆ 和 as 不一樣的是,which 引導的補述用法形容詞子句不可置於句首,而且沒有如同的意思,因此這例句若以 which 引導,意思是該名候選人贏得選舉,這是大家所期待的。

例 15 The candidate won the election, which was expected.

例 16 Tom was late for class today, as is usual with him.

例 17 Tom was late for class today, as usual.

　　　一如往常,湯姆今天上班遲到。

例 18 As is often the case, Tom was late again.

例 19 Tom was late again, as is often the case.

例 20 Tom was late again, which is often the case.

　　　這是常有的事,湯姆又遲到了。

　　　→ as 是 something like a fact that 的意思。

例 21 This winter, as is well known, there was no winter weather.

　　　今年冬天,大家都知道的,沒有冬天。

◆ than 準關係代名詞 than 用於比較級的句子,than 可以作主詞或是受詞。

例 22 There is more to it than meets the eye.

　　　還有一些是你沒看見的。

　　　→ than 是形容詞子句的主詞

例 23 We raised more money than we had expected.

　　　我們募得超出我們之前所期待的金額。

　　　→ than 是形容詞子句的受詞

比較:

例 24 Tom swam faster than was expected.

例 25 Tom swam faster than it was expected for him to swim.

　　　Tom 游得比預期來得快。

　　　→ than was expected 是副詞子句

but

◆ but 充當準關係代名詞時，句子必須是否定意涵。

but 充當準關係代名詞一般認為是舊式用法，屬於 old-fashioned English。

例 26 There is no rule but has exceptions.

例 27 Every rule has exceptions.

沒有規則是沒有例外的。

例 28 There is nobody but has his faults.

沒有人是沒有缺點的。

例 29 None came to the reception but was welcome.

蒞臨招待會的人都會受到歡迎。

比較：

例 30 It never rains but it pours.

禍不單行。

→ but 作為連接詞時，引導完整的句子。

Q07. "Jack is planning to take a trip to Singapore during the Chinese New Year, which is my must-do during the summer time." 句子中，形容詞子句的先行詞是什麼？

原來
如此　依語意，先行詞是不定詞 "to take a trip to Singapore"

◆ 限定用法的形容詞子句提供必要訊息以辨識、確認或限定先行詞，非限定用法的形容詞子句與先行詞逗號相隔，不具限定功能，僅提供訊息，先行詞除了相鄰的名詞之外，還可以是其他的組成成分，甚至是句子本身。

例1 Jack is planning to take a trip to Singapore during the Chinese New Year, which is my must-do during the summer time.
傑克正計畫春節期間到新加坡旅行，那是我夏季期間一定做的事。
→ 先行詞是不定詞 "to take a trip to Singapore"。

例2 Jack is planning to take a trip to Singapore during the Chinese New Year, when I will be traveling with my family.
傑克正計畫春節期間到新加坡旅行，那時候我正和家人一起旅行。
→ 先行詞是介係詞片語 "during the Chinese New Year"。

例3 Jack is planning to take a trip to Singapore during the Chinese New Year, which I was told two days ago.
傑克正計畫春節期間到新加坡旅行，我二天前聽到的。
→ 先行詞是整個主要子句。

例4 Jack is planning to take a trip to Singapore during the Chinese New Year, which is my dream destination.
傑克正計畫春節期間到新加坡旅行，那是我夢想的去處。
→ 先行詞是 Singapore。

◆ 非限定用法的形容詞子句的先行詞雖無限制，但為求語意清晰明確，以上各句應改寫如下：

例 5 Jack is planning to take a trip to Singapore during the Chinese New Year. In fact, I take a trip to Singapore during the summer time every year.

例 6 Jack is planning to take a trip to Singapore during the Chinese New Year, and I will be traveling with my family then.

例 7 Jack is planning to take a trip to Singapore during the Chinese New Year. I was told that two days ago.

例 8 Jack is planning to take a trip to Singapore during the Chinese New Year. Well, it is my dream destination.

> **Q08. "I'm inspired by each and every one who is speaking out against gender discrimination."這句子的 every one 搭配關係代名詞 who，正確嗎？**
>
> **原來如此** 正確，但正式文體或英語能力測驗仍以 that 為準。

◆ 先行詞包含 the only、the same、no, any、all 等表示特定指涉的語詞時，可以搭配關係代名詞 which、who，不以 that 取代，這是英美人士廣泛的用法，也常見於主流媒體。

例 1 The model is not the only thing which makes up the show.

Malta Independent Online

模特兒不是唯一撐起整個表演的東西。

例 2 The title-chaser who went to Miami isn't the same guy who will make his choice in July.

ABS-CBN News

去邁阿密的標題追求者跟七月份要做選擇的不是同一個人。

例 3 There will be no children who do not go to school.

The Herald

沒有不上學的孩童。

例 4 It's the typical reaction of any kid who gets on the ice for the first time.

Montreal Gazette

那是任何第一次上到冰塊上的孩子的自然反應。

例 5 We are making an effort to clean up all the garbage which lies in the path of better relations.

Newsweek

我們正試圖清除橫在較佳關係上的所有垃圾。

◆ 句子若分為結構及語詞二部份，結構猶如主幹，不易改變，甚至歷久不變，例如簡單句、合句、複句、複合句等句子類型；語詞猶如枝葉，用法可能因時而異，但不影響句式結構。因此，以學習的角度而言，熟捻句子結構是基礎，掌握現代語詞用法是造詣，基礎有限，造詣無盡，二者都要勞苦研習，方能有成。

Q09. 怎樣分析 94 年統測試題的句子"A balanced diet gives the body the nutrients it needs to function properly." ？

 原來如此 needs 為中心，受詞以關係代名詞填補，但省略，主詞是 it。

◆ 動詞是句子的核心，句子是其語意的投射，主詞、受詞、補語等必要成分若是缺項，語意便不完整，這是語意主導結構，結構鋪陳語意的句子特性。

例 1 Give freely to the poor and needy in your land.

舊約聖經

總要施捨給你土地上困苦窮乏的弟兄。

→ "give" 的意思是施捨，只有主詞是必要成分。

例 2 The ambassador is giving a banquet for the visiting President.
大使將舉辦宴會以歡迎到訪的總統。

→ "give" 的意思是舉行，主辦者及活動是必要成分，搭配主詞及受詞。

例 3 A balanced diet gives the body the nutrients it needs to function properly.

均衡的飲食給予身體正常運作所需的營養成分。

→ "gives" 表示「給予」，要提到「誰給的 —A balanced diet」、「給誰 —the body」、「給什麼 —the nutrients」，必要成分包括主詞、直接受詞、間接受詞。

→ "A balanced diet gives the body the nutrients" 沒有標記從屬位階的連接詞，主要子句。

→ needs 是時態動詞，子句結構，受詞缺項，只有形容詞子句有 wh- 詞移位而留下缺項，因此直接受詞是含形容詞子句的名詞片語。

◆ 名詞片語：the nutrients / it needs – to function properly

→ "needs" 的意思是「需要」，應說明「誰需要」及「需要什麼」，必要成分是主詞及受詞。needs 前面的 it 是主詞，指涉 "the body"，受詞是 "the nutrients"，但是留空（"to function properly" 是修飾語，表示目的），形容詞子句的底層結構是 "the body needs the nutrients to function properly"，受格關係代名詞 which 取代 the nutrients 並移至形容詞子句首，但是省略了：

A balanced diet gives the body the nutrients (which) it needs ---
to function properly.

◆ 再來看經濟學人 "The Economist" 雜誌中的一個句子：

例4 Some Republican governors turned down the federal money it
made available to expand Medicaid in their states.

有些共和黨的州長拒絕聯邦政府所提供要用以擴展醫療補助的那筆錢。

→ 先行詞與形容詞子句劃分如下：

the federal money / it made available to expand Medicaid in
their states.

→ "made" 的主詞是 it，依據上下文是指 "the government"；受詞缺項，
指的是 "the federal money"，關係代名詞 which 填補，也省略了。

例5 Some Republican governors turned down the federal money
which it madeavailable to expand Medicaid in their states.

The government made the federal money available to expand
Medicaid in their states.

政府讓那筆聯邦政府所提供的錢可用以擴展醫療補助。

→ 形容詞子句的意思是："made" 的受詞是 "the federal money"，受
詞補語是 "available to expand Medicaid in their states"。

Q10. "What a nice sound that is!"的感嘆句型怎麼形成的？

 原來如此 感嘆句也是 wh- 詞前移的結果。

◆ wh- 詞取代語詞，前移至語詞所在的句子或片語起首位置並留下痕跡而形成 wh- 問句、間接問句、形容詞子句、wh- to V。

(1)wh- 問句

例 1 Why did you choose your college ---?

你為什麼選擇你就讀的大學？

(2) 間接問句

例 2 I would like to know how the shuttle service works ---.

我想要知道接駁車服務是怎麼運作的。

(3) 形容詞子句

例 3 The man whom you met --- in the elevator is a dentist.

你在電梯遇見的那名男子是一名牙醫。

(4) 名詞片語

例 4 No one had to tell me when to evacuate ---.

沒有人要告訴我該在什麼時候撤離。

◆ 感嘆句也是 wh- 詞前移的變形。wh- 詞不置於句中，wh- 詞引導的感嘆訊息前移至句首，這是組成成分的移位。為了聚焦於感嘆的訊息，感嘆句的主詞及動詞大多省略。另外，感嘆句首的 what 不是疑問詞，而是限定詞，意思是「多麼的」。

例 5 What a nice sound that is ---!

那是多麼美好的聲音啊！

例 6 What a great world!

多麼棒的一個世界啊！

◆ 另一引導感嘆句的 wh- 詞是 how，意思是「多麼」，副詞性質，修飾形容詞或副詞。感嘆句的 what、how 都不具疑問目的，主詞與動詞的詞序不變。

例 7 How incredible a journey it was ---!

真是一趟不可置信的旅程！

例 8 How beautifully the girl is dancing ---!

那位女孩舞跳得真好！

Q11. "It is important to conserve energy." 句中 的主詞為什麼要用 it？

原來如此 主詞是不定詞，結構大，訊息份量重，置於句尾，符合尾 重原則。

◆ 形容詞評論一個事件，事件的訊息份量較形容詞重，置於形容詞右側，
形成訊息份量從輕至重的排列。另外，訊息份量重的語詞置於句尾，
取得句重音，凸顯訊息焦點，這是語意尾重原則。

    It is important to conserve energy.

    節約能源是重要的。

◆ "to conserve energy" 是訊息焦點，移至形容詞的右側，句首主詞
位置以 it 填補，符合句子主詞位置不可留空的句構原則。

訊息份量依序排列如下：

填補主詞	形容詞	主題
無語意訊息	份量輕	訊息焦點

◆ 相較於 important，"to conserve energy" 是不定詞，結構可再擴增，
置於右側，語詞由小而大平衡排列。

◆ it 是虛詞，分量小於形容詞，置於句首，句子形成結構升冪排列—語
詞結構由左而右漸次增大，這是結構尾重原則。若是語意與結構兩相
衝突，語意勝出，畢竟是語意主導句式。

Q12. "Help yourself to a drink, won't you?" 的附加問句為什麼是 "won't you?"

 說話者提出邀請，聽話者尚未執行，搭配 will，又以否定語氣婉轉詢問聽話者的意願，原句是 "**Won't you help yourself to a drink?**"，以 "**won't you?**" 作為附加問句。

◆ 祈使句傳達命令、禁止、請求、勸告等語氣，動作執行者是聽話者，訊息焦點是動作，置於句首且不標記時態，達到聚焦的效果。

例 1 Help yourself to a drink.

請自取一份飲料。

◆ 說話者提出邀請時，聽話者尚未執行，搭配 will，同時表示未來及意願。另外，以否定語氣婉轉詢問聽話者的意願，期望聽話者遂行，含有勸進的意味，例 1 的底層結構如例 2：

例 2 Won't you help yourself to a drink?

你不自取一份飲料嗎？

→ 縮減為 "won't you?" 以確認訊息，因此例 1 的附加問句是 "won't you?"。

◆ 祈使句表達要求或請託時，無論是肯定或否定，都以肯定語氣確認聽話者是否進行動作。

例 3 Open the door, will you?

把門打開，方便嗎？

例 4 Don't open the door, will you?

不要打開門，方便嗎？

→ 例 3、4 都是以 "Will you open the door?" 確認聽話者是否進行動作，附加問句都是 "will you?"。

◆ "Let's" 句型搭配 "shall we?" 作為附加問句，因為 "Let's" 的底層結構是 "You let us…"，如例 5，省略主詞，let 與 us 縮寫，如例 6：

例 5 You let us eat out for dinner.

你讓我們出去吃飯吧。

例 6 Let's eat out for dinner.

我們出去吃飯吧。

→ 例 6 的附加問句 "shall we?" 是 "Shall we eat out for dinner?" 的縮減，同樣是確認訊息。

"let's " 句型的主詞為何是 you，而不是 we 呢？我們可以從 let 的受詞加以驗證─主詞若是 we，let 的受詞是 ourselves，而不是 us。

例 7 We let ourselves eat out for dinner.

Q13. "The more you do, the more you can do."這句子怎麼分析？

原來如此 這是雙重比較，前句是副詞子句，表示條件；後句是主要子句，表示結果。

◆ 例 1 的意思是「愈多做，愈能做。」，擔任美國 VOGUE 主編 20 多年的 Anna Wintour 於牛津大學的精采演說！

例1 The more you do, the more you can do.
你做得越多，你能做的就越多。

→ 我們可從語意、結構及聲韻等三層面來理解雙重比較的句子。

(1) 語意層面

◆ 雙重比較平行結構的前一句是副詞子句，表示條件，the 是從屬連接詞；後一句是主要子句，表示結果，the 是副詞。例 1 的意思如例 2 或例 3：

例2 If you do more, you can do more.
如果你做得越多，你能做的就越多。

例3 When you do more, you can do more.
當你做得越多，你能做的就越多。

◆ 雙重比較平行結構的副詞子句與主要子句各自獨立，主詞不須一致。

例4 The sooner you treat your son as a man, the sooner he will be one.
你越早將你兒子當成一個男子對待，他就越早成為一個男子。

例5 The more profit the company makes, the more money the stockholder gets paid at the end of the quarter.
公司獲利越多，股東在季末獲得的錢就越多。

◆ 主詞若指涉一致，主要子句的主詞以適當的代名詞表示。

例6 The more powerful a car is, the more it costs.
一部汽車越有動力，就越值錢。

例7 The more efficient a system is, the lower it costs to operate.
一個系統越有效率，運轉的成本就越低。

例8 The more a patient engages in the treatment process, the healthier he or she will become.
一位病患越投入療程，不論性別，就越快康復。

(2) 結構層面

雙重比較平行結構包含移位及省略二變形，移位是指語詞前移至句首以形成訊息焦點，省略是指省略強調語詞之外的部分。

移位

例 4 ～ 8 可以還原為例 9 ～ 13：

例 9 If you treat your son as a man sooner, he will be one sooner.

例 10 When the company makes more profit, the stockholder gets more money paid at the end of the quarter.

例 11 If a car is more powerful, it costs more.

例 12 If a system is more efficient, it costs lower to operate.

例 13 If a patient engages in the treatment process more, he or she will become healthier.

省略

語境清楚，語意不致混淆的情況下，雙重比較句型的主詞或動詞可以省略。

省略主語與動詞

例 14 The sooner you start, the better it will be.

→ 省略：The sooner, the better.

越快越好。

省略連綴動詞

例 6 ～ 8 可省略如例 15 ～ 17。

例 15 The more powerful a car, the more it costs.

例 16 The more efficient a system, the lower it costs to operate.

例 17 The more a patient engages in the treatment process, the healthier he or she.

省略受詞

例 18 The more (things) you do, the more (things) you can do.

你做的事愈多，你愈能做事。

(3) 聲韻層面：

雙重比較平行結構的前後句子都是 the 起首，如同中文修辭學中的排比法，句子簡潔而長度相仿。另外，省略平行結構之外的語詞，不僅吸引閱聽者專注於句構，鏗鏘的聲韻效果也因應而生，猶如音節首子音重複的押頭韻，音韻悅耳，節奏分明，誠屬修辭一大傑作。

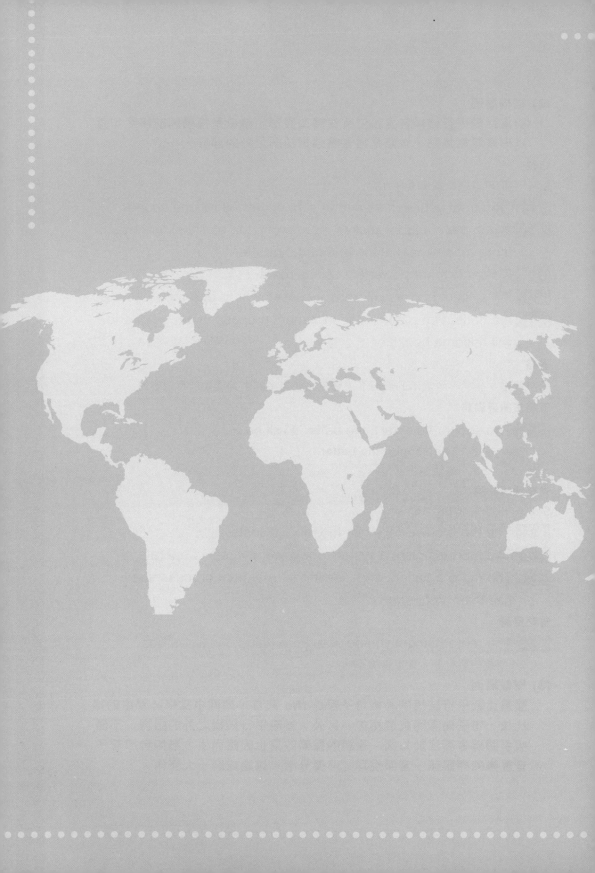

Chapter 7.
經濟原則

語意或結構不致混淆的情況下，語詞應儘量精簡，這是經濟原則，包括縮減與省略二途徑：

1. 縮減：改變結構以使訊息集中或語詞精簡。

2. 省略：結構不變，省略語詞，但語意或結構不致混淆。

Q01. May all your dreams come true!" 是疑問句嗎？

 原來如此 不是疑問句，而是表示祝願的倒裝句型。

◆ 形意搭配是英文句式的主要特徵，表達特殊語意時，除了遣詞用字，還得調兵遣將一變換詞序，才能明確表達語意。情態助動詞 may 表示祝福或願望時，為了強調祝願的語氣，may 移至主詞前，形成倒裝句型，搭配驚嘆號。

例1 May you succeed!

祝你成功！

例2 May you always be happy!

祝你永遠快樂！

例3 May your dreams come true!

願你夢想成真！

例4 May your country become strong and prosperous!

祝福貴國強大繁榮！

◆ wish 也常表示祈願，但是用法講究。wish 加接子句時，主詞可以省略，表達許願，成事在天，搭配假設語氣的動詞形式。

例5 Wish (that) I could retire tomorrow!

但願明天能夠退休！

例6 Wish (that) I could have another day of vacation!

但願能再有一天假期！

◆ 搭配間接受詞時，主詞不可省略，否則就是命令語氣，而不是祈願。

例7 I wish you a Merry Christmas!

祝你耶誕快樂！

例8 We wished him all the best!

我們祝他一切順利！

例9 Mr. Lin wishes you success in your new job!

林先生祝你新職成功！

◆ 主詞若是 "I" 或 "we"，主詞省略，wish 以現在分詞 "wishing" 呈現，常見於信件結尾語或網路貼文。

例 10 Wishing you a Merry Christmas!

= I/We wish you a Merry Christmas!

祝你耶誕快樂！

例 11 Wishing you all the best during the Chinese New Year!

= I/We wish you all the best during the Chinese New Year!

祝你春節期間一切順利！

◆ hope 也可表示祝福，主詞是 "I" 或 "we" 時，主詞可以省略，hope 或 hoping 都可以。hope 是謀事在人，可能成真，現在式表示祝福的內容。

例 12 Hope you come back soon.

祝你早日歸來。

例 13 Hoping you win the gold medal.

祝你贏得金牌。

Q02. "We want the former manager back." 句子中的 back 是動詞嗎？

原來如此 不是動詞，是副詞。

◆ want 加接的受詞及受詞補語可視為一個事件，受詞是事件的主題，受詞補語是針對主題的敘述。受詞與受詞補語可視為一個句子，受詞是主詞，受詞補語是敘述部分。want 的受詞補語有以下幾種結構：

(1) 不定詞，最常見的受詞補語形式。

例 1 Do you want me to take you to the airport?
你要我送你到機場嗎？

(2) 現在分詞，常帶有持續的意味。

例 2 We don't want you eating spicy food often.
我們不要你一直常吃辛辣食物。

例 3 I don't want you calling me late at night.
我不要你晚上很晚了還一直打電話給我。

(3) 過去分詞，表示受詞的被動狀態。

例 4 The manager wants these samples sent tomorrow.
經理要這些樣品明天寄出。

例 5 Mr. Lin wants the job done by the weekend.
林先生要這工作在周末前完成。

(4) 形容詞，說明受詞變化的狀態。

例 6 I want this pizza hot.
我要這塊披薩熱一下。

例 7 She didn't really want the killer dead.
她不是真的要兇手喪命。

(5) 副詞，省略動詞。

例 8 We want the former manager back.
我們想要前任經理回來。

例 9 We want the teenager away from gangs.
我們要那位青少年遠離幫派。

(6) 介係詞片語

例 10 The boy is annoying. I want him out of here now.
那男孩很討厭，我要他馬上離開這裡。

Q03. "play the piano" 一定要有定冠詞 the 嗎？

 不，除了 **play the piano**、**play piano**、**play a piano** 也都普遍。

◆ 一般認為表示彈奏樂器時，樂器是個人專屬物品，樂器名稱必須搭配定冠詞 **the**。

例1 play the piano

　　彈鋼琴

例2 play the violin

　　拉小提琴

例3 play the flute

　　吹長笛

◆ 事實上，play the piano、play piano、play a piano 都廣泛使用於英美地區及主流媒體。

例4 He knew how to play piano.

BBC News

　　他知道怎麼彈鋼琴。

例5 Sometimes I play piano and she sings. Sometimes she plays piano and I play accordion.

San Francisco Chronicle

　　有時候我彈鋼琴而她唱歌，有時候她彈鋼琴而我拉手風琴。

例6 We both play violin.

Ottawa Citizen

　　我們倆人都拉小提琴。

例7 In primary school he learnt to play flute.

The Times

　　上小學時，她學會吹長笛。

例8 Children learn how to play a piano.

The New Times

　　孩子學習如何彈鋼琴。

例9 You use the hands and wrists to play a piano, but only the fingers for a harpsichord.

Baltimore Sun

　　你用手及手肘彈鋼琴，但只能用手指頭談大鍵琴。

例 10 At the age of four, he said he wanted to play a violin, too.

BBC News

四歲時，他說他也要拉小提琴。

例 11 At the age of 60, she learned to play a flute.

Wall Street Journal

60 歲時，她學習吹長笛。

◆ 運動項目是抽象概念，不須搭配冠詞。

例 12 play basketball

打籃球

例 13 play volleyball

打排球

例 14 play soccer

踢足球

◆ 若是玩球的動作，而不是運動比賽，球是遊戲的工具，搭配冠詞，以 with 引介。

例 15 The boy is playing with a baseball.

那位男孩正在玩一顆棒球。

例 16 I saw Belle playing with a tennis ball.

我看見貝拉在玩一顆網球。

例 17 Let's play with the volleyball.

咱們來玩排球。

◆ 一些生活語詞跟運動一樣，抽象概念不搭配冠詞，具體物品才搭配冠詞。

例 18 go to bed

去睡覺

→ bed 是抽象概念。

例 19 go to the bed

去床那裡

→ bed 是移動的目標，具體物品，the 表示已知的物品。

例 20 I went to the museum by bus.

我搭公車去博物館。

→ by bus 表示交通方式，抽象概念。

例 21 I took a bus to the museum.

我搭公車去博物館。

→ bus 是搭乘的交通工具，具體物品，但不特指，搭配不定冠詞 a。

例 22 We are eating lunch.

我們正在吃中餐。

→ 吃午餐，抽象概念。

例 23 We had a light lunch today.

今天我們吃一頓清淡的中餐。

→ 形容詞修飾 lunch，描述某一頓午餐，搭配不定冠詞 a。

例 24 We enjoyed the nice lunch you prepared.

我們喜愛你預備的豐盛午餐。

→ 特指的一餐，搭配定冠詞。

Q04. "Doing his homework, Tom went out for a walk."這句話對嗎？

原來如此 不對，分詞構句所示的動作較早發生，搭配完成式。

◆ 分詞構句提供主要子句時間、條件、原因、讓步等訊息。

例1 Lawmakers want to ban using a cellphone while walking across the street.

立法者要禁止走路過馬路時滑手機。

例2 If provided a picture of a pet, the waiter will produce an image on your coffee.

如果提供一張寵物照，侍者將在咖啡上畫出一個圖像。

例3 There being a lot of fog, the walk uphill was tough.

由於濃霧，走路上山很困難。

例4 Though understanding no English, the customer was still able to communicate.

儘管完全不懂英文，那名客人仍然能夠溝通。

◆ 分詞構詞若較主要子句早發生，完成式呈現。

例5 Having done his homework, Tom went out for a walk.

做完他的工作之後，湯姆就出去散步。

例6 Having failed my medical exams, I took up business.

因為醫學考試未通過，我便從事商業工作。

◆ 時間有過去、現在、未來三個範疇，若要表示同一時間範疇的先後順序，搭配完成時貌。

例7 We had completed the project by the end of last quarter.

上一季結束之前我們就已完成這項計畫。

例8 The mountain climbers have left the campsite so far.

登山客目前已離開營區了。

例9 Turn left at the corner and you will have arrived at the hotel.

在角落處左轉，你便已抵達飯店了。

◆ 非限定子句也有完成式，表示較限定動詞早發生。

例 10 The painting is believed to have been destroyed.

據相信,這幅畫已遭毀損。

例 11 The assistant ignored my requests to meet with the board director, despite my having left my email with her.

助理忽略我會見董事長的要求,儘管我事先已寫電子郵件給她了。

例 12 How come they flew such planes without having checked thoroughly before flying?

他們怎麼會搭乘這種飛行前未徹底檢查的飛機呢?

補充學習

★ 不定詞的時態與語態

◆標記時態、人稱、數目的動詞是限定動詞,不標記時態、人稱、數目的動詞是非限定動詞,包括不定詞、省略 to 的不定詞、黏接字尾 ing 的現在分詞、動名詞、黏接字尾 en 的過去分詞。

以 take 為例:

to take 是不定詞

take 是省略 to 的不定詞

taking 是現在分詞或動名詞

taken 是過去分詞

◆與限定動詞相同,非限定動詞也有時態與語態,標記非限定動詞構成的事件的樣貌。非限定動詞的時態與語態的架構與限定動詞一致:

• 簡單式就是非限定動詞的基本型,表示習慣或是常態。

• 進行式是 **be 動詞加接現在分詞,凸顯當下的動作。**

• 完成式是 **have 加接過去分詞,標示較早發生。**

• 完成進行式是 **have been 加接現在分詞,標示仍然持續。**

• 被動語態是 **be 動詞加接過去分詞,而 be 動詞標示簡單或是完成。**

一、不定詞

1. 簡單式：to 動詞原形

◆ 與主動語態句子相同，主動語態不定詞以**主事者為主題**

例 1 I plan to major in linguistics in college.

我打算在大學主修語言學。

→ 限定子句：I will major in linguistics in college.

◆ be to V 用於正式的安排或計畫，相當正式的用法

例 2 The prime minister is to visit China next week.

總理將於下周訪問中國。

◆ be 動詞加接被動式不定詞，強調受事者主詞受動作的影響。

例 3 These dishes are to be washed.

這些盤子要洗了。

例 4 The cleaning is to be finished by noon.

整潔工作中午前要完成。

2. 被動語態不定詞用於強調受事者，受事者作為主詞。

例 5 The donor didn't want to be contacted.

捐贈器官者不要被聯繫，強調被聯繫的是捐贈器官者。

例 6 The desk is covered with forms to be filled in.

桌上擺滿要填的表格。

例 7 The desk is covered with forms which will be filled in.

◆ congratulate、encourage 搭配被動式不定詞，聚焦在受事者主詞。

例 8 You are to be congratulated.

你將獲得恭賀。（重點是誰被恭喜，受事者當主詞。）

例 9 This behavior is to be encouraged.

這行為該被鼓勵。（重點是被鼓勵的行為，受事者當主詞。）

◆ blame 的被動意味濃厚，主動語態表示受事者主詞受責難的狀態。

例 10 Nobody was to blame for the accident.

沒有人要為這起意外而遭受責難。

◆ 被動語態不定詞用於主事者不明確或不須提及。

例 11 Tom was hoping to be chosen for the soccer team.
　　　湯姆一直希望入選足球隊。選拔的人不明確。

◆ 被動語態不定詞常用於公告或指示。

例 12 This cover is not to be removed.
　　　這個蓋子不要移走。

◆ 訊息重點是受事者及動作，受事者作為主詞。

例 13 To be taken three times a day after meals.
　　　餐後一天服用三次。

　　　→ 限定子句：The drug should be taken three times a day after meals.

　　　→ 訊息焦點是藥該怎麼被服用，藥是明確的受事者，不須提及主事者，受事者及主事者都可不出現。

3. 進行式不定詞

◆ ing 標記存在，現在分詞凸顯當下。

例 14 It's nice to be sitting here in the park.
　　　現在坐在公園這裡很棒。

　　　→ 不定詞簡單式表示習慣或經常發生。

例 15 It's nice to sit here in the park.
　　　坐在公園這裡很棒。

例 16 I noticed that the man seemed to be smoking a lot.
　　　我注意到那名男子似乎菸抽個不停。

　　　→ 現在分詞使當下的意涵更加鮮明。

例 17 We plan to be staying in the city for longer than two weeks.
　　　我們規劃要在這城市停留兩個多星期。

4. 完成式不定詞

◆ 說話之前的動作。

例 18 I'm sorry not to have replied to your message earlier.

I'm sorry that I didn't reply to your message earlier.

很抱歉，我沒有早一點回覆您的訊息。（說話之前的動作。）

例 19 He is said to have died from losing so much blood.

It is said that he died from losing so much blood.

據說他死於失血過多。

◆ 未來某時之前將完成。

例 20 We hope to have finished the building construction by the end of August.

我們希望八月底前完成營造工程。

5. 完成進行式不定詞

◆ 截至過去某時仍持續。

例 21 She seemed to have been sitting there for an hour before I noticed her.

在我注意她之前，她似乎已在那裡坐了一小時了。

二、動名詞

1. 動名詞具有名詞詞性，扮演主詞、補語、受詞等句子必要成分的角色。

例 1 Smoking is prohibited.

禁止吸菸。

→ 動名詞當主詞，不是動作產生者，而是事件主詞，smoking 的主事者，就是吸菸者是不定指的對象。

例 2 Sorry – there's no smoking in the waiting room.

抱歉，等候室裡面禁止吸菸。

→ 「There is no 動名詞」的句型常用於公告，表示不允許。

例 3 It's no use his apologizing – I will never forgive him.

他道歉是沒有用的，我絕不會原諒他。

→ 動名詞當 it is no use 的真主詞，搭配所有格或受格。

例 4 Do you mind me smoking?

你介意我抽菸嗎？

→ 動名詞當及物動詞的受詞，動名詞的主事者是 me。

例 5 She was angry at Tom lying to her.

她氣湯姆對她說謊。

→ 動名詞當介係詞的受詞，動名詞的主事者是 Tom。

例 6 My job is arranging the agenda for the CEO.

我的工作是為執行長安排行程。

→ 動名詞當主詞補語，動名詞的主事者是 I。

2. 完成式動名詞表示較限定動詞早發生。

例 7 I remembered having met the man before.

I remembered meeting the man before.

我記得之前見過那名男子。

例 8 The man was accused of having cheated.

那名男子被控詐欺。

Tom denied having been to the pub.

湯姆否認去過那家酒吧。

3. 被動語態動名詞

◆ 形容詞或分詞不是名詞，不扮演主詞或受詞等名詞角色，必須還原 be 動詞，藉由 be 動詞形成動名詞來扮演主詞或受詞。

例 9 Being rich and famous is a dream for many people.

名利雙收對許多人來說是一個夢想。

→ being rich and famous 是動名詞片語扮演主詞

例 10 Being laid off is different from being fired!

臨時解雇不同於革職。

→ being laid off、being fired 都是動名詞片語

◆ be 動詞的完成式是 having been，過去分詞搭配 having been 形成完成式動名詞，表示較早發生的被動狀態。

例 11 The car showed no sign of having been touched.

這部汽車沒有曾被碰觸過的跡象。

例 12 Tina's angry about not having been invited.

= Tina's angry about that she was not invited.

蒂娜很生氣她沒有受邀。

◆ 動名詞常**搭配所有格以標示主事者**。

例 13 His not knowing English brought him a lot of inconvenience.

他不懂英語,這給他帶來許多麻煩。

→ 動名詞的主事者是 he

例 14 I'm sorry for my being late.

很抱歉,我遲到了。

→ 動名詞的主事者是 I。

例 15 I strongly object to your taking full-page advertisements.

我強烈反對你刊登全版廣告。

→ 動名詞的主事者是 you。

三、分詞

◆ 過去分詞無完成式或被動語態,現在分詞有完成式,及物現在分詞有被動語態。

現在分詞的時態與語態,以 do 為例。

	主動	被動
簡單式	doing	being done
完成式	have doing	having been done

1. 簡單式現在分詞表示與限定動詞同時發生。

例 1 While walking on her way home, Cindy did meet the principal and had some brief conversation with him.

在走路回家路上,Cindy 遇到校長,還跟他簡短聊了一下。

→ walking on her way home 的主事者是 Cindy,與主要子句主詞一致,因此省略。

2. 簡單式現在分詞表示較限定動詞稍早發生。

例 2 Returning to the office, she began to write an email to the client.

她回到辦公室之後，馬上寫電子郵件給那名客戶。

→ Returning to the office 的主事者是 she，與主要子句主詞一致，因此省略。

3. 完成式現在分詞明確表示在限定動詞之前發生。

例 3 Having finished his work, Tom came to help me out.

湯姆做完工作之後過來幫我忙。

→ Having finished his work 的主事者是 Tom，與主要子句主詞一致，因此省略。

4. 完成進行式現在分詞表示限定動詞之前持續發生。

例 4 Having been driving all day, I felt exhausted.

一直開了一整天的車，我累癱了。

→ Having been driving all day 的主事者是 I，與主要子句主詞一致，因此省略。

5. 被動語態現在分詞

◆ 簡單式被動語態現在分詞「being 過去分詞」，being 標記現在分詞，進行中的被動動作。

例 5 The car being repaired is also equipped with a manual transmission.

The car which is being repaired is also equipped with a manual transmission.

正在維修的那部汽車同時配備手排變速箱。

→ 過去分詞後位修飾，表示完成。

例 6 A couple of the guests invited didn't show up.

二三位受邀賓客沒有出席。

6. 完成式被動語態現在分詞「having　been　過去分詞」。

例 7 Having been thoroughly tested, the new hydrogen engine was ready to power a new line of automobiles.

徹底檢測之後，新款氫氣引擎要為一系列新汽車提供動力。

→ 若不強調動作先發生，having been 省略。

Thoroughly tested, the new hydrogen engine was ready to power a new line of automobiles.

→ 分詞構句可以擴增為副詞子句

After it had been thoroughly tested, the new hydrogen engine was ready to power a new line of automobiles.

Q05. "Tom went out shutting the door behind him."句中 shutting 是副詞子句縮減的分詞構句嗎？

原來如此 不是，**shutting** 是 "**and shut**" 縮減的分詞構句。

◆ 語意或結構若不致混淆，語詞可以省略，這是經濟原則。

(1) 語詞省略

例1 Open the door.

打開門。

→ 省略主詞。

例2 I think (that) I will take the course next semester.

我想我下學期會修那門課。

→ 省略補語連詞 that。

例3 My brother has spent years (on) building up his collection.

我哥哥花了好多年時間蒐集收藏品。

→ 省略介係詞 on。

(2) 結構縮減

(2.1) 形容詞子句縮減為分詞片語

例4 The boy playing the guitar at the end of the show is my son.

在表演結尾彈吉他的男孩是我兒子。

→ 底層結構：The boy who is playing the guitar at the end of the show is my son.

例5 The man was hit by a car while crossing the road.

男子穿越馬路時被車撞了。

→ 底層結構：The man was hit by a car while he was crossing the road.

(2.2) 合句及限定動詞也常縮減為分詞構句。

(2.2.1) and 連接主詞一致的句子，其中一句可縮減為分詞構句。

例6 The lady rushed into the police station, asking for help.

那位女子衝到警察局求助。

→ 底層結構：The lady rushed into the police station, and she asked for help.

→ 分詞構句表示連續的動作。

例 7 The warthog mother was killed, leaving three young ones surviving for themselves.

疣豬媽媽被殺，留下三隻幼豬自力求生。

→ 底層結構：The warthog mother was killed, and it left three young ones surviving for themselves.

→ 分詞構句表示結果。

例 8 Walking on tiptoe, the man carefully searched around.

踮著腳尖走路，男子仔細四處搜索。

→ 底層結構：The man walked on tiptoe, and he carefully searched around.

→ 分詞構句表示方式。

(2.2.2) 平行結構的限定動詞，表示接續或附帶動作。

例 9 Tom went out shutting the door behind him.

湯姆出去，隨手關上門。

→ 底層結構：Tom went out and shut the door behind him.

例 10 The boy went up to his mother crying.

男孩哭著往他母親那裡去。

→ 底層結構：The boy went up to his mother and cried.

例 11 They have to work wearing protective clothing.

他們必須穿著防護衣工作。

→ 底層結構：They have to work and wear protective clothing.

Q06. "The rich are not always happy." the 為什麼接形容詞 rich？

 原來如此 the 表示泛指，而泛指群體時，名詞省略。

◆ 我們常說 the 加形容詞表示具形容詞特徵的群體，泛指成員，the 搭配複數名詞。那麼，"the rich" 的名詞是什麼呢？當然就是 people---the rich people。至於 people 為什麼省略呢？因為語意明確，不致誤解時語詞可以省略，以符合能省則省的經濟原則。the 若是搭配分詞，名詞一樣可以省略，禮運大同篇的英譯就有許多例子：

THE CHAPTER OF GREAT HARMONY(TA TUNG)

Provision is secured for **the aged** till death, employment for **the able-bodied**, and the mean of growing up for **the young**. Helpless widows and widowers, orphans and **the lonely**, as well as **the sick** and **the disabled**, are well cared for.

使老有所終，壯有所用，幼有所長，鰥、寡、孤、獨、廢疾者皆有所養。

the aged 老者	the able-bodied 壯者
the young 幼者	the lonely 孤獨者
the sick 疾者	the disabled 廢者

◆ 若是明確指涉單數可數名詞或是抽象名詞，"the 形容詞" 搭配單數動詞。

例1 The accused has to be brought to justice.

該名被告必須繩之以法。

→ 被告通常是單數，the accused = the person accused。

例2 The deceased has been identified as an Italian guy.

死者經辨認是一名義大利人。

→ the deceased = the deceased person。

◆ 若是可能造成泛指或是特指的混淆，名詞不可省略。

例3 The deceased and the injured were all bus passengers.

死者及傷者全都是公車乘客。

→ The deceased 及 the injured 都是指複數的乘客。

例4 The injured driver has been removed from the vehicle.

受傷的駕駛人已被移出車輛。

Q07. "a mountain lake of blue color, round in shape" 如何使這樣的寫法更好？

原來如此 color 是贅字，blue 的語意已包含 color，而 round 就是 shape，in shape 也是贅字。

◆ 任何語詞都有語意特徵，也就是定義的要項。

> father：human、male、adult
>
> mother：human、female、adult

◆ 只有一項語意特徵相異的語詞為相反詞，例如 father ／ mother、husband ／ wife。

◆ 語詞若伴隨其語意特徵的字詞，除非必要，否則就屬贅字，應該避免，以合乎經濟原則。

例1 My father is a humorous adult. / My father is humorous.

> 我父親很幽默。

例2 My little brother is a smart boy. / My little brother is smart.

> 我弟弟很可愛。

例3 My wife is a conservative woman.

> 我太太是個保守的女人。
>
> → woman 雖是 wife 的語意特徵，但表示 conservative 的族群一員，含有歸類的意味，略帶刻板成見。

例4 She is my wife, married and beautiful. / She is my beautiful wife.

> 她是我漂亮的老婆。

◆ 寫作首重語詞簡潔、語意明確，而贅字常是遣詞用字的絆腳石，應當剔除，雖然有人認為數大就是美，多語多詞多分數，但是，字裡行間要見解多、觀點多、創意多，文字才結實強壯，否則冗長而不見論述，虛胖罷了。

以 "a mountain lake of blue color, round in shape" 為例，color 及 in shape 都是贅字。若要顧及結構，增添非語意特徵的語詞以拓化意境，應是不錯的策略。

例5 a mountain lake, bright blue and as round as a full moon

> 一座山裡的湖泊，湛藍，宛如滿月一樣地圓。

◆ bright blue 比 blue in color 更細緻、真實，full moon 不僅呈現 round 的客觀事實，更藉由明喻使文字嵌入美而傳神的意象，引出 mountain lake 的蘊含意境。

以下是一些常見的贅字例子：

actual fact
→ fact 事實
and together with
→ and / together with 一起
basic fundamental
→ basic / fundamental 基本的
blind in both eyes
→ blind 瞎的
building architect
→ architect 建築師
do exercise
→ exercise 運動
imaginary dream
→ dream 夢想
new innovation
→ innovation 發明
loud noise
→ noise 噪音

Q08. "I am afraid that I can't agree with you."句子的 that 引導的是什麼子句？

原來
如此 名詞子句，介係詞 of 的受詞，但介係詞省略了。

◆ afraid 是述語形容詞，置於連綴動詞後面，介係詞 of 引介害怕的事物，介係詞片語可視為 afraid 的補語。

例 1 I am afraid of height.
我懼高。

例 2 The little girl is afraid of speaking in public.
那位小女孩害怕在眾人面前說話。

◆ 若以子句結構表示害怕的內容，子句是介係詞 of 的受詞，既是受詞，當然是名詞子句，補語連詞 that 引導，至於 of，省略了。

例 3 I am afraid (of) that I can't agree with you.
恐怕我無法贊同你。

◆ 若是形成強調句或分裂句，of 未連接 that 子句，必須還原。

例 4 What I am afraid of is (that) I can't agree with you.
恐怕的是我無法贊同你。

例 5 It is that I can't agree with you (that) I am afraid of.
我無法贊同你是我擔心的。

◆ of 加接動名詞，表示存在，也就是害怕的內容，若要表示害怕去進行某動作，搭配不定詞，副詞性質。

例 6 The little girl is afraid to speak in public.
那位小女孩害怕去眾人面前說話。

◆ sorry、glad 等形容詞搭配的 that 子句也是名詞子句，介係詞的受詞，而介係詞省略。

例 7 I am sorry that you feel that way.
你那樣感覺，我很抱歉。

例 8 I am glad that you can join us.
很高興你能跟我們一起。

Q09. "Mrs. Lin's son died young." 的 young 怎麼分析？

 原來如此 young 表示 died 的時間，副詞子句的縮減。

◆ die 常搭配名詞、形容詞、分詞，說明死者死亡時的狀態，可視為縮減結構。

例1 The old man died a poor man.
老先生往生時是一個窮人。（身分）
→ 底層結構：The old man was poor when he died.

例2 The firefighter died a martyr at his post.
那名消防弟兄因公殉職。（原因）
→ 底層結構：The firefighter died and he was a martyr at his post.

例3 The entrepreneur died young.
那名企業家英年早逝。（年齡）
→ 底層結構：The entrepreneur was young when he died.

例4 The woman died young, leaving two little children.
那名婦人年輕時就過世，留下二名稚子。（結果）
→ 底層結構：The woman died and left two little children when she was young.

例5 The gangster died a miserable death.
= The gangster died in a miserable way.
那名幫派分子慘死。（狀態）

例6 The soldier died fighting for his country.
那名士兵為國家奮戰到最後一口氣。
→ 底層結構：
(1) The soldier fought for his country until he died.（狀態）
那名士兵為國家奮戰到最後一口氣。
(2) The soldier died from fighting for his country.（原因）
那名士兵為國捐軀。

◆ 一些動詞常搭配名詞、形容詞、分詞，說明動作發生時主事者的狀態，簡潔而流暢地增添訊息，是值得學習運用的描述技巧。

名詞

例 7 The man left his hometown a teenager and came back a senior.

那名男子離開家鄉時是青少年，返鄉時已是老年人。

例 8 The late president was born a poor black child, and died a millionaire.

已故總裁出生時是可憐的黑人小孩，過世時是一名億萬富翁。

形容詞

例 9 Tom lay ill in bed of a burning fever last week.

上星期湯姆因高燒而臥病在床。

例 10 The coach sat silent for a moment.

那名教練坐著，靜了一會兒。

例 11 The performer stood still in the corner acting like a statue.

表演者在角落站著不動，舉止像一尊雕像。

例 12 Mrs. Lin married young.

林太太很年輕就結婚了。

例 13 The soldiers have returned safe and sound from the war.

那些士兵已從戰火中平安歸來。

例 14 The criminal was captured alive.

那名罪犯被活捉。

分詞

例 15 Everyone stood listening attentively to the leader's every word until the end.

每個人都專注聆聽帶頭者的每一個字，直到結束。

例 16 A student was caught cheating on the SAT.

一位學生在 SAT 測驗時作弊被抓。

→ "cheating on the SAT" 說明被抓的原因，考試作弊是主動動作，搭配現在分詞。

◆ 補充描述主詞狀態的語詞是修飾功用，若是省略，句子仍是正確，不同於主詞補語，必要成分，若是省略，語意不完整，句子錯誤。

例 17 The man remained silent and gave no answer.

那名男子保持沉默，未給答案。

例 18 Everyone stayed calm during the earthquake.

地震期間，大家都保持冷靜。

Q10. "how come"可以代換為"why not "嗎？

 不可以。"how come" 用於詢問理由或方式，"why not" 用於提出建議或表達同意等。

◆ "how come" 詢問原因或發生的方式，相當於中文的「怎麼」，用於輕鬆的口語或聊天而不用於正式場合或寫作，語氣較 why 緩和。另外，"how come " 的底層結構是 "How did it come that…?"，come 是發生—to happen 的意思，搭配直述詞序的 that 子句是 it 的真主詞。

例1 How come you didn't come to class?

= How did it come that you didn't come to class?

你怎麼沒來上課？

（你沒有來上課這件事是怎麼發生的？）

比較：

例2 Why didn't you come to class?

你為什麼沒來上課？

（語氣較直接）

例3 How come you seem to have gained weight?

= How did it come that you seem to have gained weight?

你怎麼似乎發胖了？

（你似乎發胖了這件事是怎麼發生的？）

例4 A: I will have to be absent tomorrow.

B: How come?

A：我明天得缺席。

B：怎麼了？

（語氣帶有關心的意味）

◆ "why not? " 用法

(1) 表示建議

例5 Why not join us for a hearty lunch today?

= Why don't you join us for a hearty lunch today?

今天何不加入我們一起享用一頓溫馨的午餐？

例 6 A: I am so hungry.

B: Why not take a break and get something to eat?

= Why don't you take a break and get something to eat?

A：我好餓。

B：何不休息一下，找點吃的東西？

例 7 A: How about if we meet at Starbucks?

B: Why not (meet) at the meeting point?

A：我們在星巴克碰面好嗎？

B：何不在會面點？

→ "How about …?" 及 "What about…?" 都表示建議，尤其是提出已被忘卻的內容。

(2) 表示同意

例 8 A: May I eat out with you?

B: Sure, why not?

A：我可以跟你們一起去用餐？

B：當然，有什麼不行的？

例 9 A: Let's go to the pub after work tonight.

B: Of course, why not?

A：咱們今晚下班後去上夜店。

B：當然，有什麼不行的？

(3) 詢問否定原因

例 10 A: I will not go with you to the movies.

B: Why not? (Why will you not go with me to the movies?)

A：我不跟你們去看電影。

B：為什麼不去？

(4) 表示堅持

例 11 A: Are you really going to sue your colleague?

B: Yes, why not?

A：你真的要控告他們嗎？

B：是，為什麼不告。

◆ 相較於 "how come" 詢問過去或未來狀況的原因，"why not" 只涉及未來的話題，若是過去，助動詞 didn't 應該保留。

例 12 A: I could have called the police then.

B: Why didn't you do it?

誤 Why not do it?

A: 我那時候可以報警的。

B: 你為什麼不做？

例 13 Why didn't you call me back after the meeting?

誤 Why not call me back after the meeting?

你會議後為什麼不回我電話？

Q11. "due to"與"because of"的用法一樣嗎？

 原來如此 不一樣，"**due to**"形成形容詞片語，修飾名詞；"**because of**" 形成介係詞片語，副詞性質。

◆ 一般認為 "due to" 與 "because of" 都是片語介係詞，用法一致，但是二者形成的介係詞片語功用不同，嚴格來說，不可代換。

"due to"表示 on account of，caused by（因何而起）、resulting from（導因於）的意思，形成的介係詞片語是形容詞性質，修飾名詞、代名詞或是充當 be 動詞的補語。另外，due 是形容詞，resulting 的意思，可以搭配副詞以形成「due 副詞 to」的片語介係詞結構。

例 1 The flight delay was due to bad weather.

= The flight delay was caused by bad weather.

班機延誤是由於不良氣候。

例 2 The candidate's defeat was due chiefly to energy issue.

= The candidate's defeat was choefly caused by energy issue.

該名候選人主要由於能源議題而落敗。

◆ 一些認為 "due to" 搭配 "the fact that…" 是正式用法，但其實是贅字形式，遣詞用字仍應簡潔。

例 3 Tom was late to the meeting due to the fact that traffic was heavy.

比較： Tom was late to the meeting due to heavy traffic.

由於交通壅塞，湯姆開會遲到。

◆ 現代英語中， "due to" 片語也修飾動詞片語或置於句首修飾句子。

例 4 The flight delayed due to weather conditions.

由於天氣狀況，班機延誤了。

例 5 Due to ill health, the manager didn't attend the meeting.

由於不佳的健康狀況，經理未出席會議。

◆ "because of" 表示 for the reason that，形成的介係詞片語是副詞性質，修飾動詞、形容詞或子句，不修飾名詞或代名詞。另外，"because of" 不可代換為 "caused by"，這或許可作為檢視 "because of" 及 "due to" 差別的方式。

例 6 Tom arrived late because of heavy traffic.

湯姆晚抵達，因為車流壅塞。

例 7 The candidate was defeated because of energy issue.

因為能源議題，該候選人遭到挫敗。

例 8 The student was frustrated because of his brain injury.

由於腦部受傷，該名學生感到挫折。

◆　"due to" 雖然打破了形容詞的用法限制，但是，寫作正式文體或學術論文時，仍應準確區分 "due to" 與 "because of" 的用法時機。

Q12. "under control"為什麼表示被動？

原來
如此　**under** 表示空間上是在……下方，引申為被動。

◆ 介係詞與名詞片語構成介係詞片語，標示名詞片語的語意關聯。

in the room	→ 位置 location
to the hilltop	→ 目的地 destination
for a while	→ 期間 duration
on Sunday	→ 時間 time
for you	→ 受益者 beneficiary
with a spoon	→ 工具 instrument
with my partner	→ 陪伴 associate
by mistake	→ 方式 manner
by the police	→ 主事者 agent—doer

◆ 大多數的介係詞都有對應的字首，因此，我們可以將介係詞片語視為黏接字首的單詞。

介係詞片語：介係詞 名詞

單詞：字首 字幹

on board / a-board 在車（船、飛機）上

before room / ante-room 接待室

by the path / by-path 小路

over the head / over-head 在頭上的

above the face / super-ficial 表面的

under the ground / under-ground 地下的

under way / sub-way 地鐵

◆ under 就是字首 sub- 的意思，"under control" 表示在控制之下，當然是受控制的意思。

◆ at 的意思是「處於」，構成的介係詞片語表示處於某狀態，主動的動作。

at play / playing 正在玩

at work / working 正在工作

at table / eating 正在吃飯

at dinner / eating dinner 正在吃晚餐

◆ 包含指示詞的名詞片語分析為一個單詞，就是將指示詞視為一個字首，
例如：

　　a book 一本書

　　an eraser 一個橡皮擦

　　the number 那個號碼

　　my car 我的汽車

含字首的單詞也可視為一個片語。

　　unicorn / one horn　獨角獸

　　bicycle / two cycles 單車

　　triangle / three angles 三角形

　　quadrangle（quadrilateral）/ four sides 四角形

　　because / by cause 因為，原因所在的敘述

　　biology / study of life 生物學

　　unhappy / not happy 不快樂

　　almighty / all mighty 全能的

Q13. 為什麼 this 及 is 不可縮寫？

 原來如此 this is 若縮寫，is 的 i 省略，造成 /s/、/z/ 二嘶擦音相鄰，不易發音，也聽不清楚，因此 this is 不縮寫。

◆ 英語是拼音文字，語音主導拼字，語音表現影響拼字形式，而發音方便，聽得清晰是語音的重要原則。

◆ /s, z, ʃ, ʒ, tʃ, dʒ/ 等子音發音時產生氣流嘶擦的現象，稱為嘶擦音。二嘶擦音相鄰，發音不易，聽者容易混淆，因此，this、is 不縮寫，避免形成 "this's[ðɪsz]" 的唸音及拼寫。

二詞素黏接而造成嘶擦音相鄰時，常見三種音韻變化，一是插入響度很小的母音 /ɪ/，填補字母 e，二是省略其中一個嘶擦音，三是轉音。

(1) 插入母音 /ɪ/：

(1.1) 複數名詞

1. 名詞黏接屈折綴詞 -s 形成複數，由於母音及有聲子音等有聲音的數量最多，因此唸音為 /z/。名詞字尾若是無聲子音，/z/ 同化為 /s/，例如：

   cups 杯子

   cats 貓

   desks 桌子

2. 名詞字尾若是嘶擦音，則插入母音 /ɪ/，加上填補字母 e，例如：

   classes 班級

   dishes 盤子

   ditches 水溝

3. 名詞字尾若是不發音的 e 字母，插入的母音 /ɪ/ 對應 e，因此不增加填補字母 e，例如：

   houses 房子

   garages 車庫

   oranges 柳丁

(1.2) 單數動詞

動詞黏接屈折綴詞 -s，唸音的變化與複數名詞一致，例如：

> sips 啜飲
>
> puts 放置
>
> walks 走路
>
> closes 關閉
>
> washes 洗
>
> catches 抓
>
> judges 判斷

(2) 省略

(2.1) 省略前一單字尾的嘶擦音，例如：

> gas station 加油站
>
> Sue is swimming in the pool.
>
> 蘇正在游泳池游泳。

(2.2) 省略字幹首的嘶擦音，字母縮減，多發生在黏接字首 ex- 的單字，例如：

> expire   ex + spire 到期
>
> expect   ex + spect 期待
>
> exorcise   sorc = oath 驅除

(2.3) 省略重疊音，例如：

> excite 使興奮
>
> exsiccate [`ɛksɪˌket] 變乾

(2.4) ex- 黏接有聲子音為首的字幹時，x 字母省略，例如：

> ebullient 熱情洋溢的
>
> edit 編輯
>
> egress 出口
>
> eject 噴射
>
> elaborate 詳盡的
>
> emancipate 解放
>
> eruption 爆發
>
> evoke 喚起

(2.5) ex- 省略 /s/，保留 /k/，**ex-** 拼寫為 **ec-**，例如：

eccentric 古怪的

ecstasy 狂喜

(2.6) s 字尾的複數名詞形成所有格時，僅黏接所有格標記，以避免二個 **s** 重複，
例如：

the teachers' office 教師辦公室

a ladies' room 女生盥洗室

a girls' high school 女子中學

(2.7) 省略所有格字尾綴詞 **s** 字母，這是現代英語的趨勢，例如：

Achilles's heel, Achilles' heel
阿基里斯腱，致命傷。

Max's philosophy, Max' philosophy
馬克思哲學

my boss's car, my boss' car
我老闆的車子

(3) 轉音：/s/ 與 /ʃ/ 相鄰時，同為無聲嘶擦音，唸音過於接近，因此 /ʃ/
轉音為 /tʃ/，例如：

question 問題

suggestion 建議

Q14. cellphone 與 cell phone 的拼寫有什麼差別？

 原來如此 複合詞的形成階段不同。

◆ 複合詞是由二或數個單詞，甚至是字母及單詞所構成，形式有以下三種：

(1) 分開書寫，最先出現的複合詞形式。

cover letter 附函

dining car 餐車廂

copy machine 影印機

reading room 閱覽室

boiled water 沸水

(2) 連字號連接：三、四個單詞構成的複合詞都以連字號連接，包含字母的複合詞也會以連字號連接以避免混淆。

Jack-O-lantern 傑克燈籠

ten-year-old 十歲大的

jack-in-the-box 玩偶盒

all-you-can-eat restaurant 吃到飽餐廳

含字母的複合詞

email 電子郵件

T-bar T 霸

U-turn U 型轉彎

V-neck V 型領

X-ray X 光

(3) 合併：

blackboard 黑板

greenhouse 溫室

pickpocket 扒手

playground 遊樂場

◆ 複合詞合併拼寫之前通常先是分開書寫，或是連字號連接。

　　　e-mail → email 電子郵件

　　　cell phone → cellphone 行動電話

◆ cell phone 及 cellphone 都是正確的複合詞書寫形式，只是形成的階段不同，但二者應該一樣普遍。

Chapter 8.
語用原則

語詞的運用除了講究正確，還要考究是否合乎時宜。若是以學習為目的，語用原則包括以下幾點：

1. 學習多種用法，不以偏概全
2. 寧可語意清晰，不要繁複句構
3. 文法之外仍需文化
4. 避免古代用法
5. 留意當代用法

Q01. " It will be fun being in New York again." 正確嗎？

原來如此　正確，"it is fun" 句型可以搭配動名詞。

◆ 不定詞除了要去做、未完成的意涵，還可以表示事實。

例 1 It is fun to take a ride on a cable car
搭乘纜車很好玩。

例 2 It is important to make a plan before you start writing.
寫作之前先做一計畫是重要的。

例 3 Neil Armstrong is the first human to walk on the moon.
尼爾•阿姆斯壯是第一位在月球上步行的人類。

→ "to walk on the moon" 表示已完成的事實。

◆ 動名詞表示存在或持續，因此，"it is fun" 搭配動名詞，陳述事實或經驗。

例 4 It will be fun being in New York again.
再次待在紐約是令人愉快的。

例 5 It is fun going around London looking for old post boxes.
逛遍倫敦找尋古老的郵筒是一大樂趣。

◆ 一些形容詞搭配動名詞同樣表示事件或經驗。

例 6 I'm telling you all that it is important learning English as a second language.
我剛跟你們大家說，學習英語作為第二語言是重要的。

→ 動名詞表示「學習英語作為第二語言」這件事，而不是去做這動作。

例 7 There is no doubt it will be fun being back in the same football district as Santa Fe High School, and it will be fun to have plenty of new district foes in the other sports.

lamonitor.com

無疑地，令人愉快的是以 Santa Fe 中學的名義重返同一足球賽區，另外，要是其他運動出現大量而且新的賽區勁敵，那就有趣了。

◆ 動名詞表示經驗，不定詞表示對於未來事件的客觀立場。

Q02. "It is no use"只能搭配動名詞嗎？

 原來如此 是的，搭配動名詞合乎近代用法。

◆ "It is no use" 的意思是做某事是無益的，it 是虛主詞。

例1 I tried to get up again but it was no use.

我努力再一次起身，但是沒有用。

→ it 是指 "tried to get up again"，"no use" 評論該動作是無益的。

例2 It is no use crying over spilt milk.

= There is no purpose in crying spilt milk.

覆水難收。

→ it 不是指涉動名詞，動名詞不是移自句首，也不移至主詞位置，因此沒有 "V-ing is no use" 的寫法。例 3-5 的動名詞不是移位的結果。

例3 There's no use asking me about it, because I don't know anything.

Cambridge Dictionary

問我關於那事沒用，因為我一無所悉。

例4 It is no good using hard words among friends about the past.

The Defence of Freedom and Peace

朋友之間為過去而惡言相向是無益的。

例5 There's no point in complaining.

抱怨是沒有用的。

◆ "It is no use" 搭配不定詞是較早年代的用法，不符合現代趨勢。例 6 是十九世紀初俄國戲劇家 Nikolai Gogol 講的一段話，因為頗具寓意，廣為流傳，但也留下 "It is no use to" 的過往痕跡，我們就當作賞析題材，無須論斷，但也不宜援用。

例6 It is no use to blame the looking glass if your face is awry.

臉歪的時候，責怪鏡子是無益的。

Q03. "What does Tom look like today?" 這句話正確嗎？

原來如此 不正確。**What … like** 通常用於詢問長期的狀況。

◆ 詢問天氣有二句型：

例 1 How is the weather?

例 2 What is the weather like?

天氣怎樣？

◆ "what…like" 通常詢問長期的狀況，例如人的外貌或特質。

例 3 A: What does David look like?

B: Tall and dark, cheerful-looking.

A：大衛看起來怎樣？

B：高挑，黝黑，看起來很有精神。

例 4 A: What's Kelly like?

B: She's quiet, and a little shy.

A：凱莉怎樣？

B：安靜又有點害羞。

◆ how 通常詢問短暫的狀況，例如健康、心情或對食物的感覺等。

例 5 A: How does Tim look today?

B: Exhausted.

A：提姆今天看起來怎樣？

B：累癱了。

例 6 A: How was your steak?

B: Delicious. Very juicy and beautifully tender.

A：你的牛排怎樣？

B：美味，軟嫩多汁。

例 7 How would you like your steak? Rare, medium or well done?

你的牛排要幾分熟？一分熟，五分熟或全熟？

Q04. 可以用"How young"詢問訊息嗎？

 原來如此 可以。談話焦點是 **"young"** 時，可以用 **"how young"** 詢問 **"young"** 的程度，但不用於年齡。

◆ 就使用頻率而言，形容詞分為正向及負向二類，彼此互為程度相反詞。

正向	負向
old 老的	young 年輕的
high 高的	low 低的
wide 寬的	narrow 窄的
long 長的	short 短的
deep 深的	shallow 淺的

◆ 正向形容詞使用頻率高，該類形容詞的名稱多與其同源。

形容詞	名詞
high 高的	height 高度
wide 寬的	width 寬度
long 長的	length 長度
deep 深的	depth 深度

◆ 詢問形容詞的程度時，多以正向形容詞搭配 how 構成疑問語詞。

How old 年紀多大

How long 多長

How deep 多深

How wide 多寬

◆ 若以度量衡回答，正向形容詞置於右側，後位修飾，但可省略，結構與中文相同。

ten years old 十歲大

five miles long 五英里長

two inches deep 二英吋深

eight meters wide 八米寬

◆ 一些正向形容詞可代換為「in 同源名詞」構成的介係詞片語。

two meters in length 二米高

three inches in depth 三英寸深

nearly 100 meters in height 接近 100 米高

15 years of age 15 歲大

◆ 我們也可以形容詞片語回答。

A: How old is your dog?

B: Very old.

A：你的狗多大？

B：很老了。

→ Very young. 還很小。

◆ 負向形容詞 "young" 也可構成詢問語詞，用於 "young" 為談話主題的語境，鮮少用於詢問年齡。

A: The makeup is supposed to make you look younger.

B: Really? How young do I look now?

*How young is your dog?

A：這款化妝品讓你看起來更年輕？

B：真的嗎？我現在看起來多年輕呢？

Q05. "Mr. Lin suggests that the student speak English when making a presentation." 句中受詞子句的 speak 是省略 should 嗎？

 原來如此 不是，這是美式用法，表達重要或渴望獲得的假設語氣，搭配原形動詞，與 should 無關。

◆ 假設語氣表達可能、想望、渴望獲得等非真的敘述，以有別於直述句的動詞形式予以標記。

例1 Mr. Lin suggests that the student speak English when making a presentation.
林老師建議該名學生簡報時講英語。

例2 The judge recommended that the man remain in prison for life.
法官建議該名男子終生監禁。

例3 Our advice is that the company should invest in new equipment.
我們的建議是該公司在新設備方面加以投資。

例4 It was important that the salesperson should contact the client as soon as possible.
重要的是，行銷人員儘快和那名客戶聯繫。

◆ **原形動詞是省略 should 的形式嗎？不是，二動詞形式不是省略 should 的差別。**

1. 原形動詞大多用於美式英語的正式用法，認為想望是強制性的假設語氣，也就是現在式假設句，搭配原形動詞，標示與命令句一樣直接而強烈的指令。

例5 It is essential that our prices remain competitive.
非常重要的是，我們的價格要保持競爭優勢。

例6 The author insisted that all the charts be deleted from the article.
作者堅持所有的圖表要從文章中刪除。

2. 「should 原形動詞」是英式用法，should 標示意念尚未成真的想望，非真假設語氣。

例7 The manager recommended that Tom should move to another office.
經理建議湯姆搬到另一間辦公室。

例 8 We felt it desirable that schools should reduce class sizes.
我們覺得學校減少班級人數是好的。

◆ 補語子句搭配原形動詞或 should 原形動詞的語詞：

動詞	名詞	形容詞
1.advocate	1. appointment	1. advisable
2.agree	2. arrangement	2. determined
3.allow	3. conviction	3. imperative
4.appoint	4. decision	4. natural
5.arrange	5. decree	5. no wonder
6.ask	6. demand	6. pitiful / a pity
7.command	7. determination	7. proper
8.decide	8. insistence	8. regrettable
9.decree	9. objection	9. resolved
10.demand	10. order	10. strange
11. determine	11. preference	11. surprising
12. direct	12. proposal	12. traditional
13. intend	13. recommendation	13. urgent
14. maintain	14. request	14. vital
15. move	15. resolution	15. wonderful
16. object	16. suggestion	16. amused
17. order		17. annoyed
18. pray		18. astonished
19. prefer		19. curious
20. propose		20. depressed
21. request		21. fortunate
22. require		22. grateful
23. resolve		23. pleased
24. urge		24. proud
		25. shocked
		26. sorry
		27. strange
		28. surprised
		29. thankful

Q06. "The key opened the door." 中的 key 怎麼會自己開門？

原來如此 工具當主詞，工具無法操控動作，但對物品產生作用，具有及物性，當及物動詞的主詞。

◆ 句子可視為一段陳述或是一起事件，主詞可能是蓄意的動作產生者、受動作影響者、感官的經驗者或是其他角色。了解主詞的語意角色有助於洞悉句子所述事件的始末，理解主詞與動詞的邏輯關係，是閱讀及寫作非常重要的課題。

常見的主詞語意角色如下：

(1) 主事者：

(1.1) 蓄意產生動作的生命體

例1 Tom answered the question.

湯姆回答這問題。

例2 Hank gave me a book.

漢克給我一本書

→ Hank 又是 a book 的來源（source），而 me 是動作的目標，也是 a book 的接收者。

(1.2) 擬人化的非生命體

例3 My smartphone refused to connect to the computer.

我的手機無法連結到電腦。

(1.3) 低等生物的本能動作

例4 Under normal conditions, bacteria will divide every 10 minutes.

常溫之下，細菌每十分鐘分裂一次。

(2) 造成影響者：造成影響者伴隨受影響者，就是受詞。

(2.1) 無意志動作的物體：對受詞產生影響。

例5 A strong wind blew down the shed.

一陣強風吹倒棚子。

(2.2) 對心理狀態產生影響者

例6 The news surprised everyone.

這消息令每一個人驚訝。

(3) 經驗者：體驗感官知覺或心理狀態者，感官或心理的改變視為意志操控的動作。

(3.1) 感官動詞

例 7 I saw an armadillo in the yard.
　　　我在院子看到一隻犰狳。

例 8 I felt something crawling up my shoulder.
　　　我感覺有東西爬上我的肩膀。

(3.2) 心理動詞

例 9 Villagers admired the firefighter.
　　　村民讚賞那名消防隊員。

例 10 I love the film.
　　　我喜愛那部電影。

(4) 工具：工具當主詞，說話者規避責任。

例 11 The key opened the door.
　　　鑰匙打開那扇門。

例 12 The device will turn saltwater into drinking water.
　　　這部機器會將鹹水轉變為飲用水。

(5) 受事者主詞

(5.1) 主動式的受詞：被動語態描述受事者主詞的被動結果狀態。

例 13 The car has been towed away.
　　　那部車子被拖吊了

(5.2) 狀態改變者：搭配狀態改變的與格動詞。

例 14 The book sold well.
　　　這本書賣得很好。

(5.3) 目標：授與動詞的目標，直接受詞的接收者。

例 15 Most employees were given a lecture.
　　　大部分的員工都聆聽演講。

(6) 事件主詞：主詞是一個事件，名詞子句尤其明顯。

例 16 The match will be cancelled.
　　　比賽將被取消。

例 17 That the senator will run for governor has been known to many people.
　　　參議員將競選州長這件事已有許多人知道。

(7) 描述主詞：補語描述的主詞，搭配連綴動詞。

例 18 The manager is good at marketing.

經理擅長於行銷。

例 19 Leaves are turning yellow from the bottom up.

葉子從底部往上逐漸變黃。

(8) 時間主詞

例 20 Yesterday was Thursday.

昨天是星期四。

(9) 位置主詞

例 21 Japan is to the north of Taiwan.

日本在台灣的北邊。

(10) 虛主詞

(10.1) 無指涉對象

例 22 There are two bathrooms in the house.

房子裡有二間浴室。

例 23 It seems that Hank will lose.

似乎漢克會輸。

例 24 It rained a lot this morning.

今天早上下大雨。

(10.2) 有指涉對象

例 25 It is necessary to increase the export volume of cotton next quarter.

下一季需要增加棉花的出口量。

例 26 It is likely that it will be very cold tomorrow.

明天可能會很冷。

Q07. "You may take any type of ocean shrimp in California waters." 這句話對嗎?

 對的。限定詞 **any** 除了用於否定或疑問,也用於其他表示不確定指涉對象的句式。

◆ 字源上,any 的意思是 one、a、an、some;構詞上,any 是 an 黏接字尾 -y;語意上,any 可視為不定冠詞,指涉不確定的對象,搭配表示不確定的語詞或句式。

(1) 情態助動詞 may

例 1 You may take any type of ocean shrimp in California waters.

Los Angeles Times

你可以考慮加州水域的任何種類的海洋蝦。

(2) 情態助動詞 will

例 2 Europe will make any effort to preserve the nuclear deal.

Tehran Times

歐洲將付出任何努力維護核子協議。

(3) 祈使句

例 3 Please make any outstanding payments.

麻煩結清任何未付款項。

(4) promise 承諾

例 4 Schultz has promised to take any necessary steps to prevent this type of discrimination from happening under his administration.

Reporter Magazine

舒爾茨承諾要採取任何必要手段,以防止這類歧視不發生在他的政府底下。

(5) if 條件句

例 5 Call Crime Stoppers on 919 or any Command Centers if they have any information on the illegal drug trade.

Fiji Broadcasting Corporation

如果有任何非常毒品交易的消息,打電話到犯罪防治專線 919 或任何指揮中心。

(6) 疑問句

例 6 Do you have any TV show ideas?

Daily Beast

你有任何電視節目的想法嗎?

(7) 否定句

例 7 I don't have any extra pressure.

Yahoo Sports

我沒有任何額外的壓力。

◆ 含 any 的複合代名詞 anything, anyone, anybody 也是不確定的意思，用法與 any 一致。

例 8 He was asked if there was anything else illegal in the residence.

他被問到在這住所裡面是否還有任何其他不法的物品。

例 9 Anyone will be able to ask for a free refill.

任何人都可以要求免費再填補一次。

◆ some、any 都可搭配肯定句及否定句。以下四句都是正確，但語意不同：

例 10 I like some pop music.

我喜歡某些流行音樂。

例 11 I like any pop music.

任何流行音樂我都喜歡。

例 12 I don't like some pop music.

我不喜歡某些流行音樂。

例 13 I don't like any pop music.

任何流行音樂我都不喜歡。

Q08. "Both of my parents are not teachers." 表示「我的父母不都是老師」嗎？

 為了避免歧義，英美人士幾乎不用 "both…not" 表示「部分否定」。

◆ 溝通首重訊息明確，遣詞用字力求簡潔，避免模棱兩可而徒增困擾。以例 1 來講，英美人士幾乎只有一個解釋，就是「我父母都不是老師」，將主詞 "Both of my parents" 加以否定，但為了語意明確，他們會以例 2 表示。例 3 "Not" 在 "both" 前面，否定 both，表示「我父母不都是老師」，明確指出「我父母只有其中一位是老師」。若要表示「我父母都是老師」，一定用例 5 或例 6。

例1 Both of my parents are not teachers.

我的父母都不是老師。

例2 Neither of my parents is a teacher.

我的父母中沒有一位是老師。

例3 Not both my parents are teachers.

我的父母不都是老師。

例4 Only one of my parents is a teacher.

我的父母只有其中一位是老師。

例5 Both of my parents are teachers.

我的父母都是老師。

例6 My parents are both teachers.

我的父母都是老師。

◆ all 與 not 出現在同一句子時，not 若置於 all 後面，表示全部否定或部分否定，但會造成混淆，因此，all…not 僅用於全部否定，原因與 "both…not" 一樣。

例7 All dogs cannot fly.

所有的狗都不能飛。

例8 No dogs can fly.

沒有狗會飛。

（簡潔的講法。）

◆ 出自莎士比亞的諺語「All that glitters is not gold. 閃礫者未必都是金。」是部分否定，但那是 "old-fashioned English" ，現代英語鮮少沿用。

◆ not 置於 all 前面才是部分否定，如例 9，而例 10 是簡潔的講法。

例 9 Not all dogs eat vegetables.
  不是所有的狗都吃蔬菜。

例 10 Some dogs eat vegetables.
  一些狗會吃蔬菜。

◆ not 置於 every、everything、everyone 前面，表示部分否定。

例 11 Not every business is profitable.
  不是每一椿生意都有利可圖。

例 12 Not everything is beneficial.
  不是凡事都有益。

例 13 Not everyone comes from the same background as you.
  不是每個人都來自跟你一樣的背景。

◆ 以例 11 而言，英美人士會以例 14 表示部分否定：

例 14 Not all businesses are profitable.
  不是所有的生意都有賺頭。

Q09. "The vase broke." 這句子為什麼不是被動式？

 原來如此 break 是二格動詞，主詞是主事者時，及物性質，著重動作；主詞是受事者主詞時，不及物性質，著重狀態。

◆ 及物性是動詞的重要性質，及物、不及物是動詞主要的次分類，而及物動詞又分單賓及雙賓。

例1 The policeman caught two thieves yesterday.

那名警察昨天抓到二名小偷。

→ **單賓動詞，主事者蓄意產生及物動作並影響受事者。**

例2 My wife gave me a birthday card this morning.

我太太今天早上送我一張生日卡。

→ **雙賓動詞，搭配間接及直接受詞。**

例3 A man is standing at the entrance.

一名男子站在入口處。

→ **不及物動詞，不需受詞。**

◆ 二格動詞（ergative verbs），又稱為作格動詞或動者格動詞，兼具及物及不及物性質，同時適於 SVO 及 SV 句型。二格動詞的主詞是主事者時，及物性質，著重及物動作產生影響，如例 4；主詞是受事者主詞時，不及物性質，表示受事者主詞的狀態，如例 5。當然，二格動詞若以被動式呈現，著重受事者受動作影響而產生的被動結果狀態，常伴隨著動作產生者，如例 6：

例4 A boy broke the vase.

例5 The vase broke.

例6 The vase was broken by a boy.

◆ 受事者作為主詞的與格動詞用法非常普遍，語意也容易理解，例如：

例7 The book is selling well.

這本書正熱賣中。

例8 The door will open automatically.

門會自動打開。

例9 Has the show started yet?

表演開始了嗎？

◆ 烹飪相關的動作常有與格動詞的用法，表達的焦點是食物，例如：

例 **10** The meat was roasting in a hot oven.

肉正在熱爐子裡烤。

例 **11** Water boils at 100° Celsius.

水在攝氏 100 度沸騰。

例 **12** Make sure all food has fully defrosted before cooking.

確定所有的食物在烹調前都已解凍。

◆ 一些與交通工具有關的動作也有與格動詞的用法，例如：

例 **13** The car crashed into a tree.

那部車子撞到一棵樹。

例 **14** The car stopped at the traffic lights.

那部車子停在交通號誌的地方。

例 **15** The plane has been flying for 10 hours.

那架飛機已經飛了十小時。

◆ 商用英文中，為了使訊息明確清晰，句子都會力求簡潔，與格動詞是常見的表達風格，例如：

例 **16** The cost of the project has increased dramatically since it began.

該專案開始以來成本就一直攀升。

→ increase 及 begin 都是與格動詞的用法

例 **17** Our share of the market has decreased sharply this year.

今年我們的市占率急劇下降。

例 **18** Some music played in the background.

背景播放了一些音樂。

例 **19** The economic situation has changed significantly since that time.

經濟局勢自從那時候起已有顯著的變化。

Q10. "The film amused all the children."句中的受詞是接受動作者嗎？

 不是。受詞是經驗者，心理或情緒改變者可視為受詞。

◆ 受詞接受及物動作的影響，這是受事者受詞，也是典型的受詞角色。事實上，受詞與動詞之間還有其他的語意關聯，不僅透露事件真相，也決定句式鋪陳，值得一探究竟。

(1) 受事者：最常見的受詞，動作接收者或受動作影響者。

例 1 A boy kicked the stray dog.

一名男孩踢了那條流浪狗。

例 2 The warm water melted the snow.

這些溫水把雪融化了。

(2) 被創造者：受事者受詞在動作之前就存在，被創造的受詞是因動作而存在的。

例 3 God created the world.

神創造天地。

例 4 Dad fixed breakfast this morning.

爹地今天早上弄早餐。

(3) 經驗者受詞：生命體因心理動詞而產生的感官或心理經驗，心理的改變視為動作的影響。經驗者受詞也可以是接收者。

例 5 The film amused all the children.

這部電影令所有的孩子很開心。

例 6 The woman comforted her daughter.

那名婦人安慰她的女兒。

例 7 The film appeals to me.

這部影片吸引我。

例 8 It matters to me.

它對我有關係。

例 9 The manager insulted the hire.

經理羞辱那名新員工。

例 10 They spoiled their only child.

他們寵壞了他們的獨生子。

(4) 共同受詞：共同參與者分化而成受詞。

例 11 I met my previous colleague in the mall.

我在大賣場遇見我的前同事。

例 12 My previous colleague and I met in the mall.

我和我的前同事在大賣場遇見了。

→ 不論是事先約定或是巧遇，都是二者共同參與。

比較以下句子：

例 13 **Tom and Hank fought.**

湯姆和漢克打架

→ Tom 和 Hank 共同參與，一起當主詞。

例 14 Tom fought Hank.

湯姆打漢克

→ Tom 是主事者，Hank 是受事者。

例 15 Tom fought with Hank.

湯姆和漢克打在一起

→ Hank 是陪伴進行動作者。

(5) 位置受詞：受詞未受動作影響，只是動作的位置或目標，不適於被動語態。

例 16 We climbed the mountain last week.

我們上星期爬了那座山。

例 17 A drunken man approached me.

一名醉漢往我靠過來。

(6) 隱匿受詞：最常搭配或最易聯想的受詞可以省略，這種省略的受詞稱為隱匿受詞。

例 18 The man drank (liquor) heavily.

那名男子嚴重酗酒。

例 19 The boy loves to eat (food).

那位男孩很愛吃。

(7) 合併受詞：合併在動詞語意中的受詞。

例 20 The farmer fed the cows. (food)

那名農夫餵了母牛。

例 21 The fire has been stoked up. (wood)

火已添柴火。

(8) 同系受詞：不及物動詞的同源的名詞作為受詞時，這種受詞是同系受詞。

例 22 The singer sang an old song.
那名歌手唱一首老歌。

例 23 The injured man breathed his last breath this morning.
那名傷者今晨過世了。

→ 其他搭配同系受詞的動詞片語

dream a sweet dream
做一個甜美的夢

laugh a merry laugh
愉悅地笑

live a simple life
過一個純樸的生活

smile a little smile
掛上一抹微笑

sigh a sigh of relief
嘆了一口氣

sleep a good sleep
睡一陣好覺

(9) 慣用受詞：受詞無語意，也無指涉對象。

例 24 The old monk died a natural death the night before.
老和尚前天晚上圓寂。

例 25 Let's call it a day.
今天就到此為止吧！

例 26 Trust me; you can do it.
相信我，你可以辦到的。

Q11. "Asia is three times bigger than Europe"
表示亞洲比歐洲大三倍嗎?

 不是,是大二倍,也就是三倍大的意思。

◆ 表示二者倍數關係有以下三主要句式,例句都是 "亞洲是歐洲的三倍大":

(1) 倍數詞比較級 than

例1 Asia is three times bigger than Europe.

◆ 為了訊息明確,用語簡明,英美人士大多以「倍數 as 比較內容 as」表示二者的倍數關係。

(2) 倍數詞 as 原級 as

例2 Asia is three times as big as Europe.

(3) 倍數詞 the 比較內容 of 比較對象

例3 Asia is three times the area of Europe.

◆ 英文倍數詞中的半數是 "half",二倍是 "twice"(不是 two times),較不搭配比較級。

例4 A triangular traffic island has a base half as long as its height.

三角交通島的基底長度是高度的一半。

例5 The wildlife refuge is twice as big as France.

= The wildlife refuge is twice the size of France.

野生動物保護區是法國的二倍大。

補充學習

介係詞

◆ 介係詞常搭配名詞、動詞、形容詞等實詞，完整陳述語意，語意上，介係詞與搭配的語詞相關，學習上，若是知曉二者意涵，便能理解甚至預測搭配的介係詞。另外，介係詞的受詞的論旨角色與字源有關，介係詞的字源投射相關語意，進而構成諸多搭配語詞，這是構詞與句法相互為用的現象，也是熟習語詞的必要認知，例如：

例 1 result in / result from

→ result 的意思是 to happen or exist because something else has happened，搭配表示結果的 in 引導的介系詞片語，「結果造成」的語意，由於多是負向，因此對應中文的「導致」。

例 2 Icy conditions resulted in a couple of roads being closed.

路面結冰，導致兩三條公路封閉。

→ 若是搭配表示原因的 from 引導的介系詞片語，「因⋯⋯發生、由於⋯⋯導致」的語意。

例 3 The student's difficulty in walking results from a childhood illness.

這名學生不良於行導因於孩童時期的疾病。

→ 因此，result in / result from 的語意端視介系詞 in/from 而定，而非 result in / result from 的語意，何況介系詞片語修飾動詞，二者構成動詞片語時，不可分析為「動詞 + 介係詞 / NP」，而是「動詞 + PP」。

(1) 目標－ Goals，包括空間、時間及接收者。

(1.1) to

字源上，to 有 in the direction of、for the purpose of、furthermore 等意思，包含方向、目的、事件發展等語意，字首 ad 表示 to，衍生字可視為 to NP/ to VP 的介系詞片語或不定詞，例如：

arrive = to the river

appear = to come forth

attest = to test

(1.1.1) 空間

例 4 We're going to town on the bus.

我們要搭巴士進城。

例 5 Let's look at how to get to the office from the station.

我們來看看怎麼從車站抵達辦公室。

(1.1.2) 時間

例 6 It's twenty to six.

現在是五點四十分。

例 7 It's only two weeks to Christmas.

只再兩周就要聖誕節了。

(1.1.3) 接收者

例 8 Tom threw a ball to his dog.

湯姆將一顆球丟向他的小狗。

例 9 I lent my bike to my roommate.

我把我的單車借給我室友。

(1.1.4) to 延伸為事件的發展，成為不定詞的標記。

例 10 Do you want me to take you to the destination?

你要我送你去目的地嗎？

例 11 We can't force you to make a decision.

我們不能強迫你作決定。

(1.2) at

字源上，at 就是字首 ad，to 的意思，也表示 near。

例 12 The assisant always shouting at the children.

助理老是向著孩子喊叫。

例 13 The policeman aimed his gun at the criminal.

警察用槍瞄準那名罪犯。

(2) 來源─Source

字源上，from 是 forward─從來源朝向某處、away from in time or space--離開的意思，延伸為原料、狀態、原因、阻止（以免）等來源有關的語意。

例 14 The wind is coming from the north.

　　　這陣風來自北邊。

例 15 A：Where are you from?

　　　B：I'm from Japan.

　　　A：你來自哪裡？

　　　B：我來自日本。

(2.1) 分離

例 16 He was isolated from all the other prisoners.

　　　他被迫與所有其他囚犯隔離。

例 17 A baby baboon that got separated from its mother.

　　　一隻幼小狒狒跟牠的母親分離。

(2.2) 時間

例 18 Drinks will be served from eight o'clock.

　　　八點起開始供應飲料。

例 19 The price of petrol will rise from tomorrow.

　　　明天起油價將要上升。

(2.3) 原料

例 20 The table is made from pine.

　　　這張桌子是松木製成的。

例 21 Meringues are made from sugar and egg whites.

　　　蛋白酥是糖及蛋白所製成。

(2.4) 狀態改變

例 22 The situation went from bad to worse.

　　　局勢每況愈下。

例 23 The story was translated from Turkish to English.

這故事從土耳其文翻成英文。

(2.5) 原因

例 24 My uncle died from cancer.

我叔叔死於癌症。

例 25 She made her money from investing in property.

她靠投資不動產掙錢。

(2.6) 阻止（以免）

例 26 The driver will be banned from driving for six months.

該名駕駛將被禁止開車六個月。

例 27 The bank loan saved her company from bankruptcy.

這筆銀行貸款救了公司免於破產。

◆ 字首 ab 表示空間、時間上分離，又表示 source、origin、in consequence of，例如：

     absence = away + to be

     abduct = away from + to lead

     abnormal = away from + rule

◆ off 也有 away from 的意思，形成的片語動詞常有分離的意涵，例如：get off、put off、set off、turn off

(3) 受益者—benefactor

◆ 字源上，for 有 "in favor of" 一有利於的意思，其對象就是受益者—beneficiary。

例 28 I bought a bunch of flowers for my mother.

我買一束花送我母親。

例 29 The government will build a library for the community.

政府將為該社區興建一間圖書館。

(4) 工具－ Instrument

例 30 The mechanic took apart the device with a screw driver.

技術員以一把螺絲起子拆解這部裝置。

例 31 They spoke in Russian the whole time.

他們全程以俄文發言。

(5) 位置－ Locative

例 32 The thief hid the stolen money in a trash can.

竊賊將贓款藏在垃圾桶裡。

例 33 The janitor put the rack by the bookshelf.

管理員將置物架放在書櫃旁邊。

◆ 說明：字源上，字首 in 有 in、into、on、upon 等意涵，例如：

income = come in

input = put…in

Q12. "We drank three bottles of wine between the four of us." 這句話對嗎？

 對的，**between** 也可表示二者以上之間。

◆ 介係詞 between 由字首 "be"（處於）與字根 "tween"（two）所構成，意思是「二者之間」。

例 1 These books were written between 2000 and 2010.
這些書在 2000 至 2010 年之間寫的。

例 2 There is a screen between the bed and the door.
窗和門之間有一扇屏風。

例 3 There is a difference between the two terms when speaking ofgeography.
提到地貌時，這二詞彙之間有一差別。

◆ "in between" 是片語介係詞，表示二者之間，但也可當副詞。

例 4 The hostel is somewhere in between Taipei and Ilan.
該民宿位於台北與宜蘭之間的某個地方。

例 5 Tom ate breakfast and dinner, and didn't eat anything in between.
湯姆吃早餐及晚餐，中間沒吃任何東西。

◆ between 也可表示二者以上，數量明確的人或事物之間。

例 6 We drank three bottles of wine between the four of us.
我們四人喝了三瓶紅酒。

例 7 The City of Mozart lies between several local mountains.
莫札特市位於幾座當地山脈之間。

例 8 A study of relationship between job stress, quality of working life and turnover intention among hospital employees.
一篇有關醫院員工之間工作壓力、工作生活品質及離職意向等關聯的研究

◆ 介係詞 among 是指三者或三者以上數目不確定的對象之間，如例 8 的 "among hospital employees" 就是人數不確定。

Q13. "The boy narrowly escaped drowning." 為什麼是表示險些溺斃？

原來如此 **narrowly** 的意思是 "些微差距地"，描述 "escaped drowning" 的情況。

◆ "narrowly escape" 常解釋為「千鈞一髮」，說明驚險避開危難，喜劇收場的橋段。

例1 The taxi driver narrowly escaped a bomb explosion.
該名計程車司機驚險避開炸彈爆炸。

例2 The firefighter narrowly escaped a roof collapse during a fire.
大火時，該名消防員差點從屋頂墜落。

→ 但是，"narrowly escape" 該怎樣理解為「千鈞一髮」呢？"narrow" 原意是狹窄的，引申為勉強的、以些微差距得到結果的意思。

例3 It is a narrow passage.
它是一個狹窄通道。

例4 The school team won a narrow victory.
校隊以些微差距獲勝（險勝）。

◆ "narrow escape" 表示勉強的避開，傳達驚險的結果。

例5 The miners got out in time, but it was a narrow escape.
這些礦工及時逃出，真是千鈞一髮。

◆ "narrowly" 表示空間狹窄地，引申為 only by a small amount—僅以些微差距地，勉強地。

例6 a narrowly constructed staircase
一座蓋得狹隘的樓梯。

例7 The boy narrowly escaped drowning.
這名男孩差點溺斃。

◆ narrowly 說明 "escaped drowning" 是勉強逃過溺斃，喜劇收場。"narrowly" 若是代換為 "only just"，語意就更清楚了。

例8 The boy only just escaped drowning.
這名男孩剛好逃過溺水。

例9 We got to the station in time for our train, but only just.
我們及時抵達車站，搭上火車，剛好趕上（差一點趕不上）。

◆ "narrowly" 的橋段不一定都是喜劇收場，要看搭配的動作而定，句 9 的意思是「失之交臂」，悲劇收場。

例 10 The team narrowly missed winning the race.

= The team only just missed winning the race.

該隊就是輸掉比賽—與獲勝失之交臂。

→ 些微差距輸掉比賽，不搭配正向結果的「勉強」或「千鈞一髮」，而是以「失之交臂」來對應負向結果。

附錄：

1. 測驗試題 & 解析

恭喜你，全書學習完畢！
接下來，就用以下的測驗試題來驗收學習成
果吧！最後，再利用每一題的解析説明對所
學溫故知新，相信學習一定能更精進！
（精選國內研究所入學試題、學測指考試題句子、
大陸高考模擬試題。）

2. 不規則動詞三態記憶

___1. You look very ill today. I recommend that you_____a doctor for medical assistance.
A. seeing B. have seen   C. saw   D. see

___2. What do you think you_____five years from now?
A. do   B. are   C. are doing   D. will be doing

___3. Sara has not called me. She_____to charge her cell phone.
A. forgets   B. forgot   C. may have forgotten   D. will forget

___4. Australia and Brazil both_____affected by severe floods recently.
A. have been   B. are being   C. were to be   D. could be

___5. Jackson_____an elementary school principal for over twenty years by the time he retired.
A. will have been   B. had been   C. has been   D. was

___6. Even after the elderly retire from their jobs,_____can continue to socialize through their wisdom and experience, and by influencing the younger generations.
A. who   B. they   C. which   D. and they

___7. It seems a long time since I last_____my brother.
A. seeing   B. see   C. saw   D. to see

___8. Therefore, to make tall buildings more accessible to their users, the elevator _____.
A. invented   B. had invented
C. was invented   D. would have invented

___ 9. _____ risks every day of their lives, close to death from drowning, thirst or starvation.

A. Not only were the seamen of old terrible

B. The seamen of old running terrible

C. The seamen of old ran terrible

D. Whenever the seamen of old ran terrible

___10. _____ nearly thirty years for the planet Saturn to complete one orbit.

A. It takes   B. To take it   C. Taking it   D. Take it

___11. Why do you want a new job _____you've got such a good one already?

A. that   B. where   C. which   D. when

___12. A brain that can learn _____the beginning of intelligence.

A. possess   B. possessing   C. possesses   D. to possess

___13. When I _____ the windows, I sat down and had a cup of tea.

A. had opened   B. have opened   C. open   D. opened

___14. The secretary opened the mail which _____that morning.

A. had delivered   B. delivered

C. had been delivered   D. would have been delivered

___15. If I hadn't slipped on the ice, I _____my arm.

A. couldn't break   B. wouldn't break

C. couldn't have broken   D. wouldn't have broken

___16. Video games have long been blamed. But a recent research suggests _____also have an upside.

A. that   B. they   C. which   D. what

___17. Some people cling greedily to their possessions as if they

_____.

    A. were sure that they would never die

    B. will never die certainly

    C. almost would never die

    D. were certain that they were not to die

___18. The effect of physical and mental demands and pressures

    on the human body _____as stress.

    A. may be thought B. may be thought of

    C. may think of   D. may think

___19. Most of the countries have the law that shops _____to

    sell cigarette to underage kids.

    A. don't allow   B. shouldn't allow

    C. aren't allowed   D. not be allowed

___20. In warm weather, fruit and meat _____long.

    A . don't keep   B. can't be kept

    C. are not kept   D. are not keeping

___21. Light will not bend round corner unless _____to do so with

    the help of a reflecting device.

    A. be made B. made C. having made D. to be made

___22. The bill he had long been opposed _____at the last

    session, _____in more young men being recruited into

    the army.

    A. to being passed…just to result

    B. to be passed…only to result

    C. to was passed…resulting

    D. was passed…having resulted

___23. "Random House Webster' Advanced English Dictionary"
_____for learners of English as a foreign language,
_____the most common words and phrases in the
English language.
A. intended… covered   B. is intended…covered
C. is intended…covering   D. intended…is covered

___24. I _____while waiting for the Metro. Fortunately, my fellow
clerk woke me up in time!
A. had fallen asleep   B. have fallen asleep
C. fell asleep   D. fall asleep

___25. _____, and you'll finish your job on time.
A. Not let her to disturb you   B. Not being let her disturb you
C. Not to let her to disturb you D. Don't let her disturb you

___26. It seems that oil _____from this pipe for some time. We'll
have to take the machine apart to put it right.
A. had leaked   B. is leaking
C. leaked   D. has been leaking

___27. Generally speaking, _____according to the directions,
the drug has no side effect.
A. when taking   B. when taken
C. when being taken   D. when to be taken

___28. The behavior of gases is explained by _____the kinetic
theory.
A. what scientists call   B. what do scientists call
C. scientists they call   D. scientists call it

___29. The Mona Lisa is a name which is perhaps more recognizable to people throughout the world_____of da Vinci himself.

A. than   B. as   C. than that   D. to that

___30. Gold has been highly prized throughout the ages due chiefly to _____.

A. it is scarce   B. so scarce is it

C. scarcity of it   D. its scarcity

___31. _____ good care of the vegetables so that they can remain fresh.

A. Take   B. To take   C. Having taken   D. Taking

___32. The news reporters hurried to the airport, only_____the film stars had left.

A. to tell   B. to be told   C. telling   D. told

___33. _____CouchSurfing.org, a popular social networking site for both surfers and hosts, to gain a better understanding of how to find and contact potential hosts and begin your journey today.

A. To visit   B. Visit   C. Visiting   D. Visited

___34. The church_____ with pine trees brought from the mainland, which was quite common for the 18th century.

A. which built   B. building   C. was built   D. built

___35. Mount Kilimanjaro,_____ in Tanzania about 220 miles south of the equator in a very hot region, is the tallest mountain in all of Africa.

A. it is located   B. is located   C. which located   D. located

___36. Although_____close to the equator, Rwanda's "thousand
hills,"_____ from 1,500 m to 2,500 m in height,
ensure that the temperature is pleasant all year around.
A. locating   B. being located   C. location   D. located
A. differing   B. wandering   C. ranging   D. climbing

___37. With Wikileaks _____ secrets about governments around
the world, many countries are worried that their national
security information might be disclosed.
A. release   B. releasing   C. released   D. to release

__38. Advertising can be the most important source of income
for the media _____it is conducted.
A. through which   B. which   C. for which   D. when

___39. It was_____ late in the evening that the explorers pitched
camp.
A. before   B. when   C. till   D. not until

___40. Little is known about the criteria,_____ the committee
selects the final winners.
A. in which   B. by which   C. which   D. how

__41. _____, heat is produced.
A. The mixing together of certain chemicals
B. Whenever certain chemicals are mixed together
C. Certain chemicals mixed together
D. That certain chemicals are mixed together

측정

___42. We can say that we're lucky_____ that only soybean and cotton are the known GMOs here, but in other countries it's even scarier.
A. considered   B. considering
C. to consider   D. with consideration

___43. Whom_____ Mr. Smith saw at the entrance just now?
A. was it that   B. was what   C. was it   D. was that

___44. _____ that they were rewarded.
A. Such great suggestion was
B. So great was the suggestion
C. However great was the suggestion
D. The suggestion was great

___45. Only after he has acquired considerable facility in speaking, _____.
A. does he learn to read and write
B. then he learns reading and writing
C. finally comes reading and reading
D. he began to read and write

___46. _____his wife left him did he realize how important she was to him.
A. Only after   B. Because   C. Never   D. At no time

___47. It was between 1830 and 1835_____the modern newspaper was born.
A. when   B. that   C. which   D. until

__48. I don't think it advisable that Tom_____to the job since he has no experience.

A. is assigned
B. will be assigned
C. be assigned
D. has been assigned

___49. Not until I heard the scream _____my car nearly ran over a little girl.

A. I knew   B. did I know   C. do I know   D. I did know

___50. _____ you encounter any problems regarding the new system, please notify the tech support ASAP.

A. Might   B. Should   C. Would   D. Had

___51. _____ the lobbying groups been backing up the new protocol, but several industry labor unions are now voicing their stern support for it.

A. Not until there have   B. There have never
C. Not only have   D. If they could have

___52. Seldom _____ any mistake during my past five years of service in the company.

A. did I make
B. I did make
C. should I make
D. would I make

___53. The suggestion_____that the basketball game should be put off.

A. made
B. has made
C. has been made
D. to be made

___54. What do you think about the new office location,_____the company has chosen?

A. which   B. why   C. that   D. what

__55. The mark of heroes is not necessarily the result of their action, but_____they are willing to do for others and for their chosen cause.
A. what   B. which   C. who   D. where

__56. The custom came from the Han people_____wanted to send a peaceful message to their families and friends.
A. while   B. who   C. what   D. whoever

__57. The drummer needs to pay attention_____is going on in the plot and follow the rhythm of the characters.
A. who   B. which to   C. to which   D. to what

__58. In 1723, Franklin ran away to Philadelphia,_____he started his own newspaper.
A. where   B. which   C. when   D. what

__59. _____is often the case, we complete the task ahead of time.
A. What   B. That   C. As   D. All

__60. Less than 3 percent of the world's water is fresh, and most of_____is trapped in polar ice or buried underground in springs too deep to reach.
A. which   B. it   C. what   D. them

__61. With the help of modern technology, some supermarkets are now able to keep customers informed about_____others are buying.
A. what   B. that   C. where   D. in which

__62. The computer compared the fingerprint on the wall with all
the fingerprints in the files and told the police _____the
fingerprint belonged to.
A. where   B. that   C. whom   D. what

__63. According to the health official, the rate of increasing
number of cases is not beyond_____is expected and the
symptoms of all the patients are mild.
A. which   B. that   C. it   D. what

__64. Human rights are fundamental rights_____a person is
inherently entitled, that is, rights that she or he is born with.
A. whatever   B. to which   C. which   D. in which

__65. He will take charge of a company that is significantly bigger
and more powerful than_____he left more than a decade
ago.
A. that   B. that one   C. the one   D. which

__66. Warmer climate led to changes in the ecology of Europe,
_____the animal population and methods of hunting.
A. affecting   B. to affect
C. having affected   D. which affect

__67. 26 countries offered a flood of aids as fast as they could
_____ the buried survivors in the earthquake.
A. save   B. to save   C. saving   D. saved

__68. David, who is helpful and agreeable, is a person_____
wherever he is.
A. never to ignoring   B. never to have ignored
C. never being ignored   D. never to be ignored

__69. It made us very angry_____him talk like that.

    A. hear   B. to hear   C. having heard   D. when hearing

__70. The company opened a new factory in the State of Michigan in 1910_____ the growing demand for cars.

    A. having met   B. meet   C. meeting   D. to meet

__71. _____, the thief hid himself under the bed without daring to make a sound.

    A. Not caught   B. Not having been caught

    C. Not to be caught   D. So as not to be caught

__72. A: Was the math homework difficult?

    B: Not at all, I found_____.

    A. it very easy to be done   B. it very easy to do

    C. very easy to do   D. it very easy for doing

__73. It is said that some scientists who participated in the space program will appear before the reception_____this evening.

    A. holding   B. to hold   C. to be held   D. held

__74. What has happened here increases the chance of_____one more misfortune pretty soon. It is quoted as a saying that misfortunes never come single.

    A. there to be   B. there being   C. it to be   D. it being

__75. For there_____successful communication, there must be attentiveness and involvement in the discussion itself by all present.

    A. will be   B. is   C. to be   D. being

__76. The boy pretended_____his homework when his parents
   came back home.
   A. to do   B. do   C. doing   D. to be doing

__77. To succeed in a rough scientific research,_____.
   A. one needs to be persistent
   B. persistence is needed
   C. You need be persistent
   D. persistence is what one needs

__78. The earth seems_____part of the sun.
   A. to be   B. to have been   C. it is   D. used to be

__79. The time for a broken bone_____together again in a
   young man is usually about four weeks.
   A. grown   B. growing   C. to grow   D. grow

__80. A: What do you believe can ensure peace around the
      world?
   B:_____in that country.
   A. By talking with the national leaders
   B. Talking with the national leaders.
   C. Talk with the national leaders
   D. Being talked with the national leaders.

__81. The CEO and the designers have overcome a lot of
   difficulty_____the new project.
   A. they had developed   B. to have developed
   C. they had developing   D. having developed

__82. A. What do you think made Mary so depressed?
B._____her limousine which she spent almost all her savings on .
A. As she lost   B. Lost   C. Losing   D. Because of losing

__83. A Russian official said Chinese cooperation is the key to _____the dispute about Iran's nuclear work.
A. resolve   B. resolved   C. to resolve   D. resolving

__84. After _____, these trains are capable of attaining a very high speed.
A. technically improving   B. technically improved
C. being technically improved   D. to be technically improved

__85. The government is believed to be considering _____ a law _____it a crime to import any kind of weapon.
A. to pass…make   B. to have passed…making
C. passing…making   D. having passed…made

__86. Deforestation can also increase breeding sites for vector-borne diseases, such as_____with mosquito habitat and malaria in the Peruvian Amazon.
A. occurring   B. to occur   C. to have occurred   D. occurred

__87. The dedicated scientist died all of a sudden,_____his research project unfinished.
A. leaving   B. having left   C. to leave   D. left

__88. With more forests_____, huge quantities of good earth are being washed away each year.
A. destroying   B.destroyed   C. destroy   D. being destroyed

__89. The conference currently_____in Geneva has caught the
attention of the mass media.
A. was held   B. to be held
C. being held   D. was being held

__90. _____cold, he covered himself with a blanket, leaving only
his arms _____.
A. Felt…uncovering   B. Feeling…uncovering
C. Feeling…uncovered   D. Felt…uncovered

__91. _____more information, they could make the plan better
than it is now.
A. Having given   B. If giving   C. Given   D. To be given

__92. Active reading will result in a better understanding of what
_____.
A. is being read   B. to be read   C. to read   D. being read

__93. With land prices_____, I can't afford a piece of land big
enough to park my car on.
A. going up   B. gone up   C. go up   D. to go up

__94. English teaching at college is to a great extent _____a
language class into an information class.
A. turn   B. turned   C. turning   D. is turning

__95. The discovery of new evidence led to_____.
A. the thief having caught   B. catch the thief
C. the thief being caught   D. the thief to be caught

__96. A. What did you do yesterday afternoon?

B: I went to the bookstore,_____some books and visited
my uncle.

A. to buy   B. bought   C. buy   D. buying

__97. Few of us get the_____seven to nine hours of sleep a
night, and many who have time_____don't, for fear of
spoiling night time sleep.

A. recommended...napping   B. recommended...to nap

C. recommending...napping   D. recommending...to nap

__98. _____into French, words and phrases for congratulations at
the wedding party surely became language barriers for those
who only knew English.

A. Having put   B. Put   C. Being put   D. To put

__99. _____, her suggestion is of greater value than yours.

A. All things considered   B. All things considering

C. Considering all things   D. Considered all things

__100. In the teaching of mathematics, the way of instruction is
generally traditional, with teachers presenting formal
lectures and students_____notes.

A. take   B. to take   C. taking   D. taken

__101. Returning to her apartment late that night,_____.

A. her watch was found missing

B. her watch was nowhere to be found

C. she found her watch missing

D. she found her watch missed

__102._____with fright, the hungry fox hid himself in a small

cave,_____his tail to the rain.

A. Trembling…exposing   B. Trembled…exposed

C. Trembled…exposing   D. Trembling…exposed

__103. Having finished the first chapter, he went back over the

essay,_____spelling and grammar.

A. checking   B. to check   C. checked   D. having checked

__104. _____with a difficult situation, Arnold decided to ask his

boss for advice.

A. Being faced   B. Having faced   C. To face   D. Faced

__105. The house was very quiet,_____as it was on the side of

a mountain.

A. isolated   B. isolating

C. being isolated   D. having been isolated

__106. However, when_____how to attract young readers to

the printed press, the government said the primary

channel for the ads would be the Internet.

A. ask   B. to ask   C. asked   D. asking

__107. Do not take the medicine any more than the suggested

dosage unless_____by a doctor.

A. direct   B. having directed   C. directing   D. directed

__108. On the early morning of January 18th, people_____

standing in long lines waiting to receive the vouchers, as

they were eager to do some shopping with the vouchers.

A. find   B. found   C. were found   D. who were found

__109. They include many special safety devices and systems that help to protect the plant, the people_____in it and the public, even in the event of a serious accident.
A. worked   B. are working   C. work   D. working

__110. _____with care, this kind of flower can live for a long time.
A. Looking after   B. To look after
C. Looked after   D. Look after

__111. When hungry,_____.
A. this restaurant is the place you want to be
B. food smells so deliciously
C. your energy just goes downhill
D. one can think of nothing but food

__112. Accustomed to climbing trees,_____.
A. I had no difficulty reaching the top
B. reaching the top was not hard to me
C. the top was not difficult for me to reach
D. to reach the top was not a problem for me

__113. After spending 5 hours in the interrogation room and conferring with her lawyer, the secretary eventually confessed_____the money that had been earmarked for company travel.
A. to have stolen   B. having stolen
C. stealing   D. to stealing

__114. Road running often offers those_____a range of challenges such as dealing with hills, sharp bends, rough weather, and so on.
A. involving   B. involved   C. to involve   D. are involved

__115. It's estimated that more than 1.7 billion people make up
the world's consumer society people who have more
money to spend than_____to cover their basic needs.
A. have required   B. are requiring
C. required   D. requiring

__116. He tried to control himself, but the more he_____, the
more he laughed.
A. tried   B. had tried   C. was trying   D. did

__117. The arts of reading and writing were preserved in the
monasteries of Europe for centuries until they spread
to the general populace_____the rebirth of learning
called the Renaissance.
A. during   B. in which   C. by then   D. and

__118. Give me your telephone number_____I need your help.
A. whether   B. unless   C. so that   D. in case

__119. The Human Comedy, a sentimental story of a family in a
country at war, had special appeal because its principal
characters are children, _____its perspective is adult.
A. though   B. who   C. where   D. while

__120. The European age of discovery and the colonization of the
world _____were built on Eastern nautical technology.
A. followed   B. had been followed
C. that followed   D. that was followed

__121. Population growth _____the economic growth of a
country as well as be affected by it.
A. can affect   B. is affecting   C. affects   D. affecting

__122. The objective of the company is not so much to show a profit as it is_____that there are better ways of doing things in a business sense.
A. to demonstrate　B. demonstrating
C. of demonstrating　D. to be demonstrated

__123. Some people think that it is a good way for children to find out about things, and that_____in this way also helps children to get used to technology
A. learn　B. learns　C. learned　D. learning

__124. _____in Argentina, Brazil, or Trinidad, carnival is one of the most exciting events of the year, involving parades, parties, and dressing up in costume.
A. Which　B. That　C. If　D. Whether

__125. Some small animals have_____a high metabolism_____ they must eat several times their own weight each day to stay alive.
A. such......as　　B. either...... or
C. such...... that　D. not only......but also

__126. They believed that careful self-examination can analyze and _____ our personal characters, aims, methods and attitudes.
A. improved　B. improving　C. improves　D. improve

__127. The scientific study of the motion of bodies and the action of forces that change or cause motion_____dynamics.
A. calls　B. is called　C. are called　D. called

__128. F = ma, known widely as Newton's second law, _____a postulate of physics since the advent of Newton's masterful Principia in 1687.

A. is   B. having been   C. being   D. has been

_____129. The man_____is John.（複選題）

A. talking to me

B. talked to me

C. I talked

D. I talked to

E I talked to him

F. whom I talked

G. whom I talked to

H. to whom I talked

I. who talked to me

J. who talking to me

測驗試題解答&解析

__D__ 1. You look very ill today. I recommend that you_____a doctor for medical assistance.

A. seeing B. have seen   C. saw   D. see

> 解 recommend 表達強烈意念，祈使語氣，that 子句搭配原形動詞；事件尚未成真，又是假設語氣，that 子句搭配情態助動詞 should。

__D__ 2. What do you think you _____ five years from now?

A. do   B. are   C. are doing   D. will be doing

> 解 本題句子的變化過程如下：
> 1. You will be doing --- five years from now.
> 2. You think you will be doing --- five years from now.
> 3. What do you think you will be doing five years from now?
> 4. 未來進行式表示未來預定發生的動作。

__C__ 3. Sara has not called me. She_____to charge her cell phone.

A. forgets   B. forgot   C. may have forgotten   D. will forget

> 解 "may have pp" 表示過去的推測，或許的意思。

__A__ 4. Australia and Brazil both_____affected by severe floods recently.

A. have been   B. are being   C. were to be   D. could be

> 解 recently 搭配在現在完成式。

__B__ 5. Jackson_____an elementary school principal for over twenty years by the time he retired.

A. will have been   B. had been   C. has been   D. was

> **解** by the time he retired 搭配過去完成式，過去某時之前已發生的動作。

B 6. Even after the elderly retire from their jobs,_____can continue to socialize through their wisdom and experience, and by influencing the younger generations.
　　A. who　B. they　C. which　D. and they

> **解** 主從分明，Even after 引導從的部分，空格是主要子句主詞。

C 7. It seems a long time since I last_____my brother.
　　A. seeing　B. see　C. saw　D. to see

> **解** since 子句搭配過去簡單式，表示一段時間的起點。

C 8. Therefore, to make tall buildings more accessible to their users, the elevator_____.
　　A. invented　　　　B. had invented
　　C. was invented　D. would have invented

> **解** 空格是主要子句的時態動詞，過去被發明的事實。

C 9._____risks every day of their lives, close to death from drowning, thirst or starvation.
　　A. Not only were the seamen of old terrible
　　B. The seamen of old running terrible
　　C. The seamen of old ran terrible
　　D. Whenever the seamen of old ran terrible

> **解** 主從分明，逗號左側是主要子句，選項 A 需搭配 but 子句，選項 D 有從的標記，都不是主要子句，選項 B 無時態動詞。

A 10. _____nearly thirty years for the planet Saturn to complete one orbit.

A. It takes　B. To take it　C. Taking it　D. Take it

> 解 句子必須有主詞及時態動詞。

D 11. Why do you want a new job_____you've got such a good one already?

A. that　B. where　C. which　D. when

> 解 when 可以引導原因或理由的副詞子句，本題意思是既然你已經有那麼好的一份工作，為什麼還要找新的工作呢？

C 12. A brain that can learn_____the beginning of intelligence.

A. possess　B. possessing　C. possesses　D. to possess

> 解 that can learn 是形容詞子句，主詞的中心詞是 a brain，搭配時態動詞 possesses。

A 13. When I_____the windows, I sat down and had a cup of tea.

A. had opened　B. have opened　C. open　D. opened

> 解 when 搭配過去完成式，after 的意思，動作在主要子句之前。

C 14. The secretary opened the mail which_____that morning.

A. had delivered　　　　B. delivered
C. had been delivered　　D. was delivered

> 解 形容詞子句的動詞較 opened 早發生，搭配過去完成式，被動語態。

D 15. If I hadn't slipped on the ice, I _____ my arm.
　　A. couldn't break　　　　B. wouldn't break
　　C. couldn't have broken　D. wouldn't have broken

> **解** 過去事實相反的主要子句搭配 would have pp，would 的意思是「就」。

B 16. Video games have long been blamed. But a recent research suggests_____also have an upside.
　　A. that　B. they　C. which　D. what

> **解** that 子句主詞指涉 video games。

A 17. Some people cling greedily to their possessions as if they _____.
　　A. were sure that they would never die
　　B. will never die certainly
　　C. almost would never die
　　D. were certain that they were not to die

> **解** as if 搭配現在事實相反的假設語氣。

B 18. The effect of physical and mental demands and pressures on the human body_____as stress.
　　A. may be thought　B. may be thought of
　　C. may think of　　D. may think

> **解** think of NP-A as NP-B，認為 A 是 B。

C 19. Most of the countries have the law that shops_____to sell cigarette to underage kids.

A. don't allow   B. shouldn't allow

C. aren't allowed   D. not be allowed

> 解 that 是從的標記，引導同位語子句說明先行詞 law 的內容，shops 是主詞，加接時態動詞，not be allowed 是非限定動詞，不扮演句子的時態動詞，因此不選 D。allow 的次分類是 V:_____NP to VP，句中 NP 前移至主詞位置，應選被動語態。A、B 是主動語態，應加接受事者 -patient。

A 20. In warm weather, fruit and meat_____long.

A . don't keep   B. can't be kept

C. are not kept   D. are not keeping

> 解 1. 本題考 keep 不及物性質，V _____，意思是（of food）to stay fresh and in good condition（Cambridge Dictionary）。
> 2. keep 若表示 to (cause to) stay in a particular place or condition，V_____ Adj 或 V_____ NP Adj，例如：I like to keep busy. Close the door to keep the room warm.
> 3. 題幹中的 long 是副詞，不是補語功用的形容詞，因此 B、C 不對。

B 21. Light will not bend round corner unless_____to do so with the help of a reflecting device.

A. be made   B. made   C. having made   D. to be made

> 解 連接詞 unless 是從的標記，引導從位階的句子或片語，選項皆無主詞，unless 引導的是片語。語意上，從表示主要子句的條件 —unless light is made to do so...，結構縮減為過去分詞 made。C 選項表示較早發生，D 選項有未發生的意味，皆與必須同時發生的條件不符。

_C_ 22. The bill he had long been opposed_____at the last session,_____in more young men being recruited into the army.

A. to being passed…just to result

B. to be passed…only to result

C. to was passed…resulting

D. was passed…having resulted

解 1. 反對─be opposed to，to 是介係詞，he had long been opposed to 是 The bill 的形容詞子句，to 的受詞缺項，受格關係代名詞省略。

2. 主詞是含形容詞子句的名詞片語 – The bill he had long been opposed to

3. 主詞加接時態動詞，pass 的次分類是 V:_____NP，受事者 The bill 移至句首，被動語態。

4. 逗號後面是從─片語，result in 主動語意，說明的 the bill 的附帶結果，可改寫如下：

The bill he had long been opposed to was passed at the last session and resulted in more young men being recruited into the army.

5. being recruited into the army 說明一直被徵召的狀況，being 標記當下進行。

6. just to result 表示目的，only to resul t 表示不料，負向結果，having resulted 表示較早發生，皆與語意不符。

C 23. "Random House Webster' Advanced English Dictionary"
_____for learners of English as a foreign language,
_____ most common words and phrases in the
English language.

A. intended… covered   B. is intended…covered

C. is intended…covering   D. intended…is covered

解 依照主從分明，逗號左側是主要子句，右側是從。主要子句主詞加接時態動詞，被動語態 intend 的意思是 to have as a plan or purpose，_____ NP，例如：

The course is intended for intermediate-level students.

It was intended as a compliment, honestly!

從的部分提供主要子句主詞的附帶説明，因此省略，非限定動詞，cover, V:_____ NP，主動，covering-- 及物動詞若是加接受詞，表示主動。本題可改寫如下：

"Random House Webster Advanced English Dictionary"is intended for learners of English as a foreign language and covers the most common words and phrases in the English language.

C 24. I_____while waiting for the Metro. Fortunately, my fellow clerk woke me up in time!

A. had fallen asleep   B. have fallen asleep

C. fell asleep   D. fall asleep

解 while waiting for the Metro 的時候主事者產生的動作，過去簡單式。

D 25._____, and you'll finish your job on time.
    A. Not let her to disturb you   B. Not being let her disturb you
    C. Not to let her to disturb you   D. Don't let her disturb you

解 and 子句該配搭主要子句，祈使句具有主要子句功用，B、C 是非限定動詞，不具句子功用，否定祈使句應該搭配 Don't。

D 26. It seems that oil_____from this pipe for some time. We'll have to take the machine apart to put it right.
    A. had leaked   B. is leaking
    C. leaked   D. has been leaking

解 從 seems 得知時間參考點是現在，for some time 述及持續一段時間的事件，has been leaking 表示截至現在已完成一段時間且仍持續的動作。

B 27. Generally speaking,_____according to the directions, the drug has no side effect.
    A. when taking   B. when taken
    C. when being taken   D. when to be taken

解 主從分明，空格位於從的位階，且有連接詞 when，選項皆無主詞，表示與主要子句主詞一致 —the drug，the drug 是 take 的受事者，被動語態，題意表示根據指示服藥，答案是 B。C 選項以 being 標記當下，與表示常態的 "according to the directions" 不符。D 選項以不定詞表示目的，語意與主要子句不符。

A 28. The behavior of gases is explained by＿＿＿＿the kinetic theory.
A. what scientists call
B. what do scientists call
C. scientists they call
D. scientists call it

> **解** 介係詞 by 加接名詞片語或名詞子句當受詞，what scientists call the kinetic theory = the thing that scientists call the kinetic theory，包含形容詞子句的名詞片語當 by 的受詞。
> B 選項形成直接問句，D 選項形成直述句，都是主要子句位階，不當介係詞受詞。
> C 選項形成 scientists they call the kinetic theory，call 的次分類是 V:＿＿＿＿NP NP，但缺少 NP 移位的痕跡，C 選項不對。
> The behavior of gases is explained by what scientists call the Kinetic Theory.

C 29. The Mona Lisa is a name which is perhaps more recognizable to people throughout the world＿＿＿＿of da Vinci himself.
A. than   B. as   C. than that   D. to that

> **解** more recognizable 是比較級，搭配 than，比較的內容應該對稱，這題是二名字的比較，that 代替前述名詞 name。

D 30. Gold has been highly prized throughout the ages due chiefly to ＿＿＿＿.
A. it is scarce   B. so scarce is it
C. scarcity of it   D. its scarcity

> **解** due chiefly to 意思是主要由於，副詞 chiefly 修飾形容詞 due。
> 介係詞加接名詞片語當受詞，C 選項的 scarcity 無限定詞。

A 31._____good care of the vegetables so that they can remain fresh.

A. Take　B. To take　C. Having taken　D. Taking

解　主從分明，so that 是連接詞，引導從屬子句，搭配主要子句。句首原形動詞構成祈使句，扮演主要子句。

B 32. The news reporters hurried to the airport, only_____the film stars had left.

A. to tell　B. to be told　C. telling　D. told

解　依題意，主事者不料被告知 ....，only to 表示不料，負向結果。不定詞被動式是 to be pp。

B 33._____CouchSurfing.org, a popular social networking site for both surfers and hosts, to gain a better understanding of how to find and contact potential hosts and begin your journey today.

A. To visit　B. Visit　C. Visiting　D. Visited

解　1. a popular social networking site for both surfers and hosts 是 CouchSurfing.org 的同位語，略去不看。
2. to gain a better understanding of how to find and contact potential hosts 是表示目的的不定詞，修飾語。and begin your journey today 是句首 Visit 的平行結構。
解題技巧：句首動詞片語之後未出現主要子句，空格應以原形動詞形成祈使句以扮演主要子句。

_C_ 34. The church_____with pine trees brought from the mainland, which was quite common for the 18th century.
A. which built   B. building   C. was built   D. built

解 主從分明，空格位於主要子句。bring 次分類是 V: _____ NP PP，受事者 —pine trees 前移，被動語態，未出現 be 動詞，brought from the mainland 是修飾語，修飾 pine trees，並共同形成 with 的受詞。

The church 是主要句子主詞，加接時態動詞，又是 build 的被創造者 —created DO，搭配被動語態。

受事者 —patient 是動作發生之前即存在的人或物，因此會受動作影響；被創造者 —created DO 則是動作發生之前未存在，因動作產生而存在。

_D_ 35. Mount Kilimanjaro,_____in Tanzania about 220 miles south of the equator in a very hot region, is the tallest mountain in all of Africa.
A. it is located   B. is located   C. which located   D. located

解 句中逗號隔開部分是從，依題意為形容詞子句或分詞片語。A 選項無連接詞，獨立子句，無法成為從屬子句。B 選項的時態動詞前無主詞，錯誤結構。

C 選項是句子結構，which 兼具連接詞功用，可扮演從的部分，但 locate 的意思是使位於，V: _____ NP，Mount Kilimanjaro 是位置受詞，被動語態。D 選項是過去分詞，符合語意與結構。

D、C 36. Although_____close to the equator, Rwanda's "thousand hills,"_____from 1,500 m to 2,500 m in height, ensure that the temperature is pleasant all year around.
A. locating   B. being located   C. location   D. located
A. differing   B. wandering   C. ranging   D. climbing

解 主從分明，連接詞 although 引導從，選項無主詞，雙重標記從。選項 B 的 being 標記當下，與自然環境長時存在不符，應刪除。選項 C 的 location 無限定詞，不符名詞片語結構，應刪除。從部分無主詞，表示與主要子句主詞一致，意思是 Although Rwanda's "thousand hills are located close to the equator，被動語態，答案為 D、C。

B 37. With Wikileaks_____secrets about governments around the world, many countries are worried that their national security information might be disclosed.
A. release   B. releasing   C. released   D. to release

解 主從分明，逗號左側是從，且是介係詞引導的片語，搭配非限定動詞。空格加接受詞，符合 release, V:_____ NP 的次分類，主動語態，現在分詞。不定詞表示將要發生，無法作為主要子句的原因及背景，不選 D。

A 38. Advertising can be the most important source of income for the media_____it is conducted.
A. through which   B. which   C. for which   D. when

解 依題意，形容詞子句表示 advertising is conducted through the media。關係代名詞指涉先行詞 the media，並與介係詞一起移至形容詞子句首。

311

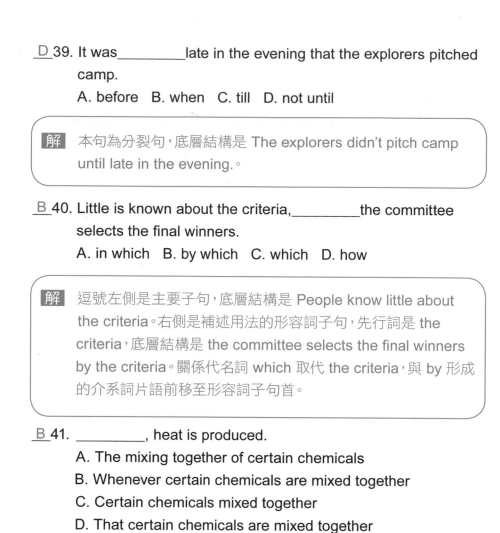

D 39. It was_____late in the evening that the explorers pitched camp.

    A. before B. when C. till D. not until

解 本句為分裂句，底層結構是 The explorers didn't pitch camp until late in the evening.。

B 40. Little is known about the criteria,_____the committee selects the final winners.

    A. in which B. by which C. which D. how

解 逗號左側是主要子句，底層結構是 People know little about the criteria。右側是補述用法的形容詞子句，先行詞是 the criteria，底層結構是 the committee selects the final winners by the criteria。關係代名詞 which 取代 the criteria，與 by 形成的介系詞片語前移至形容詞子句首。

B 41. _____, heat is produced.

    A. The mixing together of certain chemicals

    B. Whenever certain chemicals are mixed together

    C. Certain chemicals mixed together

    D. That certain chemicals are mixed together

解 主從分明，空格置於從的部分，選項 A 是名詞片語，選項 C 無連接詞，都不可作為從的部分，選項 D 是名詞子句，不具修飾句子的功用。

B 42. We can say that we're lucky_____that only soybean and cotton are the known GMOs here, but in other countries it's even scarier.
A. considered   B. considering
C. to consider   D. with consideration

解 主從分明，空格位於從的部分，considering 是從屬連接詞，引導副詞子句。選項 C 表示為了考慮，但 we're lucky 不是手段。

A 43. Whom_____Mr. Smith saw at the entrance just now?
A. was it that   B. was what   C. was it   D. was that

解 底層結構：Mr. Smith saw --- at the entrance just now.
分裂句：It was whom that Mr. Smith saw --- at the entrance just now.
疑問句：Whom was it that Mr. Smith saw at the entrance just now?

B 44. _____that they were rewarded.
A. Such great suggestion was
B. So great was the suggestion
C. However great was the suggestion
D. The suggestion was great

解 底層結構：The suggestion was so great that they were rewarded.

A 45. Only after he has acquired considerable facility in speaking,

_____.

A. does he learn to read and write

B. then he learns reading and writing

C. finally comes reading and reading

D. he began to read and write

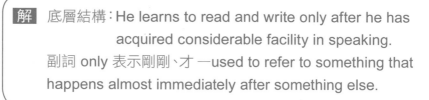

> 解 底層結構：He learns to read and write only after he has
> acquired considerable facility in speaking.
> 副詞 only 表示剛剛、才 —used to refer to something that
> happens almost immediately after something else.

A 46._____his wife left him did he realize how important she was

to him.

A. Only after　B. Because　C. Never　D. At no time

> 解 底層結構：He realized how important she was to him only
> after his wife left him.

B 47. It was between 1830 and 1835_____the modern

newspaper was born.

A. when　B. that　C. which　D. until

> 解 1. 底層結構：The modern newspaper was born between 1830
> and 1835.
> 2. 分裂句以 that 引導從屬部分。

C 48. I don't think it advisable that Tom_____to the job since he has no experience.
A. is assigned
B. will be assigned
C. be assigned
D. has been assigned

解 祈使語氣：I don't think it advisable that Tom be assigned to the job since he has no experience.
假設語氣：I don't think it advisable that Tom should be assigned to the job since he has no experience.

B 49. Not until I heard the scream_____my car nearly ran over a little girl.
A. I knew   B. did I know   C. do I know   D. I did know

解 底層結構：I didn't hear the scream until my car nearly ran over a little girl.，強調動作發生時間，not until 移至句首，主要子句首搭配助動詞。

B 50. _____you encounter any problems regarding the new system, please notify the tech support ASAP.
A. Might   B. Should   C. Would   D. Had

解 底層結構：If you should encounter any problems regarding the new system, please notify the tech support ASAP.
助動詞 should 前移至句首，省略 if。

C 51.＿＿＿＿＿the lobbying groups been backing up the new protocol, but several industry labor unions are now voicing their stern support for it.

A. Not until there have　B. There have never

C. Not only have　　　　D. If they could have

> 解 not only…but also，also 是副詞，常省略，not only 是否定副詞，常移至句首形成倒裝詞序。底層結構：The lobbying groups have not only been backing up the new protocol, but several industry labor unions are now voicing their stern support for it.

A 52. Seldom＿＿＿＿＿＿ any mistake during my past five years of service in the company.

A. did I make　　　　B. I did make

C. should I make　　　D. would I make

> 解 底層結構：I seldom made any mistake during my past five years of service in the company.

C 53. The suggestion＿＿＿＿＿＿that the basketball game should be put off.

A. made　　　　　　B. has made

C. has been made　　D. to be made

> 解 1. 底層結構：The suggestion that the basketball game should be put off has been made.
> 2. 尾重原則，同位語子句移至動詞右側，形成遠距關係。

_A_ 54. What do you think about the new office location, _____ the company has chosen?
A. which　B. why　C. that　D. what

解　關係代名詞 which 引導補述用法的形容詞子句。

_A_ 55. The mark of heroes is not necessarily the result of their action, but_____ they are willing to do for others and for their chosen cause.
A. what　B. which　C. who　D. where

解　but 連接 The mark of heroes 的平行結構，複合關係代名詞 what = the thing which。

_B_ 56. The custom came from the Han people _____ wanted to send a peaceful message to their families and friends.
A. while　B. who　C. what　D. whoever

解　介係詞 from 的受詞是一含形容詞子句的名詞片語，先行詞是人，搭配關係代名詞 who。

_C_ 57. The drummer needs to pay attention _____ is going on in the plot and follow the rhythm of the characters.
A. who　B. which to　C. to which　D. to what

解　依題意，the drummer 必須注意情景正進行的……，pay attention to 接名詞子句，what is going on in the plot = the thing that is going on in the plot。

A 58. In 1723, Franklin ran away to Philadelphia,_____he started his own newspaper.
A. where   B. which   C. when   D. what

> **解** 依題意，從的部分是 he started his own newspaper in Philadelphia，關係副詞 where 取代介係詞片語 in Philadelphia。

C 59. _____is often the case, we complete the task ahead of time.
A. What   B. That   C. As   D. All

> **解** as is often the case 表示常有的事，as 是準關係代名詞，先行詞是主要子句所述事件。

B 60. Less than 3 percent of the world's water is fresh, and most of _____is trapped in polar ice or buried underground in springs too deep to reach.
A. which   B. it   C. what   D. them

> **解** 主從分明，and 引導對等子句，主詞是 it，先行詞是 3 percent of the world's water。

A 61. With the help of modern technology, some supermarkets are now able to keep customers informed about_____ others are buying.
A. what   B. that   C. where   D. in which

> **解** 介係詞 about 加接名詞子句當受詞，依題意，該句提及其他人在買的物品，因此答案是 what，可分析為 things that others are buying。that others are buying 是形容詞子句，因此 B 選項不對；where = in which，副詞性質，無法填補 buying 的受詞。

C 62. The computer compared the fingerprint on the wall with all the fingerprints in the files and told the police_____the fingerprint belonged to.
A. where   B. that   C. whom   D. what

> 解 受格關係代名詞 whom 填補 belong to 的受詞。

D 63. According to the health official, the rate of increasing number of cases is not beyond_____ is expected and the symptoms of all the patients are mild.
A. which   B. that   C. it   D. what

> 解 介係詞 beyond 加接名詞子句當受詞，that、it 形成獨立子句，不可當受詞，which is expected 結構不完整，what = the thing that，含形容詞子句的名詞片語當 beyond 的受詞。

B 64. Human rights are fundamental rights_____a person is inherently entitled, that is, rights that she or he is born with.
A. whatever   B. to which   C. which   D. in which

> 解 形容詞子句的意思是 a person is inherently entitled to fundamental rights。

C 65. He will take charge of a company that is significantly bigger and more powerful than_____he left more than a decade ago.
A. that   B. that one   C. the one   D. which

> 解 one 指公司，the 限定是十多年前離開的那家公司。

___D___ 66. Warmer climate led to changes in the ecology of Europe,
_____the animal population and methods of hunting.

A. affecting
B. to affect
C. having affected
D. which affect

> **解** 主從分明，逗號後面是從，分詞 affecting 表示主要子句的結果，主詞與主要子句主詞一致 —warmer climate，但是 the animal population and methods of hunting 具有區域性，影響原因是 changes in the ecology of Europe，形容詞子句修飾 changes in the ecology of Europe。

___B___ 67. 26 countries offered a flood of aids as fast as they could
_____the buried survivors in the earthquake.

A. save   B. to save   C. saving   D. saved

> **解** as fast as they could 是副詞修飾語，不影響動詞加接，不定詞表示目的。

___D___ 68. David, who is helpful and agreeable, is a person_____
wherever he is.

A. never to ignoring
B. never to have ignored
C. never being ignored
D. never to be ignored

> **解** wherever he is 是條件，表示未來，搭配不定詞。

___B___ 69. It made us very angry_____him talk like that.

A. hear   B. to hear   C. having heard   D. when hearing

> **解** 不定詞是真主詞。選項 D 表示 hearing 的主詞是 it，虛主詞不產生聽覺感官。

D 70. The company opened a new factory in the State of Michigan in 1910_____ the growing demand for cars.
A. having met　B. meet　C. meeting　D. to meet

解 不定詞表示目的。

C 71. _____, the thief hid himself under the bed without daring to make a sound.
A. Not caught
B. Not having been caught
C. Not to be caught
D. So as not to be caught

解 not to VP 表示否定目的，被動語態是 not to be PP。

B 72. A: Was the math homework difficult?
B: Not at all, I found_____.
A. it very easy to be done　B. it very easy to do
C. very easy to do　　　　　D. it very easy for doing

解 it 是受詞，very easy to do 是受詞補語，to do 修飾形容詞片語 very easy。

C 73. It is said that some scientists who participated in the space program will appear before the reception_____this evening.
A. holding　B. to hold　C. to be held　D. held

解 不定詞表示即將發生，reception 是被舉行。

B 74. What has happened here increases the chance of_____
one more misfortune pretty soon. It is quoted as a saying
that misfortunes never come single.
A. there to be   B. there being   C. it to be   D. it being

解 there 搭配動名詞 being，作為 of 的受詞，說明 chance 的內容。

C 75. For there_____successful communication, there must be
attentiveness and involvement in the discussion itself by all
present.
A. will be   B. is   C. to be   D. being

解 介係詞 for 是為了引導表示目的的不定詞。

A 76. The boy pretended_____his homework when his parents
came back home.
A. to do   B. do   C. doing   D. to be doing

解 pretend 搭配不定詞，表示不存在。

A 77. To succeed in a rough scientific research,_____.
A. one needs to be persistent
B. persistence is needed
C. You need be persistent
D. persistence is what one needs

解 句首不定詞的主事者是不定指—one，主要子句主詞也應是
one。

B 78. The earth seems _____ part of the sun.

A. to be　B. to have been　C. it is　D. used to be

> 解 完成式不定詞表示較早發生。

C 79. The time for a broken bone_____together again in a young man is usually about four weeks.

A. grown　B. growing　C. to grow　D. grow

> 解 折斷的骨頭要復原的時間，不定詞表示達成的結果。

B 80. A: What do you believe can ensure peace around the world?

B:_____ in that country.

A. By talking with the national leaders

B. Talking with the national leaders.

C. Talk with the national leaders

D. Being talked with the national leaders.

> 解 1. 針對 what 回答。
> 2. 底層結構：Talking with the national leaders can ensure peace around the world.
> 3. 插入 You believe：You believe talking with the national leaders can ensure peace around the world.
> 4. 詢問動名詞：What do you believe can ensure peace around the world?

C 81. The CEO and the designers have overcome a lot of
difficulty_____the new project.
A. they had developed　B. to have developed
C. they had developing　D. having developed

> 解 have / overcome difficulty in + NP / V-ing，in 通常省略。they had 是 difficulty 的形容詞子句，不影響加接動名詞的結構。

C 82. A. What do you think made Mary so depressed?
B._____her limousine which she spent almost all her savings on .
A. As she lost　B. Lost　C. Losing　D. Because of losing

> 解 針對 what 回答，名詞性質的動名詞。

D 83. A Russian official said Chinese cooperation is the key to _____the dispute about Iran's nuclear work.
A. resolve　B. resolved　C. to resolve　D. resolving

> 解 key—關鍵，搭配介係詞 to。

C 84. After_____, these trains are capable of attaining a very high speed.
A. technically improving　　B. technically improved
C. being technically improved　D. to be technically improved

> 解 主從分明，介係詞 after 加接動名詞當受詞，被動語態動名詞是 being PP。

C 85. The government is believed to be considering _____ a law
_____it a crime to import any kind of weapon.
A. to pass…make　　　　　B. to have passed…making
C. passing…making　　　　D. having passed…made

解 consider 搭配動名詞，law 搭配分詞片語。

A 86. Deforestation can also increase breeding sites for vector-
borne diseases, such as_____with mosquito habitat and
malaria in the Peruvian Amazon.
A. occurring　B. to occur　C. to have occurred　D. occurred

解 片語介係詞 such as 搭配動名詞。

A 87. The dedicated scientist died all of a sudden,_____his
research project unfinished.
A. leaving　B. having left　C. to leave　D. left

解 主從分明，逗號後面是從，非限定動詞，表示前面動作的結果，
主動，現在分詞。

D 88. With more forests_____, huge quantities of good earth
are being washed away each year.
A. destroying　B.destroyed　C. destroy　D. being destroyed

解 主從分明，介係詞 with 引導的是從的部分，With more forests
being destroye 表示持續被破壞。

C 89. The conference currently_____in Geneva has caught the attention of the mass media.
    A. was held   B. to be held
    C. being held   D. was being held

> **解** currently 表示目前，being 標示進行，選項 C 是答案。主詞是含分詞片語的 NP—The conference currently being held in Geneva，選項 B 表示將要被舉行，與 currently 不符；選項 A、D 是限定動詞，若要形成形容詞子句，關係代名詞不可缺項。

C 90. _____cold, he covered himself with a blanket, leaving only his arms_____.
    A. Felt…uncovering   B. Feeling…uncovering
    C. Feeling…uncovered   D. Felt…uncovered

> **解** 連綴動詞以現在分詞形式表示從的部分，uncover, V:_____ NP，patient 前移，被動語態。

C 91. _____ more information, they could make the plan better than it is now.
    A. Having given   B. If giving   C. Given   D. To be given

> **解** give 表示給予時，次分類是 V:_____NP NP，該句可改寫為：If they were given more information, they could make the plan better than it is now. 選項 A 表示較早發生，選項 D 表示目的，皆與語意不合。

A 92. Active reading will result in a better understanding of what _____.
    A. is being read   B. to be read   C. to read   D. being read

> **解** 了解的是正在閱讀的素材。

A 93. With land prices_____, I can't afford a piece of land big
enough to park my car on.
A. going up   B. gone up   C. go up   D. to go up

解 主從分明，介係詞 with 搭配非限定子句，現在分詞表示地價上
漲的狀態。

C 94. English teaching at college is to a great extent_____a
language class into an information class.
A. turn   B. turned   C. turning   D. is turning

解 to a great extent 是插入語，可略去。turn 的次分類是 V:
_____ turn NP PP。

C 95. The discovery of new evidence led to _____.
A. the thief having caught   B. catch the thief
C. the thief being caught   D. the thief to be caught

解 依題意，小偷已被抓，因此選項 A、D 不選。lead to 的 to 是介
係詞，加接 NP 或動名詞，選項 B 不選。being caught 說明
the thief 被抓的事實。

B 96. A. What did you do yesterday afternoon?
B: I went to the bookstore,_____some books and visited
my uncle.
A. to buy   B. bought   C. buy   D. buying

解 三個限定動詞形成平行結構。

B 97. Few of us get the_____seven to nine hours of sleep a night, and many who have time_____don't, for fear of spoiling night time sleep.
A. recommended…napping   B. recommended…to nap
C. recommending…napping   D. recommending…to nap

> **解** seven to nine hours of sleep a night 是被建議的，搭配過去分詞 recommended。
>
> have time 搭配不定詞，表示去做什麼的時間，搭配 to nap。

B 98._____into French, words and phrases for congratulations at the wedding party surely became language barriers for those who only knew English.
A. Having put   B. Put   C. Being put   D. To put

> **解** put 的次分類是 put, V: _____ NP PP，被動語態，本題是指同一時間的因果關係，搭配過去分詞原形。

A 99._____, her suggestion is of greater value than yours.
A. All things considered   B. All things considering
C. Considering all things   D. Considered all things

> **解** 主從分明，逗號左側是從的部分。本題 consider 的次分類是 V:_____NP，刪除 B、D 選項。C 選項意指其主詞是 her suggestion，但不會產生 consider 的動作，應刪除。本句意思是：When all things are considered, her suggestion is of greater value than yours.。

C 100. In the teaching of mathematics, the way of instruction is generally traditional, with teachers presenting formal lectures and students_____notes.
A. take   B. to take   C. taking   D. taken

> **解** 主從分明，介係詞 with 二分詞構成的非限定子句，刪去選項 A。take 的次分類是 V:_____NP，刪去選項 D。二非限定子句的動作同時發生，刪去選項 B。

C 101. Returning to her apartment late that night,_____.
A. her watch was found missing
B. her watch was nowhere to be found
C. she found her watch missing
D. she found her watch missed

> **解** 主從分明，從的部分主詞缺項，表示與主要子句的主詞一致，刪去選項 A、B。missing 表示下落不明的。

A 102. _____with fright, the hungry fox hid himself in a small cave,_____his tail to the rain.
A. Trembling…exposing   B. Trembled…exposed
C. Trembled…exposing   D. Trembling…exposed

> **解** tremble 的次分類是 V: _____ PP，expose 是 V: _____ NP。

A 103. Having finished the first chapter, he went back over the essay,_____spelling and grammar.
A. checking   B. to check   C. checked   D. having checked

> **解** 主從分明，空格表示主事者接續進行的動作。

D 104.＿＿＿＿＿with a difficult situation, Arnold decided to ask his boss for advice.

A. Being faced　B. Having faced　C. To face　D. Faced

解　face 的次分類是 V:＿＿＿＿＿NP，介系詞片語不是受詞，選項 B、C 刪去。從的部分表示主要子句的背景，本題的意思是：Arnold was faced with a difficult situation and she decided to ask his boss for advice.

A 105. The house was very quiet,＿＿＿＿＿as it was on the side of a mountain.

A. isolated　　　　　　B. isolating
C. being isolated　　　D. having been isolated

解　主從分明，逗號右側是從的部分，說明主要子句主詞的被動狀態。本句可改寫為：The house was very quiet, as it was isolated on the side of a mountain.

C 106. However, when＿＿＿＿＿how to attract young readers to the printed press, the government said the primary channel for the ads would be the Internet.

A. ask　B. to ask　C. asked　D. asking

解　主從分明，空格是從的部分。ask 的次分類是 V:＿＿＿＿＿NP NP。本句可改寫為：However, when the government was asked how to attract young readers to the printed press, the government said the primary channel for the ads would be the Internet.

D 107. Do not take the medicine any more than the suggested dosage unless_____by a doctor.
A. direct　B. having directed　C. directing　D. directed

解　主從分明，unless 是從的標記，空格位於從的部分，說明主要子句的條件，搭配過去分詞原形，direct 的次分類是 V:_____NP。

C 108. On the early morning of January 18th, people _____ standing in long lines waiting to receive the vouchers, as they were eager to do some shopping with the vouchers.
A. find　B. found　C. were found　D. who were found

解　主從分明，空格位於主的部分，且是限定動詞。Find 的次分類是 V:_____NP V-ing。

D 109. They include many special safety devices and systems that help to protect the plant, the people_____in it and the public, even in the event of a serious accident.
A. worked　B. are working　C. work　D. working

解　protect 加接形成平行結構的三名詞片語作為受詞，空格是 the people 的修飾語，work 是不及物性質。

C 110._____with care, this kind of flower can live for a long time.
A. Looking after　　B. To look after
C. Looked after　　D. Look after

解　主從分明，空格位於從的部分。look after 應加接受詞；選項 D 形成祈使句，主要子句性質，搭配從的部分，與題目結構不符。

_D_ 111. When hungry, _____.

    A. this restaurant is the place you want to be

    B. food smells so deliciously

    C. your energy just goes downhill

    D. one can think of nothing but food

> **解** 主從分明，When hungry 是從的部分，主題主詞是人。

_A_ 112. Accustomed to climbing trees, _____.

    A. I had no difficulty reaching the top

    B. reaching the top was not hard to me

    C. the top was not difficult for me to reach

    D. to reach the top was not a problem for me

> **解** 主從分明，空格是主要子句，從的部分主詞缺項，表示與主要子句主詞一致。從的部分説明主要子句的背景，可改寫為 I was accustomed to climbing trees and I had no difficulty reaching the top.

_D_ 113. After spending 5 hours in the interrogation room and conferring with her lawyer, the secretary eventually confessed_____the money that had been earmarked for company travel.

    A. to have stolen   B. having stolen

    C. stealing   D. to stealing

> **解** confess to 動名詞。

B 114. Road running often offers those＿＿＿a range of challenges such as dealing with hills, sharp bends, rough weather, and so on.

A. involving　B. involved　C. to involve　D. are involved

> **解** 本題 involve 的意思是使參與，例如 It would be difficult not to involve the child's parents in the arrangements.。 offers 的受詞可改寫為 those who are involved。

C 115. It's estimated that more than 1.7 billion people make up the world's consumer society people who have more money to spend than＿＿＿＿to cover their basic needs.

A. have required　B. are requiring

C. required　　　 D. requiring

> **解** than 是連接詞，引導副詞子句 than it is required to cover their basic needs，省略 it is，C 是答案。

D 116. He tried to control himself, but the more he＿＿＿＿, the more he laughed.

A. tried　B. had tried　C. was trying　D. did

> **解** 依題意，tried to control himself 以代詞 did 取代。

A 117. The arts of reading and writing were preserved in the monasteries of Europe for centuries until they spread to the general populace_____the rebirth of learning called the Renaissance.
A. during   B. in which   C. by then   D. and

> **解** call 的次分類是 V: _____NP NP，called the Renaissance 是過去分詞片語修飾 the rebirth of learning，共同形成一個 NP，扮演介係詞 during 的受詞。

D 118. Give me your telephone number_____I need your help.
A. whether   B. unless   C. so that   D. in case

> **解** in case 的意思是以防萬一。

D 119. The Human Comedy, a sentimental story of a family in a country at war, had special appeal because its principal characters are children,_____its perspective is adult.
A. though   B. who   C. where   D. while

> **解** its principal characters are children 與 its perspective is adult 不形成因果矛盾，while 的意思是 compared with the fact that; but，然而；但是。

C 120. The European age of discovery and the colonization of the world _____ were built on Eastern nautical technology.
A. followed   B. had been followed
C. that followed   D. that was followed

> **解** 句子的限定動詞是 were built，前面是主詞部分。空格是 the world 的修飾語，選項 B 是限定動詞，應刪去。依語意，the colonization of the world 跟隨在後。

A 121. Population growth_____the economic growth of a country as well as be affected by it.
A. can affect   B. is affecting   C. affects   D. affecting

> **解**　as well as 連接平行結構，be 是動詞原形，前面動詞也應是動詞原形，can 加接動詞原形構成的 as well as 平行結構。

A 122. The objective of the company is not so much to show a profit as it is_____that there are better ways of doing things in a business sense.
A. to demonstrate   B. demonstrating
C. of demonstrating   D. to be demonstrated

> **解**　1. not so much... as 的意思是「與其說是……還不如說是……」，例如：
> They're not so much lovers as friends.（Cambridge Dictionary）
> 他們與其說是戀人，不如說是朋友。
> 2. to demonstrate 與 to show a profit 形成不定詞的平行結構。

D 123. Some people think that it is a good way for children to find out about things, and that _____in this way also helps children to get used to technology
A. learn   B. learns   C. learned   D. learning

> **解**　限定動詞 think 加接 and 連接的二 that 名詞子句作為受詞，that 引介子句，動名詞 learning 當主詞。

D 124._____in Argentina, Brazil, or Trinidad, carnival is one of the most exciting events of the year, involving parades, parties, and dressing up in costume.

A. Which　B. That　C. If　D. Whether

> **解**　or 搭配 whether，用於引出二種或多種可能性，不管……還是……；或者……或者……。

C 125. Some small animals have_____a high metabolism_____ they must eat several times their own weight each day to stay alive.

A. such……as　　　B. either…… or

C. such…… that　　D. not only……but also

> **解**　either…or、not only…but also 連接結構相同的語詞以形成平行結構，NP 與子句結構不同，刪去 B、D。包含限定詞 such 的名詞片語搭配連接詞 that，表示結果。

D 126. They believed that careful self-examination can analyze and _____our personal characters, aims, methods and attitudes.

A. improved　B. improving　C. improves　D. improve

> **解**　and 連接二結構相同的語詞以形成平行結構。

B 127. The scientific study of the motion of bodies and the action of forces that change or cause motion_____dynamics.
A. calls B. is called C. are called D. called

解　1. 空格前是主詞部分，結構是一包含 of 介系詞片語的名詞片語，中心詞是 study，介係詞的受詞是 and 連接的二 NP。
2. call 的次分類是 call: _____ NP NP，空格後只有補語，因此是被動語態。

D 128. F = ma, known widely as Newton's second law,_____a postulate of physics since the advent of Newton's masterful Principia in 1687.
A. is B. having been C. being D. has been

解　1. known widely as Newton's second law 是插入語，不影響句子結構，略去不看。
2. since 介系詞片語標示截至現在的時間起點，限定動詞搭配現在完成式。
3. F=ma 是事件主詞，等同一個名詞子句。

A、D、G、H、I 129. The man_____is John.（複選題）

    A. talking to me

    B. talked to me

    C. I talked

    D. I talked to

    E I talked to him

    F. whom I talked

    G. whom I talked to

    H. to whom I talked

    I. who talked to me

    J. who talking to me

解 A. The man talking to me is John.

→ 分詞片語修飾名詞，分詞片語擴增為形容詞子句 ─ The man who talked to me is John─ 選項 I。

B. The man talked to me is John. 誤

→ 限定動詞 talked to me 與 is John 不同連接，形容詞子句 who talked to me 不可以先行詞 the man 作為主詞。

C. The man I talked is John. 誤 / The man I talked to him is John. 誤

→ 都是獨立子句，不具形容詞子句功用，都無受詞缺項，先行詞在形容詞子句中無角色。

D. The man I talked to is John.

→ 形容詞子句省略受格關係代名詞，底層結構：The man whom I talked to is John. ─ 選項 G，含受格關係代名詞的介系詞片語可移至形容詞子句首 ─ 選項 H。

E. The man whom I talked is John. 誤

→ talked 是不及物性質，不加接受詞，因此不需受格關係代名詞，形容詞子句必須有主詞或受詞缺項。

J. The man who talking to me is John. 誤

→ 關係代名詞不搭配分詞。

◆ 不規則動詞三態記憶 ◆

◆ 動詞黏接屈折字尾 **ed 形成過去式，標記過去**，例如 worked、played、closed、stopped，黏接屈折字尾 en 形成過去分詞，**標記完成、被動**。不是黏接 ed、en 的動詞就稱為不規則動詞，若是連同原形，就是不規則動詞三態。字源上，動詞原先都是規則變化，不規則動詞是演變的結果。

動詞三態都是源自同一字源的**同源字**，除了**語意相同**之外，**字根的音節首子音**，也就是母音前面的子音字母相同。

(1) 若是單音節，母音前面的子音字母相同，例如：

catch	caught	caught
think	thought	thought
bring	brought	brought
sleep	slept	slept

(2) 若是黏接字首，字根音節首子音相同，例如：
(2.1) begin，be 是字首，gin 是字根，begin、began、begun 的字根首子音字母都是 g。
(2.2) become 的字首也是 be，come 是字根，become、became、become 的字根首子音字母都是 c。
(2.3) forget 忘記，for 是字首，away 的意思，get 是字根，take 的意思，forget 就是把事情從心裡拿走，forget、forgot、forgotten 的字根首子音字母相同。

◆ 動詞三態變化記憶技巧是**「記住原形，找出同源」**，先記住動詞原形，找出音節首子音字母相同的過去式及過去分詞，並依照唸音特性推演拼字，舉一反三，甚至三加一的節奏。另外，過去分詞著重在辨識動詞原形黏接 en 的唸音變化，也就是母音不相鄰的拼音原則。

◆ 過去分詞黏接字尾 **en**，遵循「**子音 + en**」、「**母音 + n，省略 e 字母**」的 CV（子音 母音）相鄰排列，這與**不定冠詞 a 加接子音為首的單字**，**an 加接母音為首的單字**的語音排列原則相同，例如：

eat	ate	eaten
fall	fell	fallen
write	wrote	written
forget	forgot	forgotten

(1) **been** 是因為原形 **be** 只有一個母音字母，若是省略 **e** 而變成 **ben**，與動詞原形的唸音完全不同，因此 **be** 與 **en** 的 **e** 都予以保留。

(2) 動詞原形是 **C-V-C-e** 時，過去式的母音字母是 **o** 或 **oo**，過去分詞是動詞原形黏接 **n** 字母，二個 **e** 字母不相鄰。另外，過去分詞的重音節母音字母若是 **i**，則唸短母音 **/ɪ/**

shake	shook	shaken
take	took	taken
drive	drove	driven
rise	rose	risen
give	gave	given

dive、**have**、**lose**、**make** 是例外單字。

(3) 動詞原形是 **C-V-C-e**，母音後面的子音字母 **t**、**d** 時，重複 **t**、**d** 再加字母 **n**，字重音在第一音節，封閉音節，字母 **i** 唸短母音 **/ɪ/**。

(3.1) 過去式 **i-t**

bite、bit、bitten

(3.2) 過去式 **i-d**

hide、hid、hidden

(3.3) 過去式 **o-t-e**

write、wrote、written

(3.4) 過去式 **o-d-e**

ride、rode、ridden

(4) 動詞原形或過去式是 **ow**、**aw** 字尾時，過去式都是 **ew**，過去分詞是動詞原形加 **n** 字母，**ow**、**aw** 與 **en** 的 **e** 字母不相鄰。

(4.1) 動詞原形字尾是 ow、aw

blow	blew	blown
draw	drew	drawn
grow	grew	grown
know	knew	known
throw	threw	thrown

(4.2) 過去式加 ed

mow	mowed	mown
sew	sewed	sewn
sow	sowed	sown

(4.3) 過去式 w 字尾

fly	flew	flown

(5) 過去式韻腳字母，即母音及其後的字母是 **o-C-e**（字母 **o** 子音字母 **e**）時，過去分詞是過去式加 **n** 字母，避免二個 **e** 字母相鄰，重音節是開放音節，就是母音後面沒有子音，**o** 字母唸長母音 **/o/**。

break	broke	broken
choose	chose	chosen
freeze	froze	frozen
speak	spoke	spoken
steal	stole	stolen
wake	woke	woken

(6) 過去式的韻腳字母，就是母音及母音後面的字母是 **o-r-e** 時，過去分詞韻腳字母是 **orn**，避免二個 **e** 字母相鄰。

bear	bore	born
tear	tore	torn
wear	wore	worn
swear	swore	sworn

(7) 動詞原形、過去式、過去分詞的字母對稱：

(7.1) 動詞原形是單子音字母加 **ay** 時，過去式及過去分詞變化為 **aid**、**aid**。

lay	laid	laid
pay	paid	paid
say	said	said

(7.2) 動詞原形是單子音字母加 **ind** 時，過去式及過去分詞都是 **ound**、**ound**。

bind	bound	bound
find	found	found
wind	wound	wound

(7.3) 動詞原形、過去式、過去分詞的字根母音是 $/ɪ/$ - $/æ/$ - $/ʌ/$ 的轉換。

begin	began	begun
drink	drank	drunk
ring	rang	rung
swim	swam	swum
spring	sprang	sprung

(7.4) 動詞原形母音字母是 **ee**，唸 **/i/** 時，過去式與過去分詞母音字母縮減為 **e**，唸短母音 **/ɛ/**，音節尾子音字母方面，動詞原形若是 **d**，過去式與過去分詞保留 **d**。

bleed	bled	bled
feed	fed	fed
speed	sped	sped

→ lead 的過去式及過去分詞都是 led
→ read 的過去式及過去分詞都是 read

(7.5) 動詞原形字尾若是 **t** 或其他字母，過去式與過去分詞字尾是 **t**。

deal	dealt	dealt
dream	dreamt	dreamt
feel	felt	felt
keep	kept	kept
leave	left	left
mean	meant	meant
meet	met	met
sleep	slept	slept

(7.6) 動詞原形尾字母是 **t**，過去式、過去分詞的唸音與拼字常與動詞原形一致。

cost	cost	cost
cut	cut	cut
hurt	hurt	hurt
let	let	let
put	put	put
quit	quit	quit
shut	shut	shut
spread	spread	spread

(8) 動詞若是功能轉換的結果，就是名詞或其他詞性轉換為動詞時，
沒有動詞的字源，都是規則變化。

cup	cupped	cupped
mind	minded	minded
plant	planted	planted
water	watered	watered

◆ 有些動詞有**名詞同源字**，**首子音字母相同**，一起記就是小帳加一學更多，例如：

原形	過去式	過去式分詞	名詞
drink	drank	drunk	drink
sing	sang	sung	song
give	gave	given	gift
drive	drove	driven	drive
ride	rode	ridden	ride
rise	rose	risen	rise
break	broke	broken	break
speak	spoke	spoken	speech
do	did	done	deed
build	built	built	build
buy	bought	bought	buy
catch	caught	caught	catch
dig	dug	dug	dig
feel	felt	felt	feel
leave	left	left	leave
lose	lost	lost	loss
sleep	slept	slept	sleep
win	won	won	win
pay	paid	paid	pay
sell	sold	sold	sale
sit	sat	sat	seat
stand	stood	stood	stand
think	thought	thought	thought
run	ran	run	run
cost	cost	cost	cost
cut	cut	cut	cut
hit	hit	hit	hit

語研力 *E044*

全方位英語大師：
英文文法原來如此

呈現英文的嶄新視角，引領窺見文法的義理脈絡，看見學習的明確路徑！

作　　者	蘇秦、李唯甄
顧　　問	曾文旭
編輯統籌	陳逸祺
編輯總監	耿文國
主　　編	陳蕙芳
執行編輯	翁芯俐
內文排版	李依靜
美術編輯	李依靜
法律顧問	北辰著作權事務所

印　　製	世和印製企業有限公司
初　　版	2021 年 01 月
初版二刷	2023 年 05 月
出　　版	凱信企業集團 - 凱信企業管理顧問有限公司
電　　話	（02）2773-6566
傳　　真	（02）2778-1033
地　　址	106 台北市大安區忠孝東路四段 218 之 4 號 12 樓
信　　箱	kaihsinbooks@gmail.com

定　　價	新台幣 399 元 / 港幣 133 元
產品內容	1 書

總 經 銷	采舍國際有限公司
地　　址	235 新北市中和區中山路二段 366 巷 10 號 3 樓
電　　話	（02）8245-8786
傳　　真	（02）8245-8718

國家圖書館出版品預行編目資料

全方位英語大師：英文文法原來如此/蘇秦、李唯
甄合著. -- 初版. -- 臺北市：凱信企業集團凱信企業
管理顧問有限公司, 2021.01
　面；　公分
ISBN 978-986-99669-1-7(平裝)

1.英語 2.語法

805.16　　　　　　　　109018120

你喜歡創作嗎？
出書曾經是你的夢想嗎？
或是滿腔教學理念、想法，卻找不到管道發聲嗎？
也許下一個暢銷書作家就是你！

強力徵求
暢銷書作家！

誠摯邀請有才華的你，加入作家的行列！

內容不限、新手不拘，
只要自認作品夠優秀、想法夠創新，
不論是語言學習、心靈勵志、親子教育、
醫療保健、自我成長、生活管理、人生規劃……
都歡迎與我們聯繫，讓出版能更豐富精彩！

投稿專線：(02) 2773-6566#8666
來信請到：Kaihsinbooks@gmail.com
凱信學習網粉絲專頁：https://www.facebook.com/KS.BOOKS/

讓您的作品成為人生一個漂亮的履歷，歡迎加入咬文嚼字的世界！

KAIHSIN
SINCE 1984

凱信企業集團
凱信企管 | 凱信出版 | 開企

凱信學習網粉絲專頁

凱信企管

用對的方法充實自己，
讓人生變得更美好！

凱信企管

用對的方法充實自己，
讓人生變得更美好！